In Love and Murder

An Oxford Murder Mystery

Bridget Hart Book 4

M S MORRIS

D1421603

CHAPTER 1

'By making his bargain with the devil, is Faust responsible for his own downfall?'

Dr Nathan Frost gazed out of his small, narrow window onto the college quadrangle below while his two second-year students diligently noted down the title of the essay question they would have to answer for the following week's tutorial.

It was the standard essay he always set on Goethe's *Faust*, and if considered thoroughly, went straight to the heart of the text. The question gave the academically inquisitive student a chance to explore all the major themes: the ethical responsibilities of love; the arrogance of human learning; conscience, passion, wisdom, fate. Evil.

And yet.

In thirty-odd years of teaching German literature at the University of Oxford, setting the same essay questions on the same classic texts, in an endless cycle of academic terms that had long ago started to blur into each other, Frost could count on the fingers of one hand the number of essays that had actually impressed him, and still have digits to spare.

Reluctantly, he had come to accept that most undergraduate essays were superficial and derivative. He could usually spot within the opening few paragraphs which books – if any – had been consulted for research. Students just didn't seem to have any original ideas these days. Was the internet to blame? He let out a long sigh.

This wasn't how he'd imagined the life of an Oxford academic, all those years ago when – so young and naïve – he'd been appointed to the post. He'd anticipated stimulating tutorials with the brightest and best young minds, hungry for knowledge and bursting with fresh ideas. He'd envisaged time to pursue his own researches into German Romanticism and The Age of Enlightenment, resulting in a bookshelf of critically acclaimed titles to his name, speaking engagements at universities around the world, and, in due course, a professorship.

Little of that had materialised. And what, precisely, had he learned in a lifetime immersed in academia? To paraphrase Faust himself in one of the opening scenes of the play, it seemed that the more one pursued knowledge, the more one came to the realisation that ignorance was ever man's fate. No wonder Faust had been tempted by the darker arts, and by Mephistopheles' false promises.

One of the students – was it Lizzie or Lucy? He was always getting these two muddled – cleared her throat and Frost was jolted back to the present moment, back to his room in college with its dated furniture, faded carpet and bookshelves groaning under the weight of dusty tomes by Johann Wolfgang von Goethe, Thomas Mann, Günter Grass and other German writers and philosophers. Outside the Faculty of Medieval and Modern Languages, most people had barely heard the names of these great thinkers, let alone read their words. Did that mean that his life's study was irrelevant in the modern world? Had it all been for nothing?

The students were looking at him expectantly, waiting

for him to say something more. Something profound and enlightening, perhaps. How young they looked, with their sincere expressions of belief in the value of education. Experience had not yet taught them that it would lead them to an endless cycle of bitter nothingness.

'So, if you could bring your essays with you to next week's tutorial...'

His voice trailed off as they began to gather their things together, obviously keen to be elsewhere. And why not? He wanted to say to them, 'Be gone from here! Pack your bags and find something better to do with your lives!'

'Thank you, Dr Frost,' they chorused. Then they were gone, their feet echoing down the wooden stairs, their voices chattering excitedly.

From his window, he watched them crossing Front Quad on their way to the Junior Common Room. It was five o'clock on Friday afternoon, the end of the first week of Michaelmas term.

Oxford terms were notoriously short – only eight weeks long, giving them an intense, feverish quality. A febrile atmosphere was always tangible in college at the start of a new academic year. Fresh-faced young undergraduates arrived from all corners of the United Kingdom, not to mention all around the world, so keen was the university to get its hands on the lucrative fees paid by foreign students. For them, this first week was an exciting time – a whirlwind of socialising and late-night drinking, not to mention reading the first texts of the academic year and writing the first weekly essay.

From his vantage point by the upstairs window, shielded from view by dusty, velvet curtains that had once been red but had long since faded in the sun to a dusky pink, he watched some of the current undergraduates crossing the quadrangle: scientists on their way back from the labs; arts and humanities students emerging from the library carrying armfuls of books. Some of them waved to their friends or stopped to chat, perhaps making social arrangements for the evening.

He'd seen so many students come and go over the years. Most of them had morphed in his mind into an indistinguishable mass. Like all the colleges that made up the university, Wadham College had students in every faculty, which meant there were only a few studying any given subject in each year. He only had direct contact with the three or four in each year who were studying German. Those doing other subjects were strangers to him.

But there were always one or two students who, even if he couldn't put a name to their faces, became familiar: those who drew attention to themselves by their extrovert behaviour, those who were always campaigning on behalf of some cause or other, and those who simply had a natural charisma so that, once seen, you never forgot them.

One such student stopped in the quadrangle now to speak to a couple of her friends. A final-year Psychology student, she had immediately stood out when she'd arrived at the college just over two years ago. Gina Hartman. He only knew her name because her tutor, Dr Ashley, sometimes mentioned her over a glass of port in the Senior Common Room. Not only was she reputed to be gifted academically, but she exuded a magnetic attraction with her confident personality, her long, red corkscrew curls that tumbled over her shoulders, and her full-throated laugh that echoed around the quadrangle, seeming to bring the old stones to life.

Of course, Frost had never spoken to her. Why would he? He didn't have anything to do with Psychology students, or students in any faculty other than Medieval and Modern Languages for that matter. But she absorbed his full attention whenever she walked beneath his window.

He couldn't hear the conversation between Gina and the other two girls, but from their body language, Frost got the impression they were expecting her to go with them somewhere. Gina looked at her watch and shook her head. She held up a finger as if to say she'd join them in an hour, then headed off to the neighbouring quad. Her friends exchanged a look, shrugged their shoulders then moved off in the direction of the porters' lodge. Frost was left standing behind his closed window, one of life's observers.

It was growing dark now. He checked the clock on the wall and saw that it was already nearly six o'clock. The sand was trickling through the hourglass of his life just as it had for the last fifty-odd years.

This was the time of day when his colleagues would start to gather in the Senior Common Room for pre-dinner drinks, at least those who didn't have partners and families to go home to and instead preferred to dine in college rather than admit their sad, lonely existences to themselves. He was, regrettably, one of them, never having found a woman with whom to share his passion for the works of Johann Wolfgang von Goethe. Ordinarily he would make polite conversation with the college warden over the beef bourguignon which the chef cooked every Friday, and then afterwards retire once more to the SCR to spend the rest of his evening listening to the Classics tutor droning on about Cicero as the hourglass slowly emptied, laying waste to his life.

But tonight, for once, he actually had an engagement to go to.

He withdrew from the window and went into the small adjoining room which contained a single bed, a sink and a chest of drawers. He slept in this room if there was a late-night event in college, or whenever he couldn't summon the energy to cycle up the hill to his small, terraced house in Headington.

His dinner jacket, dress shirt and bow tie were spread on the bed where he had placed them that morning in anticipation. A pair of smart, black shoes stood on the floor by the bedside locker.

Frost stripped down to his Y-fronted underpants and freshened himself up at the sink with a bar of college-issue soap and a threadbare hand towel. Then he dressed in his black tie outfit and checked his appearance in the small mirror over the sink. With a rapidly receding hairline and wrinkles starting to form around his eyes and mouth, he looked every bit the middle-aged bachelor that he was. But he was about to be transformed.

He opened a drawer in the bedside locker and removed an object, wrapped in a black velvet bag, that he had purchased at some cost from a specialist online retailer a few days previously. He unwrapped it and held it up to examine closely, his hands betraying a faint tremor at his mounting excitement.

The full-face Venetian mask he held before him was an item of unique craftsmanship and strange beauty, exquisitely decorated around the eyes and nose with a black, cream and gold diamond pattern. As was his nature, he had investigated the subject of Venetian masks at some length before making his purchase. He had decided at last on a Bauta-style mask which would cover his whole face, thereby concealing his identity while still allowing him to talk, eat and drink, thanks to the way in which the lower section of the mask protruded to a point. He tried it on and looked at himself again in the mirror.

Now he was a different man altogether.

The mask hid not only his age, but also his weariness and disappointment with life. Under the mask he might be a much younger man, a good-looking man, a man still imbued with energy and purpose. Someone who looked forward to what the future might bring.

He removed the mask and replaced it in the velvet bag. He couldn't walk around the college wearing it. He would be laughed at. He checked the clock once more. It was almost time for formal hall to begin. He crossed the quadrangle and joined the line of tutors processing from the Senior Common Room to the hall, where he found himself seated on high table next to the Classics tutor.

'Well, well,' said Dr Slater, peering at Frost's dinner jacket and black bow tie over the silver reading glasses which were permanently perched on the end of the tutor's bulbous nose, whether or not he had a book in front of him. 'It looks as if you're dressed for a night at the opera, man.'

'Not the opera,' Frost replied, 'but a... a gathering.'

Dr Slater's bushy eyebrows arched in a way that suggested he thought the idea of Frost being invited to any kind of "gathering" rather unlikely. 'A gathering?' he pried.

'Just so.'

'Well, enjoy yourself,' said Slater begrudgingly, when it became apparent that Frost had nothing more to divulge on the matter, 'and spare a thought for the rest of us poor souls spending our evening here.' After dinner, the elderly tutor hobbled off in the direction of the SCR, his pace unusually quick, no doubt with the intention of spreading this latest titbit of gossip.

Damn, thought Frost. Now his evening would be the speculation of the common room. Oxford colleges were such incestuous places, you couldn't drop a pencil without the whole college knowing about it. He wished now that he'd gone home to eat, but it was too late for that. He collected his mask from his room, then hurried through the porters' lodge and stepped out onto the street. To his relief he saw the taxi he'd arranged pulling up outside, right on time.

He climbed into the back of the mini-cab and gave the driver the address. Then he sat back and tried to recover some of the equilibrium that had been upset by his encounter with old Slater. Now there was a man who would never escape the ivory tower of academia. He would probably die in the Bodleian Library, surrounded by the works of Virgil and Homer. Frost shuddered at the thought. To live one's life in the world of books and never to experience anything at first-hand. Well, he was about to put that right.

'Fancy affair you're going to, is it?' asked the driver, a young Indian chap. He signalled right after passing the redbrick façade of Keble College and pulled onto the Banbury Road, heading north.

'I'm sorry, pardon?'

'You must be going somewhere nice, all dressed up like that,' said the driver, his eyes twinkling at Frost in the rear-view mirror.

Frost glanced nervously at the velvet bag he was clutching in his lap. 'Just a little gathering,' he said in a tone of voice which, he hoped, would put an end to further enquiries and speculation. He looked purposefully out of the passenger window to deflect any more questioning, and the driver seemed to take the hint, tuning the radio into Heart Oxfordshire, which was playing some pop music Frost didn't know.

The truth was, he had very little idea about what sort of evening he was letting himself in for. The invitation had been entirely unexpected.

He'd been taking his Sunday lunch at the Bear Inn, as he'd done every week for years, and was returning from the bar with his regulation pint of bitter, when a burly fellow knocked into him in the cramped interior of the old pub, causing him to spill some of his drink.

Frost wasn't the sort of person to cause a fuss, and would have just mopped his hand with a handkerchief and taken his glass back to his table, but the chap insisted on buying him a new pint and engaging him in conversation. Despite his usual reticence and shyness, Frost found himself drawn in by the man's ebullient manner. He introduced himself as Nick Damon and said he was in the building industry. He asked what Frost did for a living and showed polite interest when Frost admitted, in his self-deprecating manner, that he taught German literature at the university and named his college. Mention of Frost's specialism was usually a showstopper where conversations with members of the public were concerned, but Mr Damon – 'Call me Nick,' he'd said shortly into their acquaintance – turned out to be surprisingly enthusiastic. 'I can tell you're a man of great culture and learning,' he'd told Frost with a friendly slap on his back. 'You'll have to tell me all about it.'

'And you're in the building trade?' Frost enquired, wondering if he'd understood the man correctly. His experience of tradesmen was extremely limited, but he doubted that many of them had any desire to hear about German literature.

Nick smiled. 'I run my own construction company.'

The conversation had ended with Nick inviting him to a party at his house in the country on Friday evening. So here he was, dressed up to the nines, with a mask in a velvet bag on his lap, on his way to God knows where, for he knew not what.

As the taxi headed out of Oxford, Frost couldn't help indulging in the fantasy that he had become Faust, and was about to experience the sensual pleasures of life for the first time, and that Nick Damon was Mephistopheles, tempting him into a life of vice and seduction for his own evil ends. He smiled to himself at the prospect of meeting a beautiful young woman as Faust had done, falling in love with her and having a passionate affair. But then one didn't want to stretch the analogy too far. Faust's girl had come to a sticky end, poor thing, not to mention Faust himself.

Nevertheless, he was excited at the prospect of leaving behind the dry, dusty world of books and, as Nietzsche would put it, *crafting his own identity through self-realisation*. God was dead. Nietzsche had been all in favour of embracing the material world, and Frost intended to take the philosopher's advice.

The taxi wound its way through the heart of the Oxfordshire countryside, through villages built from the local yellow Cotswold stone, past isolated farmsteads and endless expanses of night-blackened fields. Mr Damon's place was certainly out of the way. Frost wondered how much longer the journey was going to take.

His mobile phone buzzed with an incoming message and he remembered that Nick had promised to send him a password for the party. Frost thought the idea faintly ridiculous, but Nick had explained that he couldn't be too careful with security. He didn't want to risk gate-crashers. Checking his phone now, Frost saw that the password for entry to the house was *Fidelio*, the name of Beethoven's only opera.

He leaned forward, trying to tell from the car's SatNav display how much further they still had to go. They seemed to be miles from anywhere, and the countryside had closed in around them, dark for as far as he could see. Then the car turned off the main road and down a winding single-lane track. He felt a sudden flutter of anxiety. Was Nick Damon luring him to a remote spot for, what? To kidnap him? That would be absurd. He wasn't a wealthy man. No one would pay a ransom for his release.

He shivered at the realisation that no one knew where he was going. Maybe he should have been more forthcoming when the Classics tutor had asked him about his plans for the evening. He might at least have left a note behind in his room. The taxi driver muttered something under his breath about *this place being in the back of beyond*. And then suddenly they were pulling up in front of a pair of wrought iron gates. A pair of brightly-lit lanterns fixed to a surrounding stone wall made a welcoming sight.

'This the place, then?' asked the driver dubiously.

'I suppose it must be,' said Frost. He hadn't envisioned anything quite so remote.

The taxi driver wound down his window and pressed the buzzer on an intercom fixed to the wall. Sitting in the back of the car, Frost couldn't catch what the voice on the other end was saying.

'They're asking for a password,' said the driver to Frost in a tone of voice that suggested he thought this was some kind of joke.

'Fidelio,' said Frost.

The driver shook his head as if to say he'd heard it all now, then repeated the password into the intercom.

The gates swung open and the driver put the car into gear, passing a small brick-and-stone cottage with a crenelated roof. A gatehouse, presumably. They continued on into the grounds of the estate.

'Blimey,' murmured the driver as the main property came into view. 'Who lives here?' He pulled up in front of a house that was much bigger than anything Frost had envisaged. It was a three-storey Jacobean mansion complete with battlements and tall chimneys. When Nick had described his business, he had clearly been understating his success.

Frost counted out six ten-pound notes and handed them to the driver. 'Keep the change,' he said, getting out of the car.

'Cheers, mate,' said the driver, 'and good luck.'

Frost stood and watched as the taxi turned and sped away back to the gates. For the first time he wondered about how he would get home later. The house was far more isolated than he'd expected. He didn't think that particular driver would be keen to make a second trip that evening. Never mind, he was here now and that was what mattered. Attempting to assume an air of nonchalance, he made his way up a short flight of stone steps to the front door where he was greeted, if that was the right word, by a tall man with a crew cut and a square jaw wearing a dark suit and tie.

'No mask, no entry,' said the man, unsmiling. It was not a very auspicious start to the evening.

'Sorry,' said Frost, taking his mask out of its bag and fumbling with the elastic as he pulled it on. Once he was suitably attired, the man on the door stood aside to let him enter.

A young woman in a silver cat mask sparkling with tiny crystals stepped forwards to greet him in the long hallway and Frost's nerves started to dissipate. The host had obviously stationed the unfriendly gate-keeper outside to keep unwelcome intruders at bay.

'Welcome,' said the woman. Beneath the mask, which covered her eyes and nose, her red-painted lips smiled at him, revealing a set of perfect white teeth. 'What name would you like to be known by, this evening?'

'Known by?' The question threw him and he didn't know how to respond.

'Yes, we leave our old identities behind here.'

'I see, well, in that case...' Frost racked his brains. And

then, perhaps because it was so similar to his own name, or perhaps because he'd just spent the afternoon teaching it, or because it seemed so fitting for the occasion, he answered, 'Faust. I shall use the name Faust.'

'An excellent choice,' said the woman. 'You may call me Cassandra.'

The woman calling herself Cassandra led him through to a spacious wood-panelled room with a high ceiling and exposed beams. About thirty masked guests were already gathered there, champagne glasses in hand. Cassandra introduced him to a tall, imposing man in a leering devil's mask who stepped forward and shook him firmly by the hand.

Once again Frost felt distinctly wrong-footed and unnerved. The painted mask, with its stern, unmoving lips, seemed peculiarly sinister. But as soon as the man behind the mask spoke, Frost recognised the voice of his host, Nick Damon. He had no doubt that Damon knew who he was as well, although he refrained from using Frost's real name. It was all very strange.

'Welcome, Faust. Please help yourself to a drink,' said Damon.

A waitress in a short black dress was circulating with a tray of champagne. She wore a small silver filigree mask over her eyes, but otherwise her facial features were clearly displayed. Damon clicked his fingers and she came over to them. As Frost put out a hand to take a chilled glass of champagne, he was shocked to see that the woman was none other than Gina Hartman, the Psychology student with the stunning red hair and deep-throated laugh, who drew admirers like moths to a light.

He gaped at her before closing his mouth in embarrassment. What would she think of him? Then he remembered that she was unable to see his facial expression beneath his mask. Had she recognised him? But why would she? He didn't think she'd ever paid him a moment's attention.

'Thank you,' he said, his voice sounding hoarse.

She stood and studied him carefully just a moment too long for comfort before moving away again into the throng of guests, leaving him gazing after her.

He was suddenly consumed by the thought that this was his chance. Just like the frustrated scholar, Faust, he had been taken in by Mephistopheles, in the guise of Nick Damon, and introduced to the woman he secretly admired. Admittedly, things hadn't ended well for Faust, but that was just a play, not real life. There was no reason why his own story should end the same way. Damon was no devil, merely the owner of a construction company.

He took a much-needed gulp of champagne and glanced around the room, searching for a glimpse of Gina's red hair. Two more identically-attired waitresses entered, carrying trays of canapés and, with a stab of recognition, he realised they were Gina's two friends from college, the ones she'd spoken to in the quadrangle earlier that evening. He turned away from them and attempted to hide himself amongst a group of revellers in a corner of the room who were laughing about something or other.

Despite being shy by nature, Frost found that the mask lent him a certain confidence, as if he were putting on a persona, like the hero of Thomas Mann's great novel *The Magic Mountain* when he dresses up on Carnival Night. Behind the mask he could move through this room of strangers unobserved, speaking to whoever he wished, becoming the man he had always wanted to be. He finished his glass of champagne and helped himself to another from a tray on a nearby table.

He mixed with the other guests, sipping champagne and consuming canapés, and soon started to relax. The company was congenial, the ambience jovial. The masks lent an air of unreality to the proceedings. He mingled with people disguised as Harlequin characters, jokers, cats and at least half a dozen Pierrots with their pantomime clown faces. Almost all the masks were colourful, patterned or adorned with jewels and feathers. One lone plague doctor cast a sombre note with his long, beak-like nose and black hat. But there was still no sign of Gina.

A number of beautiful women with statuesque figures were moving amongst the guests, in bewitching Colombina masks decorated with gold, silver and crystals. Frost goggled at their scantily-clad forms. Were these women prostitutes? They were certainly behaving in a way that was extremely friendly to all the men. His own experience of the opposite sex was limited to a brief affair as a student in the German city of Bremen with a *Fräulein* who enjoyed hiking and had a passion for Bach. She had been very serious, and their short romance had been intense, with few laughs. He hadn't been too sorry when the time came for him to return to England.

He felt a tap on his shoulder and turned around to find himself face to face with Gina Hartman again, standing before him with an empty tray. She leaned in close and whispered something which he didn't quite catch amidst the background noise of chatter and laughter.

'What was that?' he asked.

'I said, you should leave,' she repeated in a slightly louder voice. 'You don't belong here.'

Dismayed, he realised that she had seen right through his disguise and knew who he was. But then a second, more hopeful idea entered his head. *She recognises me*. Gina knew who he was! And there was no question of him leaving the party, he had only just arrived. He had waited his whole life for such an opportunity. But before he could say a word, she turned and left, vanishing into the crowd again.

Someone thrust a drink into his hand, and he drank it straight down. Then one of the women in a Colombina mask asked him if he wanted to dance and, despite never normally doing such a thing, he joined her on the dance floor in a clumsy and inexpert waltz. The woman was very attentive, and held him close. But very quickly the room began to spin and he extricated himself from her embrace, saying he needed to take a short rest. He had no idea how much he'd drunk, but clearly far more than he was used to. He stumbled out of the room and found himself at the foot of a grand wooden staircase in the hallway. As he leaned on the carved newel post, he had enough mental capacity left to tell himself that if he went upstairs he might find somewhere where he could lie down for a while. He started to climb the stairs, leaving the noise of the party behind.

★

Frost woke with a start from a strange dream. Something hard and uncomfortable was pressing into his cheek. He put a hand to his face and was disconcerted to feel the lacquered surface of a mask. He pulled it off, letting it drop to the floor. He appeared to be lying in a large, four-poster bed. Sunlight was streaming through a leaded window, casting a criss-cross shadow across the floor. He tried to sit up but his head was pounding. He fell back against the pillows.

A vague recollection returned to him of the previous evening. The curious invitation, the grand country house, the masked party. Was it real, or part of the dream?

It was then that he became aware of a shape next to him in the huge bed. He turned his head slowly and saw a woman lying with her back to him. Her long, red corkscrew curls tumbled across the pillow. It couldn't be, could it? Had he just spent the night in bed with Gina Hartman, the stunning student he had watched so many times at a distance from his college room? How had it happened? The problem was, he couldn't remember a damn thing.

Tentatively he reached out a hand and touched her bare, white shoulder. She didn't move. She didn't even seem to be breathing. He was hardly breathing himself.

He levered himself up onto one elbow and leaned over to examine her face. Her dead eyes stared blankly at the far wall and he recoiled in shock and horror.

He leapt out of bed and ran to the door, shouting for help, his head ringing like an anvil. He had no idea what had happened, but he'd woken up in bed with a dead girl beside him. The party was definitely over.

CHAPTER 2

Saturday morning at the local leisure centre was a nightmare. Detective Inspector Bridget Hart hadn't been swimming for so long that she'd forgotten just how crowded and noisy the pool could be. Fortunately there were lanes for those wishing to do lengths and avoid the mayhem in the family section. Bridget was just about able to hold her own in the medium lane with her steady, but otherwise unimpressive breaststroke. She doggedly counted off the lengths – five, ten, twenty, she was determined to make it to thirty – while the more athletic swimmers in the fast lane powered past her doing the front crawl, a stroke she had never mastered.

Her job as a DI with Thames Valley Police left little time for regular exercise and she didn't have the physique for running. But she was determined to make more of an effort to look after herself, and if she lost an inch or two from her waist, then so much the better.

She had good reason to want to improve her body image. Namely, a date that evening with Jonathan Wright who owned an art gallery on Oxford High Street. Because of the way her job kept intervening to keep them apart, their fledgling relationship had barely taken off – well, to be honest it was still taxiing along the runway, awaiting clearance from air traffic control. A recent case had ended particularly badly for Jonathan, but he was now back on his feet, thank goodness. Hopefully, tonight's date would move them on to the next stage of the relationship.

Thirty! She'd hit her goal. Even Chloe, her teenage daughter, would be impressed. Bridget had left her sleeping in bed this morning when she'd left the house. She expected her still to be in bed when she got back. She paused a moment at the shallow end of the pool to catch her breath, then heaved herself out of the water.

Once she was showered and dressed, she ordered a healthy breakfast of fruit, yogurt and muesli from the leisure centre café, studiously avoiding the tempting cooked options which all seemed to come with chips. She found an empty table in the corner, dusted away the crumbs left by the previous customer, and sat down to eat, relishing the thought of how many calories she'd saved herself through her healthy choices. Adding that to the number of calories burned swimming, she would certainly be... oh, at least a pound lighter. Maybe two. She might even fit into the dress she was hoping to wear this evening.

Her phone buzzed as soon as she'd spooned a generous portion of muesli into her mouth. She glanced at the screen, hoping to see Jonathan's name, but it was work. She should have known this would happen. At least they hadn't been able to contact her while she was in the water. She picked up the phone and listened as the duty sergeant from Kidlington HQ explained the situation to her.

A young woman found dead in suspicious circumstances in a house about six miles west of Chipping Norton. Suddenly Bridget was no longer hungry. The death of a young woman always had the power to bring her out in goose bumps. Local police from Banbury were there now, but they needed a detective inspector to take charge. Was she available?

'I'll be there as quickly as I can,' she told the duty

sergeant. 'Let me organise my team.'

The first person she called was Detective Sergeant Jake Derwent. Bridget valued the young sergeant's steady, down-to-earth approach, and liked having him at her side, even though, at six foot five he dwarfed her meagre five foot two stature.

Jake's phone rang a few times and Bridget wondered if he was still asleep. She pictured his small flat on the Cowley Road, above a launderette and sandwiched between an Indian restaurant and a Chinese takeaway. She'd picked him up from there once but had never been inside. Judging from the way he organised his desk, and the mounds of rubbish in his car, it would no doubt be a typically messy bachelor pad.

'Hello?' The voice on the other end of the line was definitely not Jake's. It wasn't even male. Instead, it had the unmistakable Welsh lilt of Detective Constable Ffion Hughes.

Well, well, well, thought Bridget, this was a new development. She'd often wondered about the relationship between those two. Sometimes it was friendly and sometimes crackling with tension. Had they finally become an item? It was ten o'clock on a Saturday morning, and she didn't think it very likely that Ffion would be at Jake's place on work-related matters. Bridget wished them well, but they made an odd couple, to say the least. Jake was easy-going and affable. Ffion was intense and prickly. But Bridget knew that it wasn't easy to meet people doing the sort of job they did, and it was inevitable that many officers hooked up with others in the force.

Bridget had bitter personal experience of how that could end. Her own marriage to a colleague had finished in divorce. Ben, her ex-, was now a highflyer with the Met in London while Bridget's career in Oxford had only just got going. The only good thing to come out of that relationship had been Chloe. She thought again of Ffion, and couldn't picture her as the maternal type.

'It's Bridget Hart here,' she said, trying to keep any

trace of surprise from her voice. A family with a crying toddler had just occupied the table next to her. She stuck a finger in her free ear to try and drown out the noise and hoped Ffion could hear what she was saying. 'Is Jake there?'

'He's just in the shower. Can I take a message?' Ffion sounded as business-like as ever and was clearly not bothered that her boss had found her staying overnight with another member of the team. But then, Ffion never seemed flustered by anything.

Bridget quickly made the calculation that she could use Ffion's objectivity and skills of perception on this new case just as well as Jake's more empathetic approach, so she explained the situation to the young DC and asked if both she and Jake could meet her at the crime scene as soon as they were ready.

'No problem.' Ffion sounded quite excited by the prospect. 'We didn't have any other plans for the day.'

Bridget wondered how else they might have been thinking of spending their weekend, if being summoned to investigate a murder was a welcome distraction, but kept her thoughts to herself. She was glad they were both available.

She took a sip of her coffee which was still too hot to drink, leaving the rest of her breakfast untouched. Then she grabbed her swimming kit and headed out to the car park. Did she have time to go home and get changed into something smarter? She decided it didn't matter. It was a Saturday, after all. People couldn't expect her to be dressed in a suit all the time. Her hair was still damp from her swim, but it would dry off in the car by the time she arrived. She sent Chloe a quick message to say where she was going, then put the address the duty sergeant had given her into the SatNav and set off, the soothing tones of Puccini's *Madame Butterfly* pouring out of the car's speakers.

She was soon heading out of Oxford and following the familiar road that would lead her through her home town of Woodstock, birthplace of Winston Churchill. This was where she had grown up, and where her own sister was buried having met her untimely death at the hands of a vicious killer. She shuddered as she passed the road that led to the church of St Mary Magdalene and focussed her attention on the journey ahead.

Her little red Mini was perfect for navigating the narrow roads of this rural part of the world. She had never been able to understand middle-class England's current obsession with SUVs the size of small tanks. Her own sister, Vanessa, ferried her two small children back and forth to their prep school in Oxford in a Range Rover that could have easily handled a cross-country track, and was far too big to park neatly at the Waitrose supermarket.

Once out of Woodstock she was in the heart of West Oxfordshire, driving past pretty villages whose stone houses gleamed yellow in the October sunlight. Recently-harvested fields stretched out around her, and the trees were starting to turn gold and brown.

After driving for nearly forty-five minutes she studied the SatNav to see how much further this place was. The house was certainly out of the way, and she wondered who lived there. The duty sergeant had been a bit vague on that point, but had said something about a builder.

Eventually she turned off the main road, passing a sign to Adlestrop, and instantly recalled the poem she had learned at school by the World War I poet, Edward Thomas. The words came tumbling back to her unbidden across the decades: 'Yes. I remember Adlestrop –' The lines invoked a pre-war age of lost innocence; of meadowsweet, and haycocks dry, and of blackbird song. Out here, at the boundary of Oxfordshire and Gloucestershire, the ghost of those innocent days seemed still to linger.

She arrived at a pair of wrought iron gates which were standing open, and turned into the driveway. Immediately to her right, a uniformed policeman was standing outside a quaint little cottage, built from local stone and finished with crenellations, exactly like a miniature castle. It was just the sort of property that Bridget would have loved to live in. She pulled to a halt and wound down her window.

'DI Bridget Hart. I'm the Senior Investigating Officer.'

'This is just the gatehouse,' explained the young policeman. 'The big house is further on.'

'Okay, thanks,' said Bridget, growing more curious all the time.

The main house, when it finally came into view, took her breath away. A three-storey Jacobean manor house, it was a wonder it was still in private hands and hadn't been acquired by the National Trust or English Heritage. The house was built from the same reddish-gold brick and stone as the gatehouse, with matching battlements on its gables and rooftops. Its leaded windows were framed in yellow stone. Immaculately-presented lawns lay to either side of the gravel drive, which turned in a wide circle before the front entrance.

A couple of marked police cars and an ambulance were parked on the driveway in front of the house. Bridget recognised two other cars: the first belonging to Dr Sarah Walker, the medical examiner she often worked with on murder cases; and the second that of Vikram Vijayaraghavan – Vik to his friends and colleagues – who was in charge of the Scene of Crime officers. Jake's bright orange Subaru wasn't there yet, and neither was Ffion's neon green Kawasaki motorbike. Bridget assumed that Ffion would come with Jake anyway, once she'd cleared the chocolate bar wrappers from the passenger seat. A row of other cars was parked off to one side of the house – a Porsche, quite a few BMWs, and a Mercedes or two. It looked like quite a gathering.

She was met at the bottom of a short flight of stone steps by a middle-aged officer in uniform who introduced himself as PC Keith Herrington, based at the Banbury station. He struck Bridget as one of those competent and reliable coppers who'd never had the ambition to get out of uniform and join CID, the sort of policeman who enjoyed walking the beat, getting to know the local community and nipping the first signs of trouble in the bud. Unfortunately, modern policing didn't really have the resources for that sort of early intervention.

'DI Hart?' he queried. 'Follow me please, we've been expecting you.'

★

PC Herrington led Bridget into a long, narrow hallway with a wooden floor and an elaborately-crafted staircase leading to the upper floors. Beyond, double doors opened into a larger room.

'Before we go any further,' said Bridget, 'could you fill me in on a few details? Who lives here? Who do all these cars belong to? And do we know who the victim is?'

'The house is owned by Mr Nick Damon,' said PC Herrington. 'He's a property developer and building tycoon.'

'He's obviously made a lot of money,' commented Bridget, glancing around at the gilt-framed pictures on the walls. A stuffed stag's head regarded her with glassy eyes.

'He's not short of a bob or two,' said Herrington, nodding. 'He employs a lot of people around here. And he's got friends in high places, if you know what I mean.'

'Such as?'

'Well, the local Member of Parliament for one thing. He was here last night as it happens, but he left early this morning before we arrived.'

'And what exactly was happening last night?'

'A party of some sort. A posh do. Not the sort of thing that ordinary folk like me get invited to. You've only got to look at the cars outside to see the sort of people who come to a place like this.'

Bridget had to acknowledge that her beloved Mini wasn't in the same league as the other cars parked on the driveway.

'So the rest of the guests are still here?' she asked.

'They stayed overnight. Lawyers, businessmen, a High Court judge, plus' – Herrington raised his eyebrows – 'a group of escorts from a London-based agency. We've got a team of local chaps taking their statements right now. But you won't have to look far to find the man responsible for the murder. Dr Nathan Frost from Wadham College was found with the poor girl dead in the bed beside him. He claims he can't remember what happened, but it's as plain as daylight. The bastard strangled her, if you'll excuse my language, ma'am. Case closed.'

'An academic?' said Bridget, surprised to hear that someone from the university had attended the party. 'What did an Oxford academic have in common with all these business types?'

Herrington shrugged his shoulders as if he hadn't given the matter any thought. Maybe that was why he'd never progressed out of uniform.

'Where is Dr Frost now?'

Herrington puffed up his chest, obviously very pleased with himself. 'Already on his way to Kidlington to be processed. He'll be ready for you to interview by the time you get back.'

'He's been arrested?' said Bridget, wondering who exactly was supposed to be running this investigation.

Herrington seemed put out by the question. 'Of course. What else were we to do with him?'

A young woman with a long mane of blonde hair emerged from one of the rooms off the hallway. She looked pale and drawn, but on seeing Bridget she immediately fixed a cheerful smile to her face with the practised air of a professional.

Her voice was just as sunny as her smile. 'Good morning. I'm Brittany Grainger, Mr Damon's PA. I was the one who called the police this morning.' Her voice carried a Northern ring, reminding Bridget of the short vowels of her own sergeant's Yorkshire accent.

'DI Bridget Hart,' she said, taking the young woman's proffered hand. 'PC Herrington was just filling me in on a few background details. Were you here last night, Miss Grainger?' She had noticed that the PA wasn't wearing a wedding ring.

'Please, call me Brittany,' said the PA, 'and yes, I was here last night. I handled the organisational details of the party.'

'Such as?'

'I booked the caterers and organised the girls who worked as waitresses...' Her voice trailed off. 'It was one of the waitresses who died. She was a student at the university.'

'What was her name?'

'Gina Hartman.'

'Which college was she at?'

'Wadham, I think.'

'And Dr Frost is from Wadham too?' Bridget didn't know Wadham College well, other than that it was a traditional Oxford college situated on Parks Road, just north of the city centre.

'That's what he told us,' said PC Herrington.

'What about the other waitresses?' asked Bridget.

'There were three of them, all from Wadham College,' said Brittany.

'Where are the other two now?'

'They went back to college last night, after the party.'

'And they didn't worry that Gina wasn't with them?'

Brittany shrugged. 'I don't know. Gina arrived some while after the other two, so maybe they thought she was leaving separately too.'

'I'll need their full names,' said Bridget. 'When my sergeant arrives you can give him all the details. He should be here soon.' The way Jake drove that Subaru, it shouldn't take him long to navigate the country roads. 'Can you supply me with a full guest list?'

'No problem,' said Brittany who looked happy to be given something to do. 'But might I ask you to be discreet? Mr Damon's guests value their privacy very highly.'

'I'm sure they do, but I can't make any guarantees.

We'll need to interview everyone who was here last night. So if you could find the list for me, that would be very helpful.'

'I'll sort it out immediately,' said Brittany, 'and can I bring you a coffee?'

Bridget thought longingly of the coffee and breakfast she'd abandoned at the leisure centre, but there would be time enough for refreshments later. Right now, she had a job to do. 'Perhaps later,' she said.

Brittany disappeared into one of the ground-floor rooms and Bridget turned back to PC Herrington who was waiting patiently by her side. 'Maybe you could take me to the dead girl now?'

'Right you are, ma'am. This way.'

He started up the stairs and Bridget followed, bracing herself for what she was going to find.

She donned a protective suit before entering the bedroom, grateful that she hadn't bothered to change out of her Saturday morning casuals. It made getting into the all-in-one coverall so much easier.

Vik, the head of the SOCO team, met her at the door. His colleagues were busy dusting the place down for prints and photographing the scene. Dr Sarah Walker, the forensic medical examiner, was checking the body of the girl on the bed.

'Morning, Vik. How's it going?'

'Not bad, although why do these murders always have to take place on my day off?' he said, lowering his face mask to talk to her. 'This must have been quite some party last night. Not the sort I ever get invited to.'

'Me neither,' said Bridget, although she didn't think she'd want to be invited to such a party. Whatever had gone on here last night, it had ended tragically for Gina.

'Mind you,' said Vik, 'we'd have been all right wearing these face masks.'

Bridget gave him a blank look. 'Whatever can you mean?'

'Didn't you know? It was a masked ball.'

'Masked?'

PC Herrington nodded in confirmation. 'Who knows what these kind of folk get up to in their big houses, eh?'

Bridget was growing tired of the constable's judgemental attitude and wondered if there was any other information he'd neglected to tell her. She would just have to make her own thorough enquiries.

'Well, at least it's a nice, clean house,' said Vik, 'so we've been able to lift some good, clear prints and collect hair samples without any cross-contamination. We'll be sending everything off to forensics as soon as we're done.'

'Excellent.'

'And we've recovered her phone too. It's bagged and ready to be sent to the lab.'

'Good work.'

These days, the victim's mobile phone was often one of the key assets in an investigation, and Bridget was glad it had been found so quickly. As ever, Vik was a complete professional, and she knew she could rely on him and his team.

She looked across to where Gina's slim body lay on the bed. She was wearing a short black dress. Even in death, Bridget could see that she must have been a real beauty, her red corkscrew curls her most striking feature. Now, her eyes stared glassily out of their sockets. Her skin had taken on a deathly pallor and there was a bluish tinge around her lips.

Bridget steeled herself for the worst. The death of a young woman always affected her more deeply than other deaths. She couldn't help it. Her own sister, Abigail, had been abducted and murdered at the age of sixteen, and with a fifteen year-old daughter herself, the idea of something like this happening to Chloe was her worst nightmare.

Dr Sarah Walker straightened up as Bridget approached. 'Ah, Bridget.'

Bridget gave the medical examiner a weak smile. For a long time, Sarah had been reluctant to call her by her first name. The doctor was a very reserved person, who took refuge in formality. Bridget decided to chalk up this small easing in relations as a win.

'Initial thoughts?' she asked.

'She was almost certainly strangled,' said Dr Walker. 'Look, you can see the bruising on her neck here.' She pointed to dark red marks around the victim's slender throat. 'She was a slim girl. It wouldn't have taken much to overpower her physically.'

'Any other signs of violence?'

'Some further bruising on the arms, legs and face.'

'What about signs of recent sexual activity?'

'I've taken swabs, but there's no obvious sign of rape.'

'Well, I guess that's something, at least. How quickly can you get the swabs analysed?' asked Bridget, conscious that the first twenty-four hours in a murder enquiry were crucial for gathering evidence.

'I'll fast-track it through the lab,' said Dr Walker. 'I should have something for you by tomorrow morning.'

'That's great. And what about time of death?'

'Well, rigor mortis is fully developed, so that would indicate that she's been dead for at least six hours.'

Bridget glanced at her watch. It was half past eleven now, so that narrowed the time of death down to the hours of darkness. She would have to wait for the post-mortem to pin it down more accurately.

'Thanks.'

She turned away as the team prepared to zip Gina's body into a bag for transferal to the morgue. Leaving Sarah and the others to get on with their jobs, Bridget left the room and removed her protective clothing.

PC Herrington was waiting for her on the upstairs landing.

'I'd like to see the owner of the house now,' Bridget told him.

*

Bridget found Nick Damon in his downstairs study, an oak-panelled room looking out onto the rear lawn and garden. The room was elaborately furnished in a period style, with antique furniture, and shelf upon shelf of leather-bound books. Bridget wondered if their owner had ever read them, or if they were just for show. She guessed the latter.

A tall, physically powerful man with black hair and fine looks, Damon was on the phone when she entered, and indicated that she should take a seat while he concluded his call. He didn't appear in the least distressed by events. It seemed to Bridget that he was negotiating a piece of business with a client, and she wondered at the sort of man who could calmly continue with his life when a woman had just been murdered in his home, at a party that he had hosted. She noted the fine cut of his suit, the crisp white shirt that he wore open at the collar, and the large diamond cufflinks on his sleeve.

A second person was also in the room, standing by the window behind Damon's desk. An older man, immaculately dressed in a navy suit and tie, he studied Bridget's jeans and casual shirt with a disdainful air, and she wished she had changed into something smarter after all.

Damon eventually put the phone down and gave her an enquiring look.

'I am Detective Inspector Bridget Hart,' said Bridget, determined to stamp her authority in this room which was bristling with the air of male power and privilege.

'Of course, Inspector,' said Damon, rising from his chair to shake her hand with a firm grip, revealing a glimpse of a heavy gold watch around his wrist. 'Nick Damon. And this' – he indicated the other man in the room – 'is my lawyer, Mr Gold.'

Bridget frowned, wondering why Damon had felt the need to summon his lawyer to the house. It was unusual for witnesses to arrange for legal representation even before the police arrived.

Mr Gold nodded at Bridget, but remained aloof by the window, saying nothing, his features devoid of expression. Bridget couldn't help being reminded of a lizard.

'Has my PA been giving you all the assistance you need?' inquired Damon. 'If there's anything we can do to help, you only have to ask.'

Nick Damon's manner was a little too smooth for Bridget's liking. Where was the concern for the murdered girl? And what exactly was his lawyer doing here?

'Perhaps you could help me out with a little background, Mr Damon. What sort of work is it you do, exactly?'

Damon grinned broadly. 'You could say that I make people's dreams come alive.' He fluttered his fingers in the air, as if showering them all in fairy dust.

'I'm sorry?' This wasn't the sort of answer Bridget had expected.

'I'm a builder by trade,' explained Damon. 'I build the homes of people's dreams. Luxury for the few, affordability for the masses. My companies do more mundane work too, of course – warehouses, offices, infrastructure – wherever there's a client willing to pay. But it's housing that's my real passion. An Englishman's home is his castle, no?' He spread his hands to indicate the room they were sitting in. 'This place is my pride and joy. It was a neglected wreck when I bought it. Holes in the roof; plasterwork peeling off the walls. Now look at it. I brought it back to life.'

'And you throw parties here?'

'Everyone longs for a little magic and excitement in their lives, don't they, Inspector? Most people's lives are so dull, so humdrum. So futile. I try to spread a little joy.'

'Your party didn't bring much joy to Gina Hartman's life,' said Bridget. 'How well did you know her?'

Damon's smile didn't falter. 'Hardly at all. Brittany deals with the staff. Why don't you ask her?'

'I'd like to know what dealings you had with her. Did you speak with her at all?'

'Maybe a few words. Just to welcome her to the house.'

'Did you see her during the party?'

'I try to pay attention to my guests, rather than the serving staff.'

'I see. Did you know that she'd gone upstairs?'

'No. I was downstairs in the great hall all evening. But people were free to move around the house, to make use of the bedrooms, if you take my meaning.'

Bridget recalled PC Herrington's reference to escorts being present at the party. 'Are you married, Mr Damon? Or perhaps you have a girlfriend?'

Damon winked at her. 'No, I'm currently available. And do call me Nick, please.'

Bridget ignored the flirtatious look on his face. 'Can you tell me why Dr Nathan Frost was present at the party?'

'He was an invited guest. I must say I don't usually have such esteemed academics at these little gatherings. The learned doctor added a welcome touch of distinction.'

Bridget frowned. The reason why Frost had been invited to the party was still a mystery to her. 'Then is he a friend?' she persisted. 'Or a business partner of some kind?'

'Let's say an acquaintance, and a very recent one at that. I met him for the first time just last weekend.'

'Really? And yet you invited him to your party.'

'Why not? Spread the magic, that's what I always say.'

Bridget was growing very tired of Nick Damon's magic and dreams. 'How often do you hold these parties, Mr Damon?'

'I like to hold them quite regularly, say once or twice a month.' He leaned forward earnestly. 'You know, when someone has the privilege of living in such a fine house as mine, I really believe that there's a duty to share it with as many people as possible.'

'As long as they drive a Mercedes or a BMW?' said Bridget. Now she was starting to sound like PC Herrington. She mustn't allow Damon to rankle her.

He grinned again. 'Sometimes they drive Aston

Martins or Bentleys, but I don't choose my guests' cars for them, Inspector. In any case, I think you'll find that Dr Frost came here by taxi.'

Bridget remained puzzled by the presence of the Oxford academic at the party, but she guessed that Damon wouldn't willingly divulge any further information on the matter.

'We'll be interviewing all your guests,' she told him, 'and I'm going to ask everyone who was present at the party to provide fingerprints and a DNA sample so that we can eliminate them from our enquiries. If I could start with you, Mr Damon…'

Mr Gold, the lawyer, spoke for the first time then, cutting her off before she could finish her sentence. 'Actually, my client is not obliged to provide fingerprints or a DNA sample unless you have reasonable grounds for suspecting him of committing a crime, so I'm going to have to deny your request.'

'Perhaps,' replied Bridget, 'I could remind you that a young woman was killed here last night. Whatever dreams Gina Hartman had, they were shattered last night, wouldn't you agree, Mr Damon?'

Nick Damon held up his hands. 'I'm very sorry, Inspector. I'd love to help you, but I always do what my lawyer tells me. Mr Gold doesn't say very much, so when he does, I'm obliged to take note.'

Right, thought Bridget, narrowing her eyes, if they're going to play difficult, then we're going to have to get tough.

'Very well. As I say, my team will be taking statements from everyone present, including staff and guests. We've already made an arrest, and it really would be in your own best interests to help us with our enquiries as much as possible. If,' she added, 'you don't want us hanging around any longer than is strictly necessary. And if you'd like us to treat your guests with discretion.'

Damon flashed his teeth at her again in a somewhat more predatory-looking smile than before. 'I understand exactly what you're saying, Inspector, and I'll help you in every possible way I can. But if Mr Gold says no DNA or fingerprints, then that's the way it's going to be.'

Behind him, the lawyer stood expressionless, staring at her with his dark eyes.

CHAPTER 3

'Aren't you going to put your foot down a bit harder?' Ffion asked as Jake drove his metallic orange Subaru sedately through the Oxfordshire countryside. 'My dad drives faster than this.'

Jake grinned. She was right, of course. He generally drove at – or sometimes over – the speed limit. But he was enjoying this time with her and didn't see any point in arriving at their destination any sooner than necessary. He and Ffion worked long hours and didn't get a lot of time to spend together. Today was supposed to be their day off, and he wondered why she had agreed so readily to go off to a crime scene. The sun was shining, and it was glorious weather for October – the perfect day for a drive through the country. It would have been nice to stop off at a pub for lunch, and to take a leisurely stroll together before heading back to Oxford. The town of Woodstock looked like a nice place to visit, and people were always telling him how pretty the Cotswolds were.

But then he thought of his boss, Bridget Hart, and immediately felt guilty. Of course they should get there as quickly as they could. He pressed his foot on the accelerator and felt the car's turbocharger kick in, sending the Subaru shooting forwards with renewed vigour.

'That's more like it,' said Ffion, her face lighting up.

Jake grinned more broadly. Ffion was a real speed demon, owning a Kawasaki Ninja H2 motorbike that made his own car look pedestrian. He still found it hard to believe that she'd agreed to go out with him.

When he'd first encountered her, Ffion's manner had been as spiky as her pixie haircut, and she had fended off all his attempts to be civil. But he'd come to realise it wasn't just him. When Ryan Hooper, one of the other detective sergeants at Kidlington, had asked her out, she'd breathed Welsh fire down his neck. After Jake had got to know her better, she'd confided in him that she tended to act defensively where men were concerned because most of them couldn't handle the fact that she was bisexual. Jake liked her all the more for her honesty, a quality which had been sadly lacking in his previous girlfriend.

He and Ffion had gone on a few dates and Jake had taken her back to his place after thoroughly decontaminating his flat and throwing out all the old beer cans, pizza boxes and takeaway food cartons. Ffion was fastidious about hygiene, and loathed disorder, Jake's usual state of domesticity. She didn't share his taste in music either, but Jake could live with that. He thought they made a good couple. And the sex was great.

'I think we're nearly there,' said Ffion, studying the map on her phone.

'Here? We're in the middle of nowhere.'

'Yeah, this looks like it,' said Ffion, pointing to a pair of wrought iron gates which appeared without warning at the roadside.

Jake hit the brakes, deftly shifted down three gears, and turned the car into the driveway. He slid to a halt next to a police car parked inside the gates, but the uniformed officer standing by its side waved them on.

'Looks like a grand place,' said Jake, as he drove along the long gravel drive lined by neatly clipped hedges. 'The grounds are huge.'

'Be sure to doff your cap when you meet the owner,' said Ffion. 'And don't speak unless you're spoken to.'

He could hear the good-natured laughter in her musical Welsh accent. Yes, even though she still liked to make fun of him at every opportunity, she had definitely softened over the few weeks they'd been together.

'Wow,' he said when they reached the house itself.

'Yeah, wow,' agreed Ffion, and even she sounded impressed by the size and grandeur of the building.

Jake parked his car behind Bridget's red Mini and jumped out. The house was a flurry of activity, with several police cars and other vehicles parked in front and at the side. Uniformed police officers were moving about, and a body was being loaded into an ambulance.

Ffion joined him at his side, taking in the busy scene. 'All right then, let's get to work.' She kissed him once, then strode ahead of him towards the house.

'Yeah, right.' At work, he and Ffion kept their relationship on strictly professional lines, but it wasn't easy, watching those long legs clad in skin-tight jeans. *Keep your mind on the job, mate*, Jake reminded himself. He followed her into the house, in search of Bridget.

A uniformed constable was standing just inside the entrance hall, directing two other officers. He turned to greet Jake and Ffion as they entered. 'I'm PC Keith Herrington from Banbury. You must be DI Hart's team.'

'That's right,' said Jake, reaching out to shake the constable's hand. 'Perhaps you could tell us where she is.'

'She's just speaking to the owner of the house, a Mr Nick Damon. Then I expect she'll be wanting to get back to Kidlington as soon as possible. We've already made an arrest.'

'Really?' said Jake, raising one eyebrow. 'That was quick work.'

Herrington regarded him suspiciously. 'Just because we're out in the countryside here, doesn't mean we work any slower than you Oxford folk.'

'No,' said Jake. 'I wasn't suggesting that you did.'

He turned over the name that Herrington had mentioned. Nick Damon. It was familiar, but he couldn't quite place it. He was about to ask what Mr Damon did for a living, when Ffion spoke.

'So, who's the corpse?' she asked, tipping her head in the direction of the ambulance outside.

Jake cringed, and wondered if he would ever get used to Ffion's coarse insensitivity. No matter how much she had softened towards him, she still had a talent for causing needless offence to others.

Herrington narrowed his eyes. 'The murder victim is a girl called Gina Hartman, a student at Wadham College.'

'And who do you think killed her?' asked Ffion.

'Dr Nathan Frost,' said Herrington. 'A tutor at Wadham.'

'This is a long way from Oxford. What were a student and an academic doing here?'

'Some kind of party.'

'Why do you think it was him?' asked Ffion, her tone of voice suggesting a low level of confidence in the constable's identification of the culprit.

'She was found dead in his bed,' said Herrington, his lip curling down in evident disapproval. 'It's not the kind of thing we expect around these parts.'

It really wasn't the kind of behaviour that was expected in any part of the country, thought Jake. He was about to intervene to prevent Ffion upsetting the local policeman any further, when he heard his name being called from across the hallway.

'Jake! Oh my God, it *is* you!'

He spun round at the sound. He would recognise that voice anywhere. Please, God, he thought, it can't be. But it was.

'Brittany. What are you doing here?'

He could feel the colour rising up his neck and his cheeks burning. Any second now the tips of his ears would be aflame.

Brittany Grainger, the girl who had once stolen his heart, and kept it for several years, before handing it back, cleaved in two. Or more accurately, smashed into a million pieces.

He had first met her at university in Bradford, and had started going out with her in his second year. He'd been studying Criminology; she'd been working towards a degree in Business and Management. He graduated first and started work in Leeds. Brittany completed her course a year later, and moved south to get a job as a personal assistant to the managing director of a construction company. She returned to the north to be with him most weekends at first, but her visits gradually became less frequent as time went by. Desperate not to lose her, he applied for a transfer to Oxford, and was assigned to Thames Valley Police Headquarters based at Kidlington police station just outside Oxford. For a while he thought they could recover the intimacy that had been lost during their year apart, but the damage had already been done. Soon after the move south, he discovered that she'd been cheating on him the whole time and was seeing someone at work. The relationship ended in tears and acrimony.

That was six months ago, in April, and he thought he'd finally got her out of his system. Now, hearing her voice again, he knew that he'd only been fooling himself.

She came up to him, hesitated for a second, and then kissed him on his cheek, which flushed a deeper shade of crimson. 'It's so good to see you again, Jake.'

Ffion was watching over the exchange like an eagle. 'I take it that you two know each other?' she said, all hint of affection gone from her voice.

Jake didn't know where to put himself. Ffion, whose green eyes never missed a trick, was looking from him to Brittany and back again, while Brittany beamed up at him, ignoring Ffion as if she had never spoken.

'Well, um, it was a long time ago,' said Jake. 'We, er...'

Now he knew where he'd heard Nick Damon's name before. He was Brittany's boss. He was the man she'd left

Yorkshire to come and work for. In a way, Nick Damon was responsible for destroying their relationship.

'It wasn't so long ago,' said Brittany, laying a hand on his arm. 'You make it sound like ancient history. Jake and I had quite a thing going for a while.'

'I get the picture,' said Ffion, her face like thunder. 'Now, we've got work to do.' She glared at Brittany. 'What's your name and what role do you have here?'

Jake wished the earth would open up and swallow him whole while he listened to Brittany blithely explaining that she worked as personal assistant to Mr Damon, the owner of the house. He could tell from the way Ffion narrowed her eyes and cocked her head to one side that she was appraising Brittany, and not liking what she saw.

It wasn't surprising. Brittany was stunningly beautiful – a match for Ffion. Jake had forgotten – or had tried to deny to himself – just what a looker she was.

Brittany was unfazed by Ffion's calculating stare. Full of charm and self-confidence, she exuded a warmth that Ffion could never match and he realised with a sense of guilt that she still exerted a strong hold over him.

He was relieved when the conversation – or interrogation – was interrupted by the arrival of DI Bridget Hart, presumably fresh from her interview with Nick Damon. She wore a grim expression on her face, and Jake guessed that she hadn't received the full cooperation she'd been hoping for from the owner of the house. Seeing Jake and Ffion in the hallway, she came over to them.

'Good, you're both here,' said Bridget. 'Has PC Herrington filled you in on the situation?'

'We know the basics, ma'am,' said Jake, hoping Bridget wouldn't notice how badly he was blushing.

'Good. Ffion, I'd like you to come with me back to Kidlington. We need to interview Dr Frost, the man who's been arrested on suspicion of murder. Did you get the guest list?' she asked Brittany.

'I have it right here,' said Brittany, holding up a couple of sheets of paper.

'Excellent. I'd like you to go through it with Detective Sergeant Derwent.'

'Um…' said Jake, ineffectually.

'I'd be delighted to,' said Brittany.

'Jake, you can stay at the house and start interviewing the guests,' said Bridget. She paused, clearly noting the atmosphere that hung in the hallway like a black cloud. She looked between Jake, Ffion, Brittany and the bemused PC Herrington, then back at Jake. 'Is everything all right?'

'Yes, ma'am. No problem,' he said, knowing he'd have a lot of explaining to do later.

'Good.'

'Come with me, Jake,' said Brittany, taking him by the arm and steering him towards the office, seeming to go deliberately out of her way to attach herself to him.

Bridget gave him an inscrutable look before making her way towards the exit.

The look on Ffion's face as she turned to follow the boss was much easier for him to decode. Even PC Herrington seemed to pick up on it.

Women, thought Jake. Why did they always have to make life so complicated?

CHAPTER 4

On the drive back to Kidlington, Bridget found Ffion to be even less communicative than usual. She quickly abandoned her initial attempts at small talk and moved instead to discussing what she'd found out about the case so far.

'The man we're going to interview, the one who woke up with the dead girl beside him, is an academic called Dr Nathan Frost. He's from Wadham College.'

'Yes,' said Ffion brusquely. 'Got all that already.'

'See if you can look him up. I want us to have some idea of who we're dealing with.'

'Okay.' Ffion's phone was quickly in her hands and she started tapping on the virtual keyboard with her thumbs at great speed. Bridget was reminded of how Chloe always complained at the slowness with which Bridget typed messages using only her index finger.

'Found him,' said Ffion. 'Dr Nathan Frost of the Faculty of Medieval and Modern Languages. Teaches German literature. He's a specialist in the eighteenth-century *Sturm und Drang* movement, meaning storm and stress. It was a Romantic movement in German literature, art and music, characterised by extremes of emotion, and was a reaction against the rationalism of the Enlightenment. Examples in literature include *The Sorrows of Young Werther* by Johann Wolfgang von Goethe, a novella of hopeless love and suicide, and his epic poem *Faust*.'

'Hopeless love and suicide? That doesn't sound encouraging. And wasn't Faust the man who sold his soul to the devil?'

'That's the one,' said Ffion.

This kind of background information was always useful before going into an interview with a suspect. It could sometimes explain how their mind worked, particularly in the case of academics, who tended to be wrapped up in their disciplines. From what Ffion had just unearthed, it sounded like Frost might not be the most well-balanced of individuals.

On arrival at Kidlington, the duty sergeant on the desk informed them that Frost was waiting in interview room number two.

'Just give me fifteen minutes,' Bridget told Ffion.

She went to her desk and looked up the website of the MP who had been at the party but had left before the police had a chance to interview him. Hugh Avery-Blanchard, the Conservative Member of Parliament for Witney, had held on to the safe Tory seat at the last election, and was from a long-established local family. His name was not much in the public eye, although that would change overnight if the newspapers found out he had attended a masked party at which a young woman had been murdered.

Mr Avery-Blanchard's website displayed a photograph of a large man with ruddy cheeks, dressed in a tweed jacket and cotton twill shirt. He was beaming at the camera in a rather self-satisfied manner, as if he had just bagged a pheasant with his shotgun. Bridget dialled his constituency office number and was answered almost immediately by a rather officious and prim-sounding woman.

'Mr Avery-Blanchard's constituency office. How may I be of assistance?'

'This is Detective Inspector Hart of Thames Valley Police. Would it be possible to speak to Mr Avery-Blanchard?'

There was a long pause before Bridget received a response.

'Mr Avery-Blanchard sees constituents between the hours of four and five on Fridays, and on alternate Saturdays between ten and eleven. Would you like to make an appointment?'

Bridget had a vision of a dragon of a woman in twinset and pearls who guarded her employer's diary like the crown jewels.

'I'm not a constituent,' she explained, although she strongly suspected that the phone dragon already realised that. 'I'm a police officer and I need to speak to Mr Avery-Blanchard on an urgent matter.'

'May I ask what this is about?'

'It's confidential.'

'I see,' said the dragon, in a tone that suggested Bridget had gone out of her way to be unreasonable. 'In that case, I will speak to Mr Avery-Blanchard myself and ask him to call you back. What is your number?'

Bridget decided that this was probably the most cooperation she was likely to get. After stressing once again the urgent nature of her call, she left her number, and then hurried over to the vending machine. There, she eyed the available choice with trepidation, and selected what she thought were the least worst options – a packet of salt and vinegar crisps, a cheese sandwich and a diet Coke. She was starving after her early morning swim and regretted not having taken five minutes to finish her healthy breakfast at the leisure centre. So much for exercising and losing a few pounds. Any weight she had lost by going swimming would probably be put back on with this hastily-taken snack. The chances of squeezing herself into that dress this evening were diminishing rapidly.

She ripped open the bag of crisps at her desk and was just stuffing a handful into her mouth when Detective Chief Superintendent Grayson walked in. She almost didn't recognise him, as he was wearing a diamond-patterned golfing jumper in pastel shades and a pair of beige slacks. By the look of it, he had just been summoned from the golf course.

He strode over to her desk and stood watching her as she munched the crisps. 'Bloody nuisance, all this happening on a Saturday morning,' he grumbled. 'I was winning too. So, what have you discovered so far?'

Grayson was clearly not in a good mood. Although, Bridget reflected, he almost never was. She swallowed the crisps and took a quick swig of diet Coke to wash them down before speaking.

'The victim's name is Gina Hartman, a student at Wadham College, although we still need to get next of kin to do a formal ID. She was found in a bedroom at a house belonging to Nick Damon, a local builder. There'd been a party there the night before – a masked ball – and Gina was working as a waitress.'

'I've heard of Damon,' said Grayson. 'He's a member of my club, although I've never actually seen him play golf. He's not your average builder, more of a property tycoon. He has building contracts with colleges and the university. Knows all the right people. Schmoozes with the local bigwigs. I expect there were a lot of important people at this party.'

'Well, maybe, but actually it all sounds a bit sleazy, sir. There were professional escorts present, apparently.'

Grayson tapped his nose. 'It doesn't surprise me. These people get up to all kinds of things behind closed doors. I expect that the masks are a way of concealing people's identities.'

Bridget wondered if Grayson ever got invited to these sorts of parties, since he seemed to know so much about them. But it was hard to picture, and she thought it better not to ask.

'Mr Damon's PA is providing us with a guest list. My team's at the house now, interviewing the guests, but the MP for Witney had already left before we arrived.'

'Hugh Avery-Blanchard?' said Grayson, knotting his eyebrows.

'It would seem so.'

'This could make things tricky. Avery-Blanchard won't want his name dragged through the mud. Neither will any of the other guests, for that matter. Make sure you keep details like that out of the press. I'm sure I don't need to remind you what happened when the press got wind of the Christ Church murder back in the summer.'

'No, I haven't forgotten that, sir,' said Bridget, wincing at the memory, although it hadn't been her or her team's fault that the media had got hold of the story. In a college environment it was almost impossible to keep a story like that under wraps, and she expected the same would be true this time too.

'What about this fellow you've got in for questioning?' asked Grayson. 'An academic, I hear. What's his connection to Damon?'

'I don't know,' conceded Bridget. 'At the moment I can't see what a lecturer in German literature would be doing at a party like this. On the face of it, he doesn't fit the profile of guests you've described, if the purpose of these parties is networking, although how much networking you can do in a mask is questionable.'

'Hmm,' murmured Grayson. He looked at his watch, presumably keen to get back to the golf course. 'Well, I won't keep you any longer, DI Hart. As always, keep me informed. And proceed with caution.'

'I will, sir.'

Grayson was already striding towards the door.

She checked the time on her phone. Her fifteen minutes were up and she hadn't even finished the packet of crisps, let alone started on the sandwich. Ffion was waiting for her, Welsh dragon mug in hand, the steam rising off one of her herbal teas. With a sigh, Bridget stuffed the remains of her lunch into a drawer in her desk, and took one last swig of the Coke. It was time to get started.

*

Dr Nathan Frost was sitting at the table in the interview room, his head cradled in his hands. A dishevelled man in his mid- to late fifties, he wore his grey hair long, the ends curling over the collar of his dinner jacket. His black bow tie hung loose around his neck and his white dress shirt was crumpled, with a wine stain by the third button. He looked up miserably as Bridget entered. His eyes were puffy, presumably after too much alcohol the night before, and his skin had a yellow tinge, not made any better by the fluorescent lighting in the interview room. Someone had brought him a cup of tea in a disposable plastic cup, but it was only half drunk. Bridget asked the officer guarding Frost to take it away.

'Dr Frost, I'm Detective Inspector Bridget Hart, and this is my colleague Detective Constable Ffion Hughes.'

Frost barely acknowledged them as they took their seats opposite him. He looked utterly dejected, and Bridget wondered whether with a little encouragement he might be ready to confess. She decided to move swiftly on with the interview, and once the preliminaries were out of the way and she'd established that he had no wish for a solicitor to be present, she asked him how he came to be at the party.

'That's a very good question, Inspector, and one which I have given considerable thought to myself.'

He was clearly a highly intelligent and articulate man, and Bridget waited for him to go on.

'While I've been sitting here,' continued Frost, 'I've been going through the circumstances which led to me being there. You see, I believed it was the result of a chance encounter, but now I have my doubts.'

'Go on.'

Frost explained how he'd literally bumped into Nick Damon at the Bear Inn in Oxford over Sunday lunch, how

Damon had caused him to spill part of his drink and had then insisted on buying him another one.

'He was unusually charming and charismatic,' said Frost. 'I couldn't help being drawn to him. I live a rather sheltered life, mostly in the confines of my college. I'm not married and I really only speak to academics and students. To enter into a conversation with a stranger in a pub is something that rarely happens to me. And he was astonishingly entertaining and well-versed in all kinds of topics. I'm ashamed to admit that it had never really occurred to me before that a man in the building trade might have so much to say that was worth listening to.'

The academic was now sitting up straighter, lips pursed, and looking Bridget in the eye. 'I must say that I was greatly impressed by him. He exercised a powerful magnetism. You might say that he cast a kind of spell over me.'

'So you'd never met Nick Damon before you encountered him in the pub one week ago, and on the back of this chance meeting he invited you to his party?' Bridget asked. It sounded somewhat far-fetched, but she was prepared to hear Frost out for the time being. Interviewing suspects was usually like trying to extract blood from a stone, and she was glad that he was at least speaking freely. In fact, he seemed unusually eager to put forward his theories.

'Yes, at least that's what I thought initially. Yet even then it occurred to me that this might not be a random meeting. In fact, the idea struck me quite forcibly that I was making a Faustian pact with the devil, and at the time I admit that I was rather excited by the idea.'

'I'm sorry,' said Bridget. 'A Faustian pact? Whatever do you mean?'

'Well, perhaps not literally,' said Frost. 'It's a literary metaphor, but one that struck me as rather apt. You see, in Goethe's *Faust*, the demon Mephistopheles appears to Doctor Faust in the guise of a human, and offers him the chance to experience the thrill of real life. As a disillusioned scholar, Faust seizes on the opportunity, but of course there's a heavy price to be paid. And just like Faust, I've spent so much of my time buried in books, I often feel that life has passed me by. The bargain seemed to me an attractive one.'

'I see,' said Bridget, beginning to doubt the reliability of the witness sitting opposite. 'So you believed that Mr Damon invited you to the party in order to experience the "thrill of real life" and that in return you would be obliged to pay some price.'

'Exactly,' said Frost. 'It seemed extraordinary, but that's exactly how it appeared to me.'

'And what kind of payment do you think might have been demanded?' asked Bridget, choosing to humour him, in the hope of getting to something more tangible.

'Well, Mr Damon – Nick, as he asked me to call him – confided in me that he was the owner of a building company. I interpreted that as a signal of what he was asking from me. You see, the college is about to put a major building project out to tender, and I assumed that Mr Damon was trying to buy my vote as a member of the college's governing body. I'm not a worldly man, as I've already explained, but I assume that this kind of thing happens.'

'Did Mr Damon make your vote a condition of you attending the party?'

'Not at all, he wasn't that crass. No kind of payment was discussed. He didn't even mention the college's building project. But you can see how his generosity might have influenced me, perhaps even unconsciously.'

'And you were fully prepared to cast your vote in favour of Mr Damon's company?'

'It really makes no difference to me which building contractor is awarded the work. I would have been more than happy to lend him my support in return for an invitation into his world.'

Bridget leaned back in her chair, wondering what to make of the academic and his bizarre theory. He seemed perfectly sincere in his belief. She glanced at Ffion, who shrugged. 'Don't you think this is all a little far-fetched?' she asked Dr Frost.

At this, Frost leaned forward and lowered his voice. 'Not as far-fetched as what I now believe to be true.'

Bridget raised an eyebrow. 'Which is?'

'In the light of what happened, I now believe that he invited me to the party in order to pin the murder on me. He needed a scapegoat, and I walked straight into his trap. I've been a gullible fool, taken in by an obvious deception. Just like Faust, I paid a high price for my foolishness. All I wanted was a bit of harmless fun and it's ended in tragedy, not least for that poor girl.'

'So now you're suggesting that Nick Damon murdered Gina Hartman?'

'I didn't say that precisely,' said Frost. 'I don't have any proof. But it's my belief that the murder was premeditated, and that he at least facilitated the crime, even if he didn't get his hands dirty himself. He's too clever for that.'

'Hmm,' said Bridget. Although she had no liking for Mr Nick Damon, and didn't trust either him or his shady lawyer, Mr Gold, Dr Nathan Frost wasn't doing himself any favours with his elaborate and unlikely theories. A jury would most likely interpret them as the ramblings of a mind that perceived the world through the distorting prism of literary ideas. She was keen to steer the interview away from literature and theory and into the concrete world of fact.

'Let's backtrack a little shall we? You've explained how you came to be at the party, but what about the woman who died? Gina Hartman. Did you know her? She was a student at your college, I believe.'

Frost's face crumpled in remorse. 'That poor, poor girl. I didn't know her exactly, I mean I'd never spoken to her before last night, but yes, I did know who she was. I'd seen her around the college...' His voice trailed off. 'You could hardly miss her,' he added almost under his breath.

Bridget recalled the strong impression she'd had when

viewing Gina's corpse of great beauty even in death. That glorious red hair, the angelic features of her face. It was understandable that a bachelor like Frost might have formed some kind of fixation on the girl, and perhaps even followed her to the party. Perhaps all this story about Damon inviting him was a ruse, or even a fantasy. It had the feel of a fiction he had created in order to justify his actions.

'So you spoke to her last night?'

'Did I say that?' he asked.

'You just said you'd never spoken to her before last night, which rather implies you had a conversation with her at the party.'

'Ah, well, that would be stretching things a bit far. It wasn't a conversation as such. I didn't say anything to her myself.'

'But she spoke to you?'

'She warned me to leave the party. I had no idea that she even recognised me at first, but then she came up to me and told me to go. But like a fool, I stayed.'

Bridget frowned, unsure whether she could believe a word Frost said. 'What did she say to you exactly?'

He screwed up his forehead in concentration. 'I think she said, *You don't belong here. You should leave.*'

'Why would she warn you to leave?'

He spread his hands in a gesture of hopelessness. 'I honestly don't know. Perhaps she had an inkling of what was about to happen. But if that was the case, she ought to have been the one to leave.'

'Did she say anything else?'

'No, I never saw her again. Not until...' He bowed his head in misery.

Bridget gave him a minute to recover his poise. 'You were found in bed with the victim the morning after the party.'

'No, that's not what happened. I woke up and found her in bed with me. Then I raised the alarm.'

'Can you tell me how you ended up in bed with her in

the first place?'

'I'm sorry, but I've absolutely no idea.'

'You don't know?'

'I don't remember.'

Bridget gave him a hard stare. 'Forgive me, Dr Frost, but that sounds rather too convenient. I find it hard to believe that you don't remember getting into bed with such an attractive young woman. Did you have sex with her?'

Frost winced at the directness of her question and averted his gaze. 'I wish I could answer that for you, Inspector. I wish I knew. I've asked myself the same question over and over.'

'Would you have liked to have sex with her?'

He rubbed his eyes with the index finger and thumb of his right hand. 'It would be foolish to deny it. Gina was the woman of my dreams, but I would never have forced myself on her, if that's what you're implying. I just wish I could remember what happened, DI Hart, I really do.'

Bridget wasn't willing to let the matter rest there. She'd been hoping for a confession, or at least to arrive at a clear understanding of events, but all she'd received was obfuscation. 'Do you have an explanation for this curious lapse in memory? Have you experienced memory loss before?'

'No. Never.'

'How much did you have to drink?'

Frost looked rueful. 'The champagne was flowing at the party and I may have had a few glasses, perhaps more than I would normally do, but that really doesn't explain my total amnesia. The only explanation I can offer you is that I was drugged. Yes, that has to be what happened.' Frost was clearly warming to this latest theory. 'Someone must have given me some kind of sleeping potion. Just like in Faust.'

Bridget was rapidly losing patience with this man. 'A sleeping potion,' she repeated, making no attempt to hide the scepticism in her voice.

'Yes, yes, or whatever the modern-day equivalent is,'

said Frost hurriedly. 'There are such drugs available, aren't there? I'd be happy to submit to a blood or urine test to prove that I'm right.'

'All right,' said Bridget. 'We'll arrange for a test. We'll also be taking your fingerprints and a DNA sample. But I have to say that unless some new evidence turns up, we'll be charging you with murder.'

CHAPTER 5

Jake wished he could have gone back to Kidlington with Bridget to interview the prime suspect rather than having to stay in the house and deal with his ex-girlfriend. That look that Ffion had given him as she left! He knew that however bad he might feel now, he would be feeling even worse once Ffion had given him a piece of her mind. It would be a large piece, no doubt, with sharp edges.

While the rest of the team began taking statements and DNA samples from the party guests who had stayed overnight, Brittany invited him into her office on the ground floor. The pleasant wood-panelled room overlooked a rose garden at the back of the house. Jake immediately noticed Brittany's own personal touches: a row of house plants in brightly painted pots on the windowsill, a collection of silk scarves hanging on a coat stand, and a lingering smell of the perfume she always wore. The slightly heady scent evoked a sudden memory of the two of them when they'd been a couple. Jake had been besotted with her. But the scent also brought painful memories of her betrayal. She'd cheated on him and left him devastated. He tried to block the thoughts from his mind and concentrate on the task in hand. He was here in a professional capacity as part of a murder investigation. There was nothing between him and Brittany anymore. Besides, he was very happy with Ffion.

'Would you like a coffee?' asked Brittany, switching on a high-tech coffee machine in the corner of the room.

'Um...' Jake was wary of accepting too much hospitality from his ex-girlfriend, and afraid of sending her any unintended messages that might encourage her to flirt with him even more than she was already. But a shot of caffeine would help him focus. 'Yes, please,' he said.

She smiled at him indulgently. 'White with two sugars?'

She clearly hadn't forgotten the way he liked it. 'Please,' he said, keeping his voice neutral.

While Brittany busied herself with the machine, Jake took in more details of the office. A state-of-the-art Apple Mac displaying a dolphin screensaver stood on a mahogany desk. Behind it, files were neatly arranged on a bookcase. Brittany had always been efficient and organised. He was willing to bet she made a top-class PA.

He ought to have realised that Nick Damon was her boss as soon as he heard the name. He'd known that she worked for the owner of a construction company, and she'd often spoken about the big house in Oxfordshire, and about the corporate entertainment she organised as part of her job, but he'd tried to blot the details from his mind. The last thing he'd wanted in the days and weeks following the break-up was to dwell on what had happened, and how easily he'd been fooled. Brittany had loved her job, and the long, unsociable hours had enabled her to have an affair with some guy at work. Seeing her in her professional environment first-hand, it all started to make a lot more sense to him now. He began to wonder who the other guy was, and whether they were still together. She'd never even told him his name. He'd never asked.

'Here you are,' she said, passing him the coffee. 'Just how you like it.'

She stood very close to him as she handed him the cup. Too close for a professional encounter between a witness and an investigating police officer. Her hand brushed against his for a fraction of a second and she gave him one of her warm smiles as she looked into his eyes. Jake could feel the tips of his ears starting to tingle again. He jerked his hand away, spilling a few drops of coffee into the saucer.

'We'd better make a start,' he said. 'Shall we sit down?'

'It's comfortable over here,' said Brittany, indicating two tub chairs in brown suede, angled close together by the window.

Jake would have preferred to interview her across the desk, to put a bit of distance between them – not to mention a solid barrier – but she was already taking her coffee over to the comfy chairs and sitting down. He took the other chair and placed his coffee on a low table. Brittany crossed one leg over the other, causing her short skirt to ride up her thigh.

Jake averted his gaze, turning his head to look out of the window. Outside, beyond the rose garden, a man was opening the bonnet of a black Mercedes S-Class. He was tall, with a muscular build and closely-cropped hair. He leaned inside the car as if preparing to tune the engine.

'It's really lovely to see you again,' said Brittany. 'You know, I'm so sorry about what happened between us. I never meant to hurt you, Jake. I often think about you and wonder what you're doing.'

'I'm just doing my job,' he said. 'Now, if we could make a start –'

'You look very well,' continued Brittany. 'Does that mean there's someone special in your life right now? What about that attractive young police woman you arrived with?' She leaned over and tapped him playfully on the arm.

'DC Ffion Hughes?' said Jake, shifting in his seat. 'She's… a colleague.'

He was definitely not going to go into details about his

relationship with Ffion. 'Now, I really do have to ask you some questions about last night.'

'Sure,' said Brittany. 'Fire away, DS Derwent.'

Jake wished she would take this more seriously. After all, a young woman had died at a party which Brittany had helped organise. But Brittany had always had a warm and bubbly personality. It was one of her most endearing features. The trouble was, she'd been warm and bubbly with another man behind his back.

'Let's start with the victim,' he said, taking out his notebook and pen and turning to a clean page. 'Who was she, and how did she come to be working here?'

Brittany sobered up at the mention of the dead girl and for a moment her eyes welled with tears. She pulled a tissue from a pink box on the table, dabbed her eyes, blew her nose daintily and took a deep breath, recovering her composure.

'Gina Hartman. I hired her myself. Gina and the other two girls, Miranda Gardiner and Poppy Radley, were students from Wadham College. They answered an advertisement on Instagram for waitresses to work at a private party. It's the sort of casual work that students like. Cash in hand, you know.'

'Had they worked for you before?'

'A few times.'

'And what did their job involve exactly?'

'Just serving drinks and canapés.'

'Is that all?'

'Sure. What are you getting at?'

'I'm just trying to establish the full extent of their duties, given that Gina was found in bed with one of the guests.'

Brittany gave a little laugh at his suggestion. 'The students weren't expected to entertain the guests in that kind of way. We hired professionals to do that.'

'What?' said Jake, his ears growing hot again. 'You mean prostitutes?'

'You make it sound so salacious when you put it like

that,' said Brittany, chiding him with another gentle tap on the arm. 'It was nothing like that. These women – and men, I might add – are highly intelligent professional escorts who can hold conversations with clients on just about any topic from politics to business to culture.'

'Really,' said Jake sceptically. Brittany had never discussed any details of the "corporate hospitality" events she had organised. Now he was beginning to understand why. As far as he was concerned, these escorts were really just posh sex workers, but he decided to leave that for now.

'What time did the three waitresses arrive last night?'

'Miranda and Poppy arrived first, at about seven o'clock, to help get things ready. Gina got here later, perhaps about nine.'

'They didn't all travel together then? Even though they were coming from the same college?'

Brittany shrugged. 'I don't know why they didn't arrive together. Perhaps Gina had a late tutorial, or something. Miranda and Poppy both left together as well.'

'At what time?'

'I think it was around one o'clock in the morning.'

'And how did they get here? Did they have their own transport? This place is pretty out of the way if you're coming from central Oxford.'

'Tyler gave them a lift here and back.'

'Tyler?'

Now it was Brittany's turn to blush. 'Nick's driver and general handyman,' she said, pointing out of the window at the guy who was tinkering with the engine of the Mercedes. Despite the autumnal air he'd stripped down to a tight-fitting black T-shirt, and even at this distance Jake could see that his arms were heavily decorated with tattoos.

Jake frowned, an unwelcome thought occurring to him. As he watched, Tyler straightened up, stretched his torso and glanced towards the window. He looked fit and muscular, but he was too far away for Jake to make out the expression on his face.

'Was Tyler here throughout the party?' he asked.

'Yes, he was on the door making sure that all the guests gave the right password.'

'Password?'

'For security,' explained Brittany. 'Tyler's also in charge of security for Nick.'

'And what about the guests?' asked Jake. 'What time did they arrive?'

'Any time from eight thirty onwards. I think the last guest arrived at about ten. I wasn't watching the clock so I can't tell you precisely.'

'And how many people stayed overnight?'

'Most of them,' said Brittany. 'About thirty. Like you say, we're a little out of the way here. No one wants to drink and drive these days.'

'Did you stay overnight too?' asked Jake.

For the second time in their conversation Brittany looked a little uncomfortable. She twisted in her seat and smoothed out a wrinkle in her skirt with her fingers. 'Well, I live here now, Jake.'

'You live in the house?' Jake stared at her open-mouthed. Was Brittany saying that she lived with Nick Damon? Was he the man she'd had an affair with?

'No,' she said hurriedly. 'I live in the grounds. After you and I split up I had nowhere to go. Nick's a very generous employer. He provides accommodation for me on-site.'

Jake remembered the gatehouse he'd driven past on the way in. 'You live in the cottage by the gate?'

'Yes.' The one-word answer was clipped and short.

'And did you go back there last night?'

'Not until gone one o'clock, after the last guest had either left or retired upstairs.'

There was something Brittany wasn't telling him about the cottage. He regarded her suspiciously, but she averted her gaze. There was an obvious question he ought to be asking her about her living arrangements, but he didn't want to know the answer. Instead, he decided to try another line of questioning.

'What exactly was your role during the party?'

'Well, I made all the arrangements for catering, sending invitations, hiring staff. I was on the door greeting the guests as they arrived and dealing with any issues that came up.'

'Did any issues come up?'

'No.'

'Did you notice anything unusual about any of the guests?'

She shook her head. 'No, I don't think so.'

'What were Mr Damon's movements during the evening?'

'Nick was chatting with his guests. He always makes sure he talks to everyone, but he's good at stepping back and giving people privacy too. He's a great host.'

'I see. What time did he go to bed?'

'He went upstairs at the same time I left for the night.'

'What about Dr Frost? Did you have anything to do with him during the evening? Did you notice who he was talking to, for example?'

'It's not easy when everyone is wearing a mask,' said Brittany. 'That's really the whole point. All I can tell you is that he gave the name "Faust" as his alias.'

'His alias?'

'Everyone adopts a new identity for the evening. It's Nick's idea. He says it liberates people and let's them open up and enjoy themselves.'

'I see. So why was Dr Frost invited to the party?'

'I don't know. Nick gives me a list of names and I send out the invitations.'

'Do you have that guest list for me?'

'Sure, it's right here.'

She got up and walked over to the desk, leaning across it so that her pert bottom was pointed in Jake's direction. He looked down and studied his notes.

'Here you go.' She handed him the sheet of paper with a smile. 'Is there anything else I can do for you?'

'Yeah. Could you show me around the outside of the property? I'd like to check if there are any ways someone might have gained entry, other than as an invited guest.'

'Of course,' said Brittany, beaming at him. 'I'd be delighted. Follow me.'

Jake tried to keep a professional distance from her as they strolled around the outside of the house, but Brittany had a habit of constantly brushing up against him. He hoped none of the other detectives, who were inside taking statements from the guests, would notice. He inspected the many windows and doors of the house, rattling a few to see if they could be opened, but they all seemed reasonably secure. There were no signs of a forced entry.

'Do you have a burglar alarm fitted?'

'Of course,' said Brittany.

They rounded the corner of the house where a line of expensive-looking cars was parked along the gravel drive, and bumped into the guy who had been working on the Mercedes. Tyler. He closed the bonnet of the car as Jake and Brittany approached, and wiped oil off his fingers with a rag. The man seemed to radiate an air of aggression and barely-restrained hostility.

He moved towards Brittany and slid an arm around her waist. 'Hey, sweetheart, everything okay? The police not bothering you, are they?'

Jake experienced a feeling like a sharp blow to the gut. Tyler must be the guy Brittany had left him for, the man she had met at work. Even though he'd had his suspicions, he was caught off guard by the strength and suddenness of his emotional reaction. He had to restrain himself from giving Tyler a punch in the face.

Brittany seemed embarrassed by her boyfriend's behaviour. 'Hey,' she said, pulling away from him. 'You'll get oil on my coat.'

Tyler grimaced and shot a look of dislike in Jake's direction.

Jake narrowed his eyes, wondering if Tyler knew that he was Brittany's former boyfriend. But of course he did. The aggressive way that Tyler was regarding him, the way he had tried to demonstrate his possession of her, were all calculated to stake his claim to her.

Jake had to remind himself that he and Brittany were no longer a couple, and that she had chosen Tyler over him. Though why she had made that choice wasn't the least bit clear to him. Tyler was a good-looking guy, with a ripped torso and movie-star features, if you liked the bad-boy look. But he was clearly a thug. Jake had dealt with guys like Tyler before, and knew the type well. He couldn't help wondering if he had ever tried to hit Brittany. If he had...

Brittany had moved a couple of feet away from her new boyfriend, positioning herself between the two men. 'Tyler, this is Detective Sergeant Derwent. He's helping to investigate last night's murder.'

Tyler grunted something in response.

'Jake, do you have any questions for Tyler?' enquired Brittany.

Plenty, thought Jake. And for Brittany, too. But he would confine his queries to a professional nature.

'I understand from Miss Grainger,' he said, 'that you're Mr Damon's driver, and that you also deal with security matters.'

'Yeah,' agreed Tyler, his tone surly and unhelpful.

'You drove the waitresses here last night, and took two of them back to their college again.'

'Yeah.' Tyler managed to inject a surprising amount of aggression into the monosyllable.

'Can you tell me why they didn't all travel together?' asked Jake. 'And why you didn't take Gina back to college?'

Tyler thrust his dirty hands into the pockets of his old jeans. 'I just do what I'm told round here. All right?'

'Was there a reason you picked up Gina separately?' persisted Jake.

'Not that I know of.'

'And didn't you wonder why she wasn't returning to Oxford at the end of the night?'

'No.'

'Did you ask her why she was staying behind?'

'I didn't see her.'

Tyler jutted his chin in Jake's direction as if challenging him to think of a question that might elucidate some useful information.

'Just one final question for now, Mr...'

'Dixon. It's Tyler Dixon.'

'Mr Dixon, where did you go after you'd dropped the other two waitresses back in Oxford?'

'I came back here.'

'And then what?'

'I stayed the night.' Tyler sneered. 'Where else did you think I might go? I live here, don't I?'

'Where, precisely?' asked Jake, although he was certain he knew the answer already.

'In the gatehouse. With Brittany.'

CHAPTER 6

With Frost back in the cells for the time being, Bridget decided that her next move should be to speak to Gina's friends in college. Jake and the other detectives were still at the house, so she would have to take Ffion with her. The young DC had sounded all right on the phone first thing, but was definitely in a strange mood now. Bridget wondered if something had happened between her and Jake. But as long as Ffion continued to behave professionally, Bridget didn't feel it was her place to poke her nose in. She took five minutes to finish the crisps and cheese sandwich that she'd hidden in her desk drawer, and then they set off for central Oxford.

Occupying a relatively quiet spot on Parks Road next door to the King's Arms, Wadham wasn't a college that attracted much attention to itself, although Bridget recalled that a few years previously, two skeletons had been unearthed by workmen digging near a gate leading into the Back Quad. Despite a sensational headline that had appeared in a student newspaper about a "bullet-ridden body", the discovery had turned out to be one for the archaeologists rather than the police. The skeletons were believed to date from the medieval period. It was a reminder of Oxford's long and complicated history. But it also demonstrated to Bridget that sometimes justice could never be obtained for the victim, which was a depressing thought.

Bridget had phoned ahead before leaving Kidlington, and made an appointment to speak to the warden of the college, Lord Bancroft, a Queen's Counsel and now a life peer in the House of Lords. A quick search on Wikipedia informed her that Lord Bancroft, CBE, QC, had led a distinguished career as a defence barrister before taking over the wardenship of Wadham.

She and Ffion signed in at the porters' lodge where the staff were sorting through the day's mail deliveries. Undergraduates were coming and going, checking their pigeon holes, congregating by the noticeboard and making plans for the evening, as yet blissfully unaware that one of their fellow students had been murdered.

It was the start of a new academic year and there was a palpable excitement in the air. Bridget remembered all too well her first few weeks at Merton College twenty years earlier – the thrill of being immersed in a world of centuries of learning, surrounded by dreaming spires and secluded quadrangles and cloisters, combined with the whirlwind of new friendships and social gatherings fuelled by copious alcohol consumption.

When news of Gina Hartman's death got out it would shatter the Oxford dream for her friends and fellow students, leaving a scar that might never fully heal.

The porter accompanied Bridget and Ffion to the Warden's Lodgings where they were met at the door by the housekeeper, a middle-aged woman who introduced herself as Mrs Watkins.

'The Warden's waiting for you just through here,' said Mrs Watkins, leading them through to a room lined with bookshelves, overlooking a well-tended garden. The room had the musty, comforting smell of age. Against the wall, an antique grandfather clock ticked slowly, beating out the steady march of time in much the same way as it had done for centuries.

Lord Bancroft rose from his desk and came forward to greet them. Bridget estimated the warden to be in his early seventies. His face was round, and his hair white. Tall, upright, and broad-shouldered, he leaned forward to shake Bridget's hand.

'DI Hart, DC Hughes, please take a seat.'

He indicated a leather sofa and chairs arranged around a low table strewn with copies of *The Times*, *The Telegraph* and *The Economist*. 'Can I offer you a cup of tea or coffee?'

'We're fine, thanks,' said Bridget as she and Ffion sat down on the sofa.

Lord Bancroft took the armchair opposite. 'So, how can I help you? You mentioned on the phone that this was a matter involving one of the college's students. I do hope they are not in some kind of trouble?'

He spoke with a deep, confident voice, well-versed in public speaking. His pace was measured, his words carefully chosen.

Bridget had dealt with a few college heads in her time as a detective inspector – the Dean of Christ Church sprang to mind, as did the Warden of Merton College who she had encountered more recently – but she had found none of them to be as immediately likeable as Lord Bancroft who seemed genuinely concerned about the welfare of his students and keen to help. She detected none of the arrogance or self-interest she had noted in the other heads of college she had encountered. Instead he exuded a quiet dignity.

'I'm very sorry to have to inform you,' she said, 'that one of your undergraduates was found dead this morning at a house in West Oxfordshire. Her name was Gina Hartman.'

'Good God,' said Bancroft. 'Do you have any idea what happened?'

'The details are unclear at this time,' said Bridget, 'but we are treating it as a murder.'

'How absolutely dreadful,' said Bancroft with obvious dismay. 'The poor girl. What can you tell me at this stage?'

'Well,' said Bridget, 'I can tell you that Miss Hartman was employed by the owner of the house as a waitress at a private party. Two of her friends were also working at the party.'

'Were her friends also students at the college? Has anything happened to them?'

'Yes, Miranda Gardiner and Poppy Radley are both students here but we have no reason to believe they've come to any harm. I would like to speak to them, if you don't mind.'

'Of course, of course.' Lord Bancroft leaned his large head in one hand. He seemed to be considering his next words carefully. 'This is all very tragic, and will need careful handling. The students will require counselling to come to terms with something like this. If at all possible, I would like to keep this out of the media until I've had a chance to make a formal announcement to students and staff myself.'

'I think that would be the right course of action,' agreed Bridget.

Lord Bancroft's concern for his students' wellbeing rather than the college's reputation was making Bridget like this man more and more. Which only made it harder for her to break the next piece of news to him.

'There's something else you should know. We're currently talking to a suspect with regard to Miss Hartman's murder. I'm afraid to tell you that he's one of your tutors, Dr Nathan Frost.'

'Frost?' Bancroft appeared shocked to the core by this latest news. He gripped the armrests of his chair tightly. 'Was Dr Frost present at this party too?'

'Yes, he was.'

'I must say I find that mystifying. As far as I am aware, Dr Frost has no social life outside the college. He's a virtual recluse, wedded to German literature. What on earth was he doing there?'

'We're keeping an open mind about that for the moment,' said Bridget, recalling Frost's various conspiracy theories. 'I have to admit, it's something of a mystery.'

'Hmm,' said Bancroft. He stared into the fireplace for a moment or two, deep in thought. Then he collected himself and turned back to Bridget with a brisk, business-like manner, acquired, no doubt, from his years as a barrister. 'What about Miss Hartman's parents? Have they been informed yet?'

Bridget turned to Ffion. 'Any news on that?'

As always, Ffion had the facts at her fingertips. 'They live in Manchester and local officers have spoken to them this morning. They'll be bringing them to Oxford.'

'Please assure them that the college will provide accommodation in one of our guest suites,' said Bancroft. 'For as long as necessary, of course.'

Bridget smiled her thanks. 'Thank you. That's very kind.'

'It's the least we can offer under the circumstances. Now, what can I do for you next? Would you like to speak to Gina's two friends?'

'We would, and we'd also like to talk to anyone who knew Gina well.'

Bancroft nodded. 'Her tutor, perhaps. That would be Dr Ashley. I'll take you to him now.'

★

While Ffion went off in search of Gina's friends, Miranda and Poppy, Bridget accompanied the warden to Dr Ashley's room across the quadrangle.

Lord Bancroft rapped smartly on the door and waited until it was opened by a good-looking young man with floppy brown hair and blue eyes. He seemed to Bridget to be too young to be a tutor – in his late twenties perhaps, or early thirties at most. If she'd passed him in the quadrangle she would have taken him for a graduate student. But then, what did she know? According to Chloe, she was already well into middle-age and completely past it, whatever "it" was exactly.

Dr Ashley wore a casual shirt, open at the neck, teamed with a pair of slim-fitting dark jeans. When the warden explained the reason for their visit, his face paled and his mouth fell open.

He gestured weakly into the room. 'Please, come in.'

The warden took his leave and Bridget thanked him once again.

Dr Ashley removed a pile of books from a sofa which was probably where his students sat during their tutorials. 'Take a seat, and please excuse the mess. I was just in the middle of marking a pile of essays.' He sat down opposite her, leaning forward with his elbows on his knees. 'Gina dead. My God. I can't believe it. When did it happen?'

'Some time last night.'

'Do you have any idea who did it?'

'We're speaking to a suspect at the moment, but I can't say more than that.'

'Right, of course not. So, what can I do to help?'

The young tutor appeared devastated to hear about Gina's death, and only too keen to assist. Bridget was struck again by the caring community that seemed to exist at Wadham.

'Maybe you could start by telling me a bit about Gina,' she said. 'What was she like as a person?'

Dr Ashley sat back and gazed out of the window as if trying to picture his dead student. 'Gina was very bright, very likeable. Outgoing, but not in a pushy way, and she had lots of friends. She came from a relatively modest background, I believe. I remember she made a very strong impression at her interview and continued to perform well throughout her university career. She was due to take her Finals next summer, and I think she would almost certainly have got a first-class degree.' He shook his head and looked back at Bridget. His eyes were glistening. 'Such a tragic waste of a young life.'

'You teach Psychology, I understand,' enquired

Bridget.

Psychology, that's right.' Dr Ashley drew a handkerchief out of his pocket and blew his nose. He took a moment to recover his poise before continuing. 'The study of the mind and human behaviour. Of course, everyone's an armchair psychologist these days, but there's a lot more to the subject than just Freud's theories on sex. Gina was especially interested in human behaviour and social interactions between people. I think she would have liked to continue into post-graduate research, perhaps here or elsewhere.'

'What about a boyfriend?'

The tutor smiled weakly. 'Gina was a beautiful girl. I imagine that a lot of guys would have liked to be her boyfriend. But she never mentioned anyone in particular. Perhaps her friends would know more.'

'Were you aware that she and two of her friends had part-time jobs working as waitresses at private house parties?'

Dr Ashley nodded cautiously. 'Yes, she did mention something about that. I had my doubts about the suitability of such a job, but she assured me that she could take care of herself. In fact, she told me that she saw it as an opportunity.'

'An opportunity? For what?'

'Gina wrote articles for one of the student newspapers. I don't know how serious she was about it, but she wanted to apply the skills she was learning in her degree course to the real world of human behaviour in all its complex forms. I think she saw these parties as a chance to mix with some influential people. Perhaps she hoped to expose some of the dirty secrets behind their public personas.'

'Did she say how she was planning to do that?'

'No, but I imagine she could have used her phone to take photos or videos.'

Bridget thought of the politician who had been at the party but who had left early that morning and wondered if Gina had had him in her sights. 'Did she mention anyone in particular that she was hoping to expose?'

'No. I never asked.'

There was one more question Bridget wanted to ask. 'Can you tell me anything about Dr Nathan Frost?'

Dr Ashley looked bewildered. 'Who? The German lecturer?'

'Yes.'

'I hardly know him. He keeps himself to himself.'

'Did he have any kind of relationship with Gina?'

'Dr Frost and Gina? Well, not to my knowledge.'

'Okay, thank you,' said Bridget, rising to her feet. She gave him her card. 'If you think of anything else that might be relevant, please get in touch.'

'I will,' said Dr Ashley. He opened the door for her. 'Good luck, Inspector. Please catch whoever did this. Gina was a good student and a lovely individual. She didn't deserve to die like this.'

*

Ffion received no answer when she knocked on Poppy Radley's door, and instead made her way in the direction of Miranda Gardiner's room, following the directions that the porter had given her. She was glad that Bridget had decided to interview Gina Hartman's tutor herself, leaving her to track down and talk to Gina's two friends. She could use some time on her own to think over what had happened this morning.

Although Jake had sometimes mentioned the girlfriend he'd known since his university days and who was the reason he'd come to live and work in Oxford in the first place, he had never shown any desire to talk about her, and Ffion hadn't been keen to press him for details. All he'd told her was that very soon after he came to live in Oxford, he discovered that she was cheating on him, and they'd split up. That had been months before Ffion had even met him, and she'd never expected to hear anything about this ex-girlfriend again, let alone come face to face with her.

And on a murder investigation too.

Arriving at the house this morning and discovering that her new boyfriend's ex-girlfriend was Mr Damon's personal assistant had given her quite a shock. To be fair, Jake had seemed taken aback too. Only Brittany herself had handled the situation with any degree of aplomb, something which hadn't the least bit endeared her to Ffion.

There was something about Brittany Grainger that Ffion instantly and instinctively mistrusted. Whether it was her bright self-confidence, her overt femininity, or her obvious delight at seeing Jake again, Ffion acknowledged that she'd experienced a strong visceral and emotional response, and the name of that emotion was jealousy. It wasn't a pleasant feeling.

Ffion hated not being in control of a situation. She didn't enter into new relationships easily, and had deliberately kept Jake at a distance for several months before gradually softening towards him. First, she'd confided in him about her bisexuality. Then she'd offered him some encouragement, to see if he could win her over. Finally, she'd dropped the last of her defences and had given herself to him entirely. He was only the second man she'd ever slept with, and she hoped she wouldn't live to regret it.

As she crossed the college quadrangle, her thoughts drifted inevitably to Jake's unconventional looks: a little too tall for comfort, with arms and legs that seemed needlessly and pointlessly long; his gigantic feet; the wiry hair that sprouted from his head; and the beard that spread like ginger fur over his face. She had to suppress a smile. The guy was charming, and she'd fallen for him hard.

Then the image of Brittany Grainger appeared unbidden: Brittany, with her manicured nails, long blonde hair, short skirt and high heels. A snake seemed to uncurl in Ffion's heart and a deep-seated fear gripped her. She would never allow that treacherous woman to steal Jake from her.

She located Miranda's staircase and went in search of

her room, pushing all thoughts of Jake and Brittany from her head as she climbed the steep stairs. She had a job to do, and needed to regain her usually unwavering focus. Hearing two female voices inside Miranda's room, she rapped loudly on the door. The voices fell silent and the door opened to reveal a long-haired girl dressed in a pair of ripped jeans and a college sweatshirt.

'Miranda Gardiner?' enquired Ffion.

'Yes?' The girl stared back at her. 'What is it?'

'I'm Detective Constable Ffion Hughes from Thames Valley Police.' She flashed her warrant card. 'Can I come in?'

'Um, sure.' Miranda stepped back so that Ffion could enter.

A second girl was in the room, sitting cross-legged on the edge of the bed. She wore black leggings and boots, with a bright yellow jumper. She and Miranda exchanged mystified glances.

'Are you Poppy Radley?' asked Ffion.

The girl on the bed nodded. 'Yes. What's going on?'

'Can you both confirm that you worked as waitresses last night at a party in a house in West Oxfordshire?'

'Yes,' answered Miranda. 'What's this about?'

Ffion scrutinised the two girls' faces for any indication that they already knew what had happened to Gina, but they both seemed genuinely puzzled by the arrival of a police detective. She softened her voice in an effort to take the sting out of what she was about to reveal.

'I'm very sorry to have to tell you that Gina Hartman's body was found this morning in one of the bedrooms at the house.'

'What?'

'No!'

The two girls' shock seemed genuine enough. Miranda sank onto the bed next to Poppy, putting her arm around her, and pulling her close.

Tears sprang to Poppy's eyes. 'Oh my God. What happened to her?' Her voice sounded small and scared.

'That,' said Ffion, 'is what we intend to find out. But I can tell you that we're treating the death as murder.'

'Oh my God,' said Poppy. 'I can't believe it.'

The tears that filled Poppy's eyes began to run down her cheeks and Ffion gave her a moment to recover her composure.

'I'd like to ask you both some questions about the party,' she said. 'Firstly, can you tell me how long you and Gina have worked for Mr Damon?'

'We started last term,' said Miranda. 'Gina spotted an online ad for occasional work, and the pay was good, so we decided to give it a try. At first we weren't sure what to expect, but Mr Damon seemed all right, and his assistant, Brittany, was really nice and friendly, so we decided it was safe enough to continue.'

Poppy nodded her agreement.

Ffion narrowed her eyes at the mention of the blonde PA. This wasn't exactly what she'd been hoping to hear, but the two girls seemed sincere in their praise of the personal assistant extraordinaire. She really must try not to let her jealousy cloud her judgement in this investigation.

Poppy was still dabbing her eyes with a tissue but seemed to have recovered from her initial shock. 'The set-up was a bit weird, though. All the guests wore masks. And the place was right out in the middle of nowhere, a huge house like something out of a film. And Tyler, the guy who picked us up and brought us back was a bit of a creep.'

'Tyler drove you to the party last night?'

'Yes,' said Miranda.

'At what time?'

'About six.'

'And what time did he bring you back?'

'I think we left about one in the morning.'

'Just the two of you?'

The girls exchanged glances again. 'Yes,' said Poppy in a weak voice.

'Why didn't Gina come back with you?'

The two girls glanced down at their hands. It was

Miranda who looked up first. 'Gina always did her own thing. She went to the party separately too. She said she had work to complete before leaving college, so Tyler had to drive us to the house and then come all the way back to pick her up. We thought it was a bit cheeky, to be honest, but that's what Gina was like. So when it was time to leave we weren't too surprised she didn't come with us.'

'When was the last time you saw Gina?'

'Um, sometime before midnight?' said Poppy. She looked to Miranda, who nodded her confirmation.

'Weren't you worried about leaving her behind?' Ffion asked. 'Did she say what she was planning to do?'

'She said she might stay overnight if she got the chance,' said Miranda, refusing to make eye contact with Ffion.

'What kind of chance?' She looked from one to the other.

A guilty look washed over Poppy's face. She evaded Ffion's question, saying, 'We should never have left her behind.' She burst into fresh tears and Miranda leaned over to comfort her again.

'What kind of chance?' repeated Ffion, beginning to exhaust her supply of sympathy for the two girls.

'Gina was always snooping around,' said Poppy, wiping her eyes. 'You know, listening in to people's conversations, taking photos when she thought no one was looking.'

'Why would she do that?'

'She fancied herself as a bit of an investigative journalist,' said Miranda, somewhat scornfully. 'I mean, she was only writing for the student newspaper, but she saw the parties as a chance to do some undercover work and poke her nose into the lives of the guests.'

'That's right,' agreed Poppy.

Ffion was starting to get the impression that while Miranda and Poppy were very close, Gina hadn't been such a close-knit member of the trio.

'We tried to tell her not to,' said Miranda.

'We were worried she'd get caught,' said Poppy, 'and

that we'd all lose our jobs. It's a really easy way to earn good money.'

'But Gina wasn't content just to earn a bit of cash,' said Miranda. 'She always had to push things to the next level.'

The girls fell silent, perhaps realising that they were sounding rather resentful of their dead friend.

'Was Gina following anyone in particular?' asked Ffion.

They shook their heads in unison.

'We didn't ask,' explained Poppy. 'We told her that we didn't want to know anything about it.'

'She told us that it was up to her what she did,' said Miranda. 'And that if she got caught, that was her problem.'

'We had a bit of an argument about it, actually,' said Poppy. 'We said that if she got caught, it would become our problem too. We didn't want to lose our jobs.' She began to cry again. 'And now she's lost her life. Oh my God, I still can't believe it.'

'When was this argument?'

'Last night. It was the last time we saw her.' Poppy dissolved into yet another flood of tears.

Ffion waited impatiently a moment while Miranda consoled her.

'Did Gina have a boyfriend?'

'No,' said Miranda. 'She went out with one of the biologists in her first year, but that didn't last long. Gina was a hard worker. She didn't really have time for boys.'

'So, was working as waitresses a regular gig?'

'This was the first time this academic year,' said Miranda. 'We'd done it a few times last term. Mr Damon throws a lot of parties, usually one every couple of weeks.'

'What do you know about Mr Damon?'

'Not much,' said Miranda. 'He told us he runs a building company. He's obviously very rich.'

'And were your duties at these parties strictly limited to waitressing?'

'What do you mean?' asked Poppy.

'She means,' Miranda explained, not making any effort

to conceal the resentment in her voice, 'were we required to provide sexual favours to the guests?'

'God, no,' said Poppy. 'Of course not. What do you take us for?'

'And yet a number of women were employed from an escort agency to entertain the guests.'

'Well, yeah,' said Miranda. 'We knew about that, obviously. But we had nothing to do with any of it.'

Poppy concurred vigorously, nodding her head. 'Mr Damon was a good employer. He always treated us well. And Brittany was really good too. She told us we didn't have to put up with any sexual harassment from the guests, and to tell her if any of them tried anything.'

Ffion bristled at this further unsolicited praise of Brittany, but stayed focused on her questions. 'And did any of the guests ever try anything on?'

'After a few drinks some of them could get a little over-friendly,' admitted Miranda, 'but you were okay if you just kept moving. We didn't stand still long enough for them to get their hands on us.'

'What about Gina?'

'What about her?' asked Miranda.

'Did she ever become involved with any of the guests?'

The girls exchanged glances. 'Gina tended to make use of her good looks to get what she wanted,' said Miranda. 'I don't want to say anything bad about her, but she knew how men looked at her, and she wasn't afraid to turn that to her advantage.'

'How?'

'Well, if she needed a guy to do something for her, or if she wanted to find out some information, she might flirt a bit to get what she wanted.'

'But she wouldn't have slept with any of them,' blurted Poppy. 'I mean, she'd have had to be really desperate. They were all middle-aged men.'

'Tell me about them. Do you know who any of them were?'

The girls looked at each other as if trying to decide

whether or not to reveal something. Eventually it was Miranda who spoke.

'Look, we're not supposed to know anything about the guests. Brittany gave us strict instructions never to ask them any personal questions. We're just supposed to smile and be helpful.'

'And they wear those masks too,' said Poppy. 'They don't even use their real names.'

'Exactly,' continued Miranda. 'But we're not stupid. One of them is a politician.'

'And one's a judge,' said Poppy.

'I think the rest are all Mr Damon's business contacts.'

'There was someone a bit closer to home present at the party last night,' said Ffion, watching their faces.

'You must mean Dr Frost,' said Poppy.

'Yes, Gina spotted him,' said Miranda. 'We were in the kitchen fetching trays of canapés, and she came in and said, "You'll never guess who's here." I thought she was going to name someone really famous, like an actor, but then she said, "Dr Frost." I had to ask her who she meant and she said that he's the German lecturer, here in college.'

'Had you seen Dr Frost at one of these parties before?'

Both girls shook their head.

'What do you remember about his behaviour at the party?'

'Not much,' said Miranda. 'Obviously, after Gina told us, we both went to see for ourselves. It was him, all right, wearing a Venetian mask. I think he'd had rather too much to drink.'

'And did Gina mention him again? Or did you see him with her?'

'No.' Miranda frowned. 'What's all this about Dr Frost?'

'He was found in bed with Gina's body this morning.'

'What? Oh my God!' Poppy threw her hands into her face once more.

Miranda looked stunned. 'But why –'

'That's what we're investigating,' said Ffion shortly.

'What do you know about him?'

'Not a lot. Poppy and I are studying English, and of course Gina was studying Psychology, not German. I've seen him walking between his room and the Senior Common Room, and he's always on high table at formal hall, but I've never spoken to him.'

'Me neither,' said Poppy. 'I know a couple of people studying German and they've never said anything about him either.'

That will soon change, thought Ffion. Frost's reputation as the college's nonentity would end forever once word got out that he'd been found in bed with a murdered student.

Somehow, Ffion couldn't quite picture the German tutor as a killer. He might be a bit of a nutter and a conspiracy theorist, but he'd been surprisingly direct and frank in his interview that morning, which wasn't how guilty people tended to behave. She suspected that he'd most likely found himself in the wrong place at the wrong time. Perhaps it had even been a deliberate set-up, as he claimed. In that case, the murderer must be one of the other party guests, or perhaps the host himself. The devil, in other words, in the guise of Nick Damon.

She thanked Miranda and Poppy for their time and told them that the police might need to speak to them again. 'Let me know if you think of anything,' she added. Then she headed back to the porters' lodge to meet Bridget.

CHAPTER 7

After taking her leave of Gina's tutor, Bridget headed back to the gatehouse to wait for Ffion. The MP for Witney had not yet returned her call, so while she waited she rang his constituency office for a second time.

A familiar haughty female voice answered after three rings. 'Mr Avery-Blanchard's constituency office is now closed for the weekend. If you would like to make an appointment to see Mr Avery-Blanchard between the hours of –'

Bridget hung up. If the MP didn't return her call, she would have to try his home number the following morning.

When Ffion arrived, they swapped notes on their respective interviews, and Bridget offered to give her a lift to wherever she wanted to go. It had been a long day and there was little more they could do now. In the morning, it would be time for a team meeting and the laborious task of bringing together all the various witness statements and forensic evidence that had been gathered during the first twenty-four hours. They would need to take a view on whether or not to charge or release Frost. And Bridget would have to meet Gina's parents and take them to the morgue to formally identify the body. But that was all for the following day.

Ffion declined Bridget's offer of a lift, setting off at a brisk pace on her long legs in the direction of the city centre. Bridget assumed she had plans for the evening ahead, presumably involving Jake.

Bridget, too, had firm plans. It was Saturday night, and she was determined not to let Jonathan, her date for the evening, down again. So many times she'd had to cancel their plans at the last minute, or had been called away on urgent business, sometimes even during a date. She wasn't going to let that happen tonight.

She checked her watch. Five o'clock. Enough time to go home, take a shower – she worried that the odour of chlorine from the pool that morning still clung to her skin, making her smell like a public bathroom – and put on something more attractive. She clambered into her Mini, turned up the volume on Mozart's *The Marriage of Figaro* and headed home.

The village of Wolvercote in North-West Oxford had been almost subsumed into the city but still retained a feeling of separateness, shielded from relentless urban encroachment by the protective barrier of the Oxford Canal and the railway tracks. The common ground of Port Meadow lay to the south, and to the north and west, mile upon mile of farmland stretched out. Bridget and Chloe occupied a tiny terraced house overlooking the village green. It was just big enough for the two of them. Her sister, Vanessa, who was married to a wealthy businessman, lived in a huge detached property on Charlbury Road in leafy North Oxford. While Vanessa employed a small army of cleaners, gardeners, painters and decorators to keep her house in show-home condition, Bridget made do with her own somewhat lackadaisical efforts at keeping the house clean and presentable. But she had made slightly more of an effort in anticipation of tonight's date, in the hope that Jonathan would come back with her afterwards. She was pleased to be met by the scent of wood polish and lemon air freshener as she let herself in at the front door.

Chloe was spending the night at a friend's house, which meant that Bridget and Jonathan would have the place to themselves. At fifteen, Chloe was growing up fast. She was now in Year Eleven and would be sitting her GCSE exams next summer. Bridget had been trying to impress upon her the importance of the coming year at school but she worried that the message hadn't yet fully sunk in.

'There's more to life than taking exams,' was Chloe's usual retort. Or, 'It's ages yet, Mum. Chill.'

But it wasn't just concern about Chloe's grades that was bothering Bridget. Her own younger sister, Abigail, had started to go off the rails at precisely this age. Once a promising student, Abigail had got in with the wrong crowd. She'd started staying out later and later, defying their parents' requests to come home at a reasonable time. And then, at sixteen years old, Abigail had been found strangled in Wytham Woods, her killer never caught. This tragic event was the defining moment of Bridget's life, shaking her comfortable, middle-class existence to the core. It was what had driven her to join the police, to try and make a difference in the world. While Vanessa cocooned herself from the outside world with her coordinating soft-furnishings, Bridget strove after justice for those who couldn't get it for themselves. It wasn't surprising that she was hyper-sensitive to Chloe's behaviour.

She called Chloe's mobile now, and was reassured to learn that she was at Olivia's house and they were planning to get a home-delivered pizza and then watch a film.

'Are you going on your date, Mum?' asked Chloe.

'I'm just about to get ready.'

'Don't screw it up this time,' said Chloe with a sigh. 'You know what always happens. You have to cancel or leave early because of work. You're not in the middle of a murder case right now, are you?'

'Well…'

'Mum!'

'Don't worry. I won't mess up this time,' said Bridget. 'I promise.'

'Okay, then. Have fun.'

'You too.'

She ended the call. Chloe knew her only too well. She checked her watch and realised with a shock that she only had half an hour to get ready. She jumped in the shower and scrubbed her body with a mesh sponge doused in lavender gel in an attempt to remove any lingering scent of *eau de chlorine*. Then she put on her best underwear and what she hoped was a stylish dress. It showed off her curvaceous figure, and Chloe had assured her that it was suitable for a date. To her relief, it still fitted. She applied a quick layer of foundation and a smear of nude lipstick, then ran a comb through her bobbed hair, but it was still damp at the ends when the doorbell rang. She rushed to get the door.

It was Jonathan, wearing a dark coat over smart trousers and a burgundy shirt. 'You look lovely,' he said, leaning forward to plant a kiss on her lips. 'Are you ready?'

'I'm ready,' said Bridget. 'Let's go.'

*

After leaving Wadham College, Ffion chose to walk rather than to accept Bridget's offer of a lift. She'd planned to go for a run this morning, but they'd been called to the house in West Oxfordshire instead. Now she was missing it. For Ffion, running wasn't merely physical exercise, it was moving meditation. Being alone and outdoors gave her the mental space she needed to think.

She walked south from the college, crossing over Broad Street and passing the Radcliffe Camera, the circular domed building that formed part of the Bodleian Library. From there she turned left onto the High Street and headed towards Magdalen Bridge. Her gear was still at

Jake's place where she'd spent the previous night.

She'd been seeing Jake for a month now and it had been going well. Ffion had enough self-awareness to know that she was a complex character, and could be difficult to get on with at times. Jake had rebuked her once or twice for being short with him, or for failing to show due consideration, and she hadn't minded. Jake had a natural gift for empathy that Ffion knew she sometimes lacked, and she was willing to learn and to change. A relationship was a continuous two-way flow, and no doubt she'd forced some changes on Jake too. There was less football in his life these days, and less beer. But a lot more sex.

Leaving the dreaming spires of central Oxford behind her, she darted across the Plain roundabout, dodging the buses, cars and cyclists that jostled for space, and headed east down Cowley Road. This was where Oxford changed from a city dominated by medieval quadrangles, Gothic towers and eighteenth-century libraries to a multi-ethnic, bustling community packed with diverse restaurants, bars and small shops. Ffion liked the alternative vibe in this part of town. Now that the new term had started, the road was bustling, as freshers headed out for the evening, keen to explore some of Oxford's lesser-frequented pubs and eateries.

She soon arrived outside the launderette below Jake's one-bedroom flat. The washing machines were all whirring away, emitting a warm, soapy smell from within. The Indian restaurant next door was just opening up for the evening. The Chinese takeaway on the other side was already doing a brisk business with people popping in to buy dinner on their way home. Ffion fished in her pocket for the key that Jake had given her and unlocked the door that led in from the street. She scooped up the day's mail that had landed on the mat – mainly advertisements for pizza delivery services and taxi companies – and climbed the narrow staircase up to his flat.

'Hi! It's me!' she called, but was disappointed to find that Jake wasn't yet home. Surely he couldn't still be at the house with Brittany. She called his phone, but the call went straight through to voicemail. 'Hi, where are you?' she said, unable to keep the irritation from her voice. 'I'm in your flat.'

She dumped the mail on the table in the living room and glanced round in despair at the general clutter and mess. She was sure she'd tidied up the previous evening, but it looked just as bad as ever. Since she'd started spending nights here she'd laid down a few rules, and Jake had begun to make a little more effort, but he still tolerated a far messier environment than she ever could. One of the first things she'd done was to buy him a laundry basket so she wouldn't have to bear the sight of his dirty clothes heaped in the corner of the bedroom. She insisted that they wash up after eating so that they didn't have to face the dirty dishes the next morning. And she had forbidden him from ever leaving the cap off the toothpaste in the bathroom. But even so, the flat was far too disorganised and dirty for her to sit and relax while she waited for Jake to come home.

They'd been called out this morning before they'd had a chance to wash up, so she set about clearing away the breakfast things and scraping the encrusted food off the plates. Having done that, she decided to tackle the bathroom, and began wiping down the surfaces, removing all traces of ginger hair from the glass shelves and white wall tiles.

The task was comforting, yet as she worked, she couldn't help reflecting on the differences between herself and Jake. It wasn't simply their divergent approaches to household hygiene. Ffion took a great deal of care over her own appearance, going to great lengths each morning to select coordinating outfits. Jake, on the other hand, didn't seem to care if he couldn't find two matching socks. She was into healthy eating, whereas he was happy to pig out on takeaways. She lived and breathed exercise, but Jake's idea of a workout was a stroll to the pub. They didn't even like the same music. He listened to indie rock bands, while she liked techno and trance...

What was going on?

She put down the bathroom cleaner and scouring pad and realised that she had worked herself up into a frenzy. She was breathing so hard she was almost hyper-ventilating. She took a few long breaths to calm herself down.

She knew exactly what was happening here. It wasn't her and Jake's differences that were bothering her. In every relationship, the two partners had to make compromises and learn to live together. To make it work, both sides had to search for common ground, not dwell on their differences.

No, the problem was the morning's encounter with Brittany Grainger. The blonde PA had got under Ffion's skin more than she ought to have.

But what was she really worried about? That Jake might leave her and go back to his ex-girlfriend? That hardly seemed likely. Jake had clearly been highly embarrassed by meeting Brittany at the house. And he had told her that the relationship finished months ago. She needed to trust him.

And yet that look on Brittany's face when she'd first laid eyes on Jake had been predatory. For all her surface charm and warm smiles, Brittany Grainger was a hunter, and she had fixed her sights firmly on Jake. Did he have the strength to resist?

Ffion waited thirty seconds, then dialled his phone again. It still went to voicemail.

She put the cleaning things away and returned to the table in the main living area. Grabbing a pen, she wrote a quick note on the back of one of the taxi leaflets: *Back at my place. See you tomorrow.*

Then she let herself out of the flat, retracing her steps back down the Cowley Road towards her own house in Jericho, west of the city centre. Out in the open air, away from the clutter and the mess of Jake's flat, she found she could breathe easily again.

*

Bridget was enjoying a lovely evening, and it wasn't over yet. First, she and Jonathan had been to Brown's for a quick bite to eat, and Bridget had chosen a wholefood salad to make up for her dietary misdemeanours during the day, while Jonathan selected steak frites. Then they'd gone to a concert in the Holywell Music Room.

She and Jonathan had recently been to a performance of *Hamlet*, and had planned to see *La Bohème* together, but she'd had to cancel at the last minute. Until this evening, she'd had no real idea what kind of music Jonathan liked. It turned out that he had a passion for German *Lieder*, especially songs from the Romantic period. At the recital, a talented young tenor performed the song cycle *Dichterliebe*, or poet's love: the perceptive words of the poet Heinrich Heine set to exquisite melodies by Robert Schumann. Although opera was Bridget's usual preference, she found herself in complete agreement with Jonathan that there was no better expression of the bitter-sweet sorrow of unrequited love.

An unwelcome echo of Dr Nathan Frost's voice fluttered briefly through her mind as she listened to the songs, following the translation in her programme, but she nudged the memory of the German lecturer firmly aside. She was definitely not going to allow work to intrude on her plans this evening.

'That was beautiful,' she told Jonathan as they walked hand in hand back to his car in Broad Street. The music had soothed away the strains and stresses of the day.

'I'm so glad you enjoyed it.'

They drove back to Wolvercote talking about the music, Bridget's heart beginning to beat slightly faster as they approached her house.

'So,' she said, when they pulled up by the village green. 'Would you like to come inside for a drink? Chloe's at her friend's house tonight,' she added. 'So we have the place to ourselves.'

'That would be lovely.'

Heart now pounding, Bridget led him into the kitchen and took a bottle of Chardonnay out of the fridge. She poured two glasses, splashing a little on the kitchen counter.

Why was she so nervous? She felt like a teenager on a first date. Well, it had been a long time since she'd been with a man. *Thirteen years.* She couldn't believe there hadn't been anyone in all that time.

She passed one of the drinks to Jonathan. 'Cheers,' she said, clinking her glass with his. She swallowed a large gulp of wine.

Jonathan sipped his, looking thoughtful.

Then he took her wine and set both glasses down. Clasping her hands in his, he pulled her to him. 'Why don't we save the wine until later?' he whispered.

Suddenly Bridget didn't feel nervous anymore. She knew there was nothing to be afraid of. Jonathan was a good man, and she cared for him deeply.

'The bedroom's this way,' she said, leading him towards the stairs.

★

It was late by the time Jake arrived back at his flat. After talking to Brittany and Tyler, he'd remained at the house, helping DS Ryan Hooper and the rest of the team take statements from all the guests who'd stayed overnight. They weren't the usual kind of witnesses you found in a murder case, consisting of company executives, finance directors, local government officials, and even a judge – a rather pompous man who insisted on being referred to as the Honourable Mr Justice Neville, even though on closer questioning his first name turned out to be Graham. Everyone he'd spoken to seemed to hold a very high opinion of themselves, and they were an uncooperative bunch, making the job take far longer than necessary.

Brittany had refused to leave him alone, and had kept

popping in to see him all day long. Ryan had made some lewd remarks about her, and DS Andy Cartwright had commented on how helpful the PA was, but Jake knew she was just trying to get his attention.

Maybe things weren't too good between her and Tyler. She hadn't been pleased when he'd put his oily hand around her, but then Brittany had always had a thing about looking her best. He found himself hoping that the couple were about to split up. Tyler was obviously a jerk. He wasn't good enough for her.

But why did he still care?

Was it possible that part of him still longed to have her back in his arms? No matter how hard he tried to convince himself otherwise, he knew he still wasn't free of her hold. The quicker this investigation could be wrapped up, the better.

'Do you think it was Frost who killed Gina?' he'd asked Ryan during his mid-afternoon tea break.

Ryan laughed. 'Let me think about that for a millisecond. You mean the creepy old guy who was found in bed with her dead body? Duh! Of course he did, you nutter!'

Jake hoped so. He checked his phone to see if Ffion had tried to call him, but there was no phone signal here at the house. The place really was miles from anywhere.

By the time he left for the evening and drove back to Oxford, he was starving. The launderette was closed and dark but the Indian restaurant was packed, a pungent aroma of spices and garlic wafting into the street. He debated whether or not to go inside, but decided instead to nip into the Chinese next door, where he ordered a large portion of Kung Po chicken in garlic with sweet chilli sauce, egg-fried rice and a side portion of prawn crackers. It would keep him going until later. With any luck, Ffion would be back and they could go out for a proper meal together.

He unlocked his front door and raced up the stairs. 'Hi! Are you home?' he called, but the flat was dark and silent.

He dumped the food onto the table and flicked on the light switch.

He was half-hoping to find Ffion sitting cross-legged in the dark, some music on her headphones, meditating or whatever weird thing she did when he wasn't around, but there was no sign of her. The place looked unnaturally tidy, however, and there was some mail on the table, so he guessed she must have been there.

He checked his phone and found two voicemails. Frowning, he listened to them. Then he noticed the handwritten note on the table. He debated whether or not to call Ffion back, but the Welsh dragon could be impossible when she was in a bad mood.

The dark clouds that had appeared on the horizon that morning seemed to be gathering into a full-blown storm, and he was at the centre, while the two women in his life rained down hail and thunder all around.

Sighing, he unwrapped the food and began to spoon chicken and rice straight out of the foil cartons. A guy still had to eat, right?

CHAPTER 8

Bridget awoke the next morning feeling happy and calm. She'd anticipated a night of passion, and hadn't been disappointed. But something much more important had happened. Last night had healed something inside her that had been broken for a very long time, ever since the disintegration of her marriage to Ben, perhaps even longer. Perhaps even since the death of her sister.

Deep down she'd doubted that she was ever capable of giving or receiving love again, but now she knew that she could.

She rolled over and found the other side of the bed empty.

'Jonathan?'

She sat up, and that was when she noticed the smell of cooking wafting up the stairs.

She smiled. A man who could cook, and who had taken care to creep out of bed without disturbing her. Jonathan really was a treasure.

But then a fresh worry struck her. What would Jonathan find if he started rummaging around in her fridge? The out-of-date pots of yoghurt, the lettuce curling at the edges, the rather mouldy cheese. There might be even worse horrors hiding at the back. Although she'd taken care to replace the bedding with newly laundered sheets, she hadn't thought of buying in groceries for the following morning. Her planning rarely stretched that far ahead.

She climbed out of bed, pulled on her dressing gown, and made her way downstairs after quickly checking her appearance in the bathroom mirror. Her hair wasn't sticking out too much and at least her eyes were bright and sparkling instead of their usual early-morning red and puffy look.

'Just in time,' said Jonathan, as she entered the kitchen. He looked up from the gas hob where he was stirring something in a frying pan, and smiled.

'It smells wonderful,' said Bridget, coming up behind him and wrapping her arms around him. 'What is it?' she asked, intrigued.

'This is my speciality – scrambled egg with herbs.'

Somehow Jonathan had managed to locate jars of dried oregano and basil that Bridget didn't even know she owned. She must have bought them in a burst of enthusiasm after receiving an Italian cookery book from Vanessa one Christmas. But the book was collecting dust on the kitchen shelf, the ingredients long abandoned.

'Did you check that the eggs are still fresh?' she asked anxiously.

He chuckled. 'I think we'll get away with it. But they needed using up. It's just as well you invited me round.'

He spooned the scrambled egg mixture onto two plates just as the toast popped up out of the toaster.

Bridget was starving, and tucked in with relish. The scrambled eggs were the best she'd ever tasted. Once Vanessa discovered Jonathan's culinary skills, she might actually be jealous of Bridget for the first time ever. She made a silent vow to herself. *I must never lose this man.*

But it wasn't just his skill in the kitchen – or the

bedroom – that made Bridget's heart feel so light this morning.

He makes me happy.

She realised how long it had been since she'd really felt that deep-down glow of contentment. It had been so long, she'd almost forgotten what it was like.

If only she could spend the whole day with Jonathan. It would be perfect to take a walk together across Port Meadow, have lunch at The Perch, then enjoy the evening listening to music. But she knew that this shared moment with him would very soon be over. She was in the middle of a murder enquiry and needed to go into work. And she also had to collect Chloe from Olivia's house.

'I need to phone Chloe,' she told Jonathan after she'd finished eating. 'Vanessa's expecting us at her place for lunch, but obviously I'm not going to be able to make it.'

'Obviously,' he said, with a wry smile.

The traditional Sunday roast was something of a sacred family ritual, a talisman against the unpredictability of life, and a way for Vanessa to prove to the world that she had everything under control. Bridget secretly wondered if her sister should see a therapist.

It was at one of Vanessa's Sunday lunches that she and Jonathan had first met, but – typically – Bridget had needed to dash off to get back to work. It seemed that she had a habit of inadvertently undermining her sister's attempts at perfection.

She dialled Chloe's number and waited for her daughter to answer. 'What time is it?' she asked.

'Nine o'clock.'

'Already? I'm going to be late!'

The phone rang for ages before Chloe picked up. 'Mum?' Chloe's voice sounded rough, as if she'd had a late night out partying rather than staying in to watch a film with Olivia.

'Are you ready for me to come and collect you?' asked Bridget.

'What, now?' said Chloe. 'It's a bit early.'

'Aren't you up yet?' asked Bridget with dismay. 'I need to drop you off at Aunt Vanessa's and then go into work.'

Chloe groaned.

Jonathan leaned over to her. 'I can get her,' he said. 'I don't mind.'

'Really?'

'Of course.'

'Thanks,' said Bridget. 'Is it okay if Jonathan comes to pick you up instead?' she asked Chloe.

'Wait, Jonathan's at home with you now?' asked Chloe, her question managing to convey a whole world of speculation and suggestion.

'Um, yes.'

'Cool,' said Chloe. 'Then Jonathan and I can go to lunch without you. Aunt Vanessa won't mind. She likes Jonathan.'

'I suppose so,' said Bridget, simultaneously pleased and aggrieved that she was apparently so easily replaceable. 'Would you mind going to lunch at Vanessa's too?' she asked Jonathan.

'Would I mind? I'd be delighted!'

Having been to Vanessa's house several times already, Jonathan obviously knew what to expect. No doubt Vanessa would fuss over him and make it an occasion to remember.

'That's settled, then, I suppose,' said Bridget.

'Cool, Mum. See you later.' Chloe ended the call.

'You know,' said Jonathan. 'Since you can't make it to lunch, why don't you come round to my place tonight for dinner?'

Bridget had so far never visited Jonathan's home. She was delighted to be asked, especially now that he had revealed his prowess in the kitchen. She was already beginning to imagine what delights he might have in store. 'But what about Chloe?' she asked.

'I'm sure she'll be all right on her own for a few hours. She's fifteen now.'

The prospect of dinner with Jonathan was certainly a

very tempting one, especially if she was going to miss Sunday lunch. 'Okay, but I can't stay all night. I'll have to get back to Chloe.'

'Of course. Then I'll see you at seven?'

*

Bridget wasn't sure if she should feel guilty or relieved at having dumped the responsibility of looking after Chloe on Jonathan. Neither of them had seemed to mind in the least, but somehow that just made her feel worse. It seemed that however well things went in her life, she always contrived to heap a mountain of blame on her shoulders.

She permitted herself a brief recollection of the highlights of the previous evening to bolster her mood, and had to stifle a smile. She must be positively glowing after her night of passion, and wondered if anyone at work would notice any change in her appearance.

'Thank you all for coming into work on a Sunday morning,' she said, taking her place in front of the whiteboard in the incident room.

The assorted members of the team had gathered for the briefing, none of them looking as bright-eyed and bushy-tailed as she felt. Judging by the tired expressions on many of their faces, their evenings hadn't been quite as pleasurable as hers. Ffion sat behind her computer screen, drinking one of her herbal teas and looking stony-faced. Jake sat on the other side of the room, chewing sullenly on a bacon roll. DS Ryan Hooper looked as he always did after a Saturday night – red-eyed and blinking under the harsh fluorescent lights of the office. DS Andy Cartwright was rubbing his eyes and attempting to bring himself back to life with a coffee. Only DC Harry Johns looked properly alert. His hair was still damp, as if he'd only just emerged from the shower. He sat at the front, notebook in hand, pen poised ready to write.

'Right then, let's get started,' said Bridget, trying to inject some of her energy into the room. After her puzzling interview with Dr Frost the day before, and the somewhat unenlightening chats with Gina's tutor and friends, she was hoping that the team she'd left behind at the house had gathered something that would shed more light on the case.

She began by reviewing what they knew so far: Gina Hartman was a third-year Psychology student at Wadham College who had worked as a waitress at a house party hosted by local building magnate, Nick Damon. Two other girls from the same college had also worked as waitresses that night: Miranda Gardiner and Poppy Radley. Gina had been found dead by Dr Nathan Frost yesterday morning when he'd woken up beside her in one of the bedrooms. So far, so simple.

Yet Frost claimed to have no memory of how he'd ended up sharing a bed with Gina, let alone how she'd died. He'd also spun an extraordinary theory of devils and conspiracies that seemed to bear little relationship to the facts.

'The most urgent question right now,' said Bridget, 'is whether we have enough evidence to charge him. He's been in custody for nearly twenty-four hours. The case isn't completely watertight, but unless we've turned up something that casts doubt on his guilt, I say we go ahead and charge him.'

She looked expectantly at her team, most of whom had spent the previous day taking witness statements at the house.

'We spoke to everyone who stayed overnight,' said Jake. 'I've got the full guest list here,' he added, handing her a sheet of paper.

'Is this the list that Mr Damon's PA supplied?'

'Um, yeah,' said Jake, moving on rapidly to consult his notes. 'Nobody was able to tell us anything about Frost. None of the guests had ever met him before and they had no idea who he was. A few people remembered him by his mask, but he doesn't seem to have made much of an impression during the party.'

Bridget was scanning the names on the list. 'Have you spoken to everyone listed here?'

'All of them except the MP, Hugh Avery-Blanchard.'

Bridget nodded. The Member of Parliament for Witney had certainly proven to be very elusive, and Bridget didn't think that was because he was busy with his constituents. 'I called his constituency office yesterday and left a message, but I'll give him another call today. Ryan, do you have anything to add?'

The young detective sergeant shook his head, still bleary-eyed. 'No, that's about it, ma'am. What Jake said.'

'Ffion? Would you like to summarise how you got on with Miranda and Poppy?'

'Well, they were shocked to hear what had happened to Gina.'

'They weren't concerned that she hadn't left the party with them last night?'

'Didn't seem to be. Gina went to the party separately, too. I got the impression that she often did her own thing. The girls said that Gina was planning to use the opportunity to snoop on some of the guests. They didn't know who she was interested in, or why, but apparently Gina used to write articles for the student newspaper. I don't think the other two approved of what she was doing. They were worried she might get into trouble and they'd all lose their jobs. Perhaps they didn't like Gina all that much. They told me they argued about it with her last night.'

'An argument?' queried Bridget. 'Could that have turned violent?'

Ffion shook her head. 'I don't think so. They weren't angry, just a bit miffed. Poppy was very upset, actually.'

'How did they get to and from the party?'

'Some guy called Tyler drove them there and back.'

'I met Tyler,' interjected Jake. 'He's Mr Damon's driver and odd job man. He's also in charge of security.'

'What did you make of him?' asked Bridget.

'He's a bit of a thug, to be honest, ma'am,' said Jake,

his ears beginning to glow pink.

'Capable of violence?'

He shrugged. 'I don't know. Maybe.'

'Okay,' said Bridget. 'Anything else?' she asked Ffion.

'The girls said that Mr Damon was a good employer. And when I asked them about Frost, they said they'd seen him at the party, but they didn't really know anything about him. They didn't think he knew Gina.'

Bridget nodded. Much of what Miranda and Poppy had told Ffion tallied with what Dr Ashley, Gina's tutor had said. There was no reason to think they were lying.

'Okay, thanks,' said Bridget.

The various witness statements had proved frustratingly free of detail. No one, it seemed, had noted anything suspicious. And the comment repeated most often was that nobody knew anything about Frost. The warden had described him as a recluse and found his presence at the party baffling. Dr Ashley clearly considered the German lecturer to be an irrelevance, perhaps even a joke. Even Nick Damon claimed to barely know him. It was as if the man had moved invisibly through his own life.

'Ma'am,' said Andy, 'we got the results of the swab tests from the victim, and the blood and urine tests carried out on Frost back from the lab this morning.'

Thank God, thought Bridget. Perhaps here was something tangible at last. She wondered why Andy hadn't mentioned the results sooner. Although to be fair, she hadn't asked him. Initiative was never Andy's strongest suit.

'Yes,' he said, rising to his feet, and thumbing through the first report. 'This one is from the tests carried out on Dr Frost. They've found traces of Rohypnol in his system.'

'Really?'

Rohypnol was a powerful tranquiliser, prescribed for the treatment of severe insomnia. It was one of the classes of medicines used as a "date rape" drug because of its ability to sedate and incapacitate victims. It was also known to cause memory loss. If Dr Frost had been administered Rohypnol in a drink, then perhaps this was the "sleeping potion" he had so anachronistically referred to.

'That does put a different slant on things. It lends some weight to Frost's theory that he was set up. If that's the case, I think we'll have to let him go. We just don't have enough to hold him on a murder charge.'

Andy was reading from the second report. 'There's more, ma'am. The swab test from the victim confirms recent sexual activity. But the semen doesn't match Frost's DNA. There's no match to the criminal intelligence database either.'

Bridget nodded slowly. 'Then we have to work on the theory that someone else at the party had sex with Gina, and that they are most likely her killer.'

It seemed that Dr Frost had been telling the truth, however unlikely it seemed, and that he was an unwitting victim.

'Jake, Ryan, did you manage to get DNA samples from everyone you spoke to yesterday?'

'Yes,' said Jake. 'A few of the guests were reluctant to let us take samples, but we managed to persuade them that it was in their best interests to cooperate.'

'So let's get them over to the lab and see if we can find a match.'

'I'll do that,' volunteered Andy.

'Good. And then you, Jake and Harry can start working through all the witness statements. See if anything jumps out at you in light of this latest information.'

'Okay.' Andy held up a plastic bag. 'We've also got Gina's phone back from the lab. Forensics dusted it for prints, but the only ones they could find were Gina's.'

'Would you like me to take a look at the phone?' asked Ffion. 'If Gina was snooping on people at the party, it's possible that she might have taken some photos or videos that will tell us something.'

'Yes, please,' said Bridget. 'Check all her calls and messages too. Jake and Ryan, were there any witnesses you didn't get a chance to take a full statement from yesterday?'

'Well,' said Ryan, a smile spreading across his face, 'we had a word with the girls from the escort agency, but they weren't very willing to talk. Perhaps if we tried again...'

'All right,' she said. 'Why don't you arrange to go and talk to them in London? In the meantime, I need to go and meet Gina's parents. They travelled down from Manchester last night. I also need to see if I can track down Hugh Avery-Blanchard, the MP for Witney. I want to take a statement from him, and also a DNA sample.'

'You think he'll be willing to give one?' asked Ryan.

'He'd better do,' said Bridget. 'If he thinks he's special just because he's a politician, he has a lot to learn.'

There was, of course, one other person who hadn't yet given a DNA sample – who had, in fact, refused outright to give one. Nick Damon, the man who Dr Frost had accused of setting him up for Gina's murder.

'But before I go hunting for an MP,' she said, half to herself, 'I'm heading back to the house. I have unfinished business with Mr Nick Damon.'

★

Bridget was making her way back to her desk when she encountered Chief Superintendent Grayson. 'DI Hart, come to my office, please.'

His tone seemed friendly enough, but Bridget was on guard. If the Chief Super was in on a Sunday, it couldn't possibly be good news.

'Progress so far?' he asked, taking up his seat behind his desk.

Bridget summarised the state of play. 'And so we're releasing Frost, but we now know that Gina had sex not long before she was killed, and it's only a matter of time before we find a DNA match. If we can find out who had sex with her, we've almost certainly got our man.'

'Hmm,' said Grayson, regarding her inscrutably. 'Do you have a full list of guests, yet?'

'Yes, sir.' She passed him a copy of the list Jake had given her.

Grayson studied it, his face growing longer with each name, his thick eyebrows occasionally rising a notch. 'This is a problem,' he concluded. 'It's not just an MP you're going to have to deal with. Some of the people on this list are company directors, finance directors, public officials... there's even a judge.'

'Nobody is above the law,' said Bridget.

'I am well aware of that fact, DI Hart,' snapped Grayson. 'My point is that the investigation may prove to be a lot more difficult than you seem to realise. Have you received full cooperation from every person present at this party?'

'No,' admitted Bridget. 'Damon refused to give a DNA sample, and we haven't been able to talk to Hugh Avery-Blanchard yet.'

'That doesn't surprise me.' Grayson slid the list back across the desk. 'No one on this list will want you prying into their private affairs. They will do everything they can to protect their privacy and keep their name out of the newspapers.'

'They may not want to help,' said Bridget indignantly, 'but a woman has lost her life. Surely that's more important than vested interests?'

Grayson let out a long sigh. 'DI Hart, in case you haven't realised, I am trying to be helpful. What I mean to say is that if you have problems getting any of them to cooperate, come and see me, and I'll see what I can do.'

*

Bridget returned to Wadham College in a subdued mood. Gina's parents had been driven down the previous evening from Manchester, and true to his word, Lord Bancroft had put them up in one of the college's guest suites and assigned them to the care of Dr Ashley, Gina's tutor.

Dr Ashley met Bridget in the porters' lodge and

accompanied her through the quadrangle. The college seemed unnaturally quiet, as if cast in a shroud of grief. Obviously, everyone would now have heard of Gina's tragic death. Bridget remembered that Dr Ashley had described her as a popular student.

'I know it's not really my place to ask,' said Dr Ashley in a hushed voice, 'but there are rumours flying around about Dr Frost, the German tutor.'

'What sort of rumours?' asked Bridget guardedly.

'Well, people are saying that he was at the party last night and that he's been arrested.'

It hadn't taken long for the news of Frost's arrest to leak out and spread around the college community. These things were inevitable in such a small world. Bridget thought of Grayson's instruction to keep things under wraps, but Grayson had been warning her about the other guests on the list, not Frost himself.

'Dr Frost has been helping us with our enquiries,' said Bridget. 'But he is not currently a suspect.' She might have said *he's no more a suspect than everyone else who was at the party*, but she kept quiet.

'Well, that's good to hear,' said Dr Ashley.

'So how are Gina's parents?' asked Bridget.

'As you'd expect,' said Dr Ashley. 'Shocked. Angry. Still in some denial, of course. I expect you're familiar with the Kübler-Ross cycle of grief?'

'Of course,' said Bridget. She was no stranger to the devastating effects of sudden and tragic death. This was an event from which Gina's parents would never fully recover, just as Bridget's own parents had never got over Abigail's death. Meeting bereaved relatives, especially parents, was the hardest part of Bridget's job and one that she always faced with a sense of trepidation, no matter how many times she did it.

They arrived at a ground-floor room and Dr Ashley knocked on the door. A man in his early fifties opened the door, his face ashen. He looked as if he hadn't slept a wink all night. He nodded mutely and stood aside to let Bridget and the tutor enter.

A woman was sitting on the bed, presumably Gina's mother. She was pale and thin with red hair like Gina's, the grey roots showing at her parting and at the temples. She rose slowly to her feet as if it were a huge effort.

'Mr and Mrs Hartman?' Bridget held out a hand. 'I'm Detective Inspector Bridget Hart and I'm leading the investigation into Gina's death. I'm so sorry for your loss.'

The parents each gave her a wan smile before sinking back down onto the bed, seeming unsure where else to sit.

'Can I fetch anyone a coffee?' asked Dr Ashley.

Mr and Mrs Hartman both shook their heads.

'We're good, thanks,' said Bridget.

'Then would you like me to stay?' asked the tutor.

'If I could speak to Mr and Mrs Hartman in private for a moment, please?'

'Of course,' said Dr Ashley, retreating towards the door. 'I'll be in my room if you need me.'

Bridget waited for the door to close before speaking.

'I realise this must be a terrible shock for you both. Has the college been looking after you? Have you been kept fully informed?'

'Yes,' said Mrs Hartman, speaking with a strong Mancunian accent. 'Everyone's been very kind.'

'What can you tell us, Inspector?' asked Mr Hartman. 'About our Gina. What happened to her?'

Bridget wondered how much to tell the grieving parents. She knew from experience that while it was hard to tell the truth, it was better for them to hear what she knew. 'We don't yet know all the circumstances of her death,' she said, 'but it would appear that Gina was strangled.'

Mrs Hartman let out a small cry, and her hands moved to her throat in a protective gesture.

'Do you know who did it?' demanded Mr Hartman.

'Not yet. But we don't think it will be long before we make an arrest.'

Mr Hartman nodded grimly.

'How much did you know about Gina's life in Oxford?' asked Bridget. 'Did she talk about her friends, or the people she knew here?'

Mrs Hartman answered, her voice hoarse. 'Not much, really. Oxford isn't our world. But we were so proud of Gina when she got in. She were the first person in our family to come to university.'

Mr Hartman echoed his wife's sentiments. 'She were a bright lass, our Gina. She wanted something better for herself.'

Bridget recognised the pride of working class people who'd loved their daughter dearly.

'So, when can we see her?' asked Mr Hartman.

'I'll take you to see her body now,' said Bridget.

CHAPTER 9

The visit to the morgue was one of the most heart-
breaking of Bridget's career. Both parents wept
openly over the body of their dead daughter. Mrs
Hartman, in particular, was racked by violent sobs and had
to be supported by her husband. Bridget lingered nearby,
her gaze averted, feeling irrationally guilty about her own
personal happiness. What right had she to feel good about
life when Gina had lost hers, and her parents' world had
been so utterly devastated? Seeing them so distraught
made her more determined than ever to find out who had
killed their daughter.

Afterwards, she drove them back to the college and
handed them over to the solicitous care of Dr Ashley. The
young tutor seemed to be going out of his way to make sure
they had everything they needed. But the one thing they
truly wanted – the life of their daughter – he was unable to
give them.

With Andy, Jake and Harry fully occupied in poring
over the witness statements, Ryan eagerly tracking down
the women from the escort agency, and Ffion examining
Gina's phone, Bridget decided to go to see Nick Damon

alone.

She was relieved to escape the chilly confines of the morgue and her awkward, stilted attempts at conversation with Gina's parents. Back on the open road, she turned her music up loud and sang along to *The Marriage of Figaro* as she sped ever deeper into the Oxfordshire countryside.

If she hadn't been working on this investigation, she would have been heading to Vanessa's house right now, in anticipation of Sunday lunch. But at least she had dinner with Jonathan to look forward to this evening. That more than made up for lunch at her sister's. She just hoped that Jonathan and Chloe were getting on all right in her absence.

It was late morning by the time she pulled up in the driveway of the big house. A young man with cropped hair and bare, tattooed arms was at the side of the house, shampooing Nick Damon's black Mercedes S-Class. This was presumably Tyler Dixon, who had driven Gina to the party, and later taken her two friends back to Wadham College. Tyler glanced up at her briefly, then returned to his work, sloshing soapy water over the car with a large, yellow sponge. But Bridget felt his eyes on her back as she climbed the steps to the front door.

She rang the bell and was answered a few moments later by Brittany Grainger, Mr Damon's PA. 'Oh, good morning, Inspector,' said Brittany, displaying some surprise at Bridget's unannounced arrival. 'We weren't expecting you back again today.'

'I'd like to speak to Mr Damon, if I may. Is he at home?'

Bridget detected a certain reluctance on the PA's part to let her in. She looked tired and drawn. No doubt she'd hoped for a rest after her busy day dealing with the police. But she quickly recovered her poise and welcomed Bridget into the long hallway. 'I'll just go and tell Nick that you're here,' she said brightly. 'Do you mind waiting a moment?'

'Not at all.'

She left Bridget standing at the foot of the staircase with its elaborately carved banister. Now that all the party guests, police and scene of crime officers had disappeared, the house felt huge and very empty. Perhaps one of the reasons Nick Damon threw such lavish parties was to fill the otherwise cavernous space. The house seemed absurdly grand to accommodate one person.

Brittany's heels reverberated on the wooden floor as she returned. 'Nick will see you now,' she said. 'This way please.'

Nick Damon was once again closeted in his study, and Bridget was struck by the similarities with the warden's room at Wadham. The oak panelling on the walls, the well-stocked bookcases, the glimpse of a garden through the leaded windows – they seemed deliberately cultivated to create the same effect. Unlike the warden of Wadham, Nick Damon was no lord, but he clearly longed for the respectability that the house conferred. Perhaps that was the true reason for him living here. By clothing himself in a layer of decorum, he imagined that he could buy his way to the top.

He rose from his chair as Bridget entered, and came to greet her, holding out a hand. 'Inspector Hart, this is an unexpected pleasure. How can I help you this time?'

Today he was wearing a black turtleneck sweater in fine cashmere, the sleeves pushed up a couple of inches to reveal his expensive gold watch and the fine dark hairs that covered his arms. His lawyer, Mr Gold, was also present, dressed as before in a sombre suit and tie. He stood by the window, studying Bridget's movements like a snake poised to strike.

Bridget felt her flesh creep as his cold eyes rested on her. She wondered what kind of dealings might require these two men to meet on a Sunday. Perhaps a businessman like Nick Damon never stopped building his empire. Then again, maybe the lawyer had come to the house in anticipation of Bridget calling round to ask more questions. Her visit may not have been unexpected at all.

Damon gestured for them both to take a seat on a pair of Chesterfield sofas arranged next to a low table in front of the fireplace. Mr Gold remained standing in front of the window, profiled against the grey light outdoors, his face in partial shadow.

Bridget sat down in the seat that would best allow her to keep both men in sight. 'I'd like to ask you a few more questions about the party.'

'Of course,' said Damon. 'In that case, I'll ask Mr Gold to stay with us.'

'If you feel you need a lawyer,' said Bridget.

At that, Mr Gold smiled, although his face didn't soften. 'Everyone needs a lawyer, DI Hart, but not everyone realises it.'

Damon spread his hands. 'Mr Gold is right. He can be desperately dull at times, but he's never wrong.'

He sat down opposite her, crossing one leg over the other and resting one arm along the back of the sofa, trying perhaps a little too hard to appear relaxed.

There was a tap at the door and Brittany reappeared carrying a silver tray with cups and saucers, a cafetière of coffee, a small jug of cream and a plate of shortbread. Bridget waited while she fussed with the cafetière, served them all coffee, and offered Bridget a shortbread. Tempted though she undoubtedly was, Bridget declined, keen to move on with the interview.

'Mr Damon,' she said, once Brittany had left, 'I'd like to know if you have any idea who might have murdered Gina Hartman.'

Nick Damon raised an eyebrow in puzzlement. 'Surely you already know the answer to that? That man you arrested yesterday. Frost. He was the one who was found in bed with Gina's body. I doubt that a jury would have much difficulty finding him guilty. What do you think, Mr Gold?'

But Mr Gold said nothing.

'New evidence has come to light,' said Bridget, 'and we're expanding our enquiry to consider other suspects.'

'Like who?'

'That's the question I just asked you,' said Bridget.

'Ah, I see. You're looking for suggestions.' Damon rested his hand against his chin, as if deep in thought. 'No, sorry,' he said after a moment. 'I really can't help you. All my guests are highly respectable pillars of the community.'

'And yet one of them committed a murder.'

At that, Mr Gold interjected. 'No, Inspector,' he said firmly. 'That is pure speculation.'

'Really?' said Bridget. 'Then how else would you explain the fact that Gina Hartman was found dead in this house?'

'It's not my job to explain that,' said Gold. 'Nor is it my client's. So if that's the reason for your visit, I suggest you bring this interview to a close.'

'I don't think so,' said Bridget. 'I have plenty more questions to ask. For a start, I'd like to know why Mr Damon invited Dr Frost to the party. He was the only academic on a guest list comprising business people, public officials and even a Member of Parliament – all of them influential people. What was Frost doing here?'

'As I already told you,' said Damon, 'I met him at a pub in Oxford. I thought he seemed like an interesting person, and so I invited him to my party. Now I wish I hadn't. I hardly feel like any further explanation is needed.'

'I would suggest to you that it's in your best interest to provide as much explanation as possible,' said Bridget. 'Otherwise I will be obliged to go and re-interview all your guests.'

Damon sighed, and Bridget detected a change, albeit slight, in his relaxed demeanour. 'All right, then. I admit that I like to socialise with people who might be useful to me in my business dealings one day. That surely can't come as a surprise to you.'

'And how might an Oxford don be useful to you?'

'The colleges are always putting building projects out to tender. It's good to have friends on the inside. You know, someone who might swing the decision my way.'

'That sounds a lot like bribery to me.'

'Not at all,' said Damon, sounding angry for the first

time during the interview. 'No money has changed hands. No improper demands have been made. I simply throw parties and my guests have a good time. If that makes them favourably disposed towards my business interests, then it's all to the good. No hard feelings if they don't.'

Damon's account of his true motivation for holding these lavish parties tallied with what Frost had suggested during his police interview. Out of the corner of her eye, Bridget detected a movement by the window as the lawyer shifted position. He was almost on the brink of intervening once more. Bridget pushed on.

'Why the masks?' she asked. 'Why the false names?'

'Just a bit of fun,' said Damon. 'Everyone likes to dress up now and again. And people are more willing to open up when their identity is concealed. It helps introverts to mingle more easily. It's a fascinating psychological insight, don't you think?'

'It also makes it easier to commit murder when your identity is hidden,' said Bridget. 'Mr Damon, I must ask you, apart from hosting the party, what precisely were you doing on Friday night?'

'You're accusing me of the murder?'

'I'm asking you to account for your movements.'

Damon glanced at Mr Gold, who nodded his assent. 'Well, obviously I was here the whole time. I circulated among my guests all evening, making sure everyone was enjoying themselves. I must have gone to bed around two o'clock in the morning, after all the guests had gone upstairs and I'd sent the staff home.'

'Did you go upstairs at any time during the earlier part of the evening?'

'No.'

'What time did you last see Dr Frost?'

'I really can't remember.'

'And Gina?'

'Well, I suppose it might have been around midnight. I remember now that she wasn't around when the other two girls were ready to leave. There was some discussion about what had happened to her, but her friends seemed to think that she'd decided to stay overnight. If they'd expressed any concern for her welfare I would have looked into the matter.'

'And did you notice any unusual behaviour amongst the guests during the evening?'

'Not at all. Everyone was enjoying themselves.'

'Not Dr Frost apparently. We have evidence to suggest that he was drugged. Do you know anything about the use of Rohypnol at the party?'

'Drugs? I never touch them myself,' said Damon, 'but I can't guarantee that someone didn't bring something to the party. It's not an activity I encourage, but I can't be held responsible for what my guests do.'

'And what about Gina?'

'What about her?'

'What was your relationship with her?'

'I didn't have a *relationship* with her,' said Damon. 'I hardly even spoke to the serving staff. They were hired by my personal assistant.'

Questions about the party were sliding off Nick Damon like water off a duck's back. Bridget decided to try a different tack.

'Were you aware that Gina and Frost were at the same college and knew each other by sight?'

'No. I didn't know which college Gina was at.'

'Did you know that, according to Frost, Gina recognised him at the party and warned him to leave?'

'Warned him? Whatever for? What did she think might happen to him?'

'In view of what actually did happen, that's a very interesting question, isn't it?'

Nick Damon pursed his lips, momentarily lost for a reply.

'I don't see what relevance this has to the matter in hand,' said Mr Gold, stepping away from the window and moving to stand behind Damon like a guardian angel. 'My client has no knowledge of private conversations that may or may not have taken place between third parties. Do you have any further questions that relate directly to him, or are we finished here?'

Bridget addressed herself once more to Nick Damon. 'I'm going to ask you again if you'll agree to supply a DNA sample so that we can eliminate you from our enquiries?'

She was expecting another outright refusal, but to her surprise the lawyer raised no objections this time, and Damon himself concurred.

'Thank you,' she said when she'd finished taking the swab. 'That will help us a great deal.'

'I do hope so, Inspector,' said Damon. 'And I trust that you'll now be able to get to the bottom of this tragic affair with the least possible fuss and publicity. You must understand that it could be very damaging to my business and to the affairs of my friends if this turned into a scandal.'

'Believe me, I don't want any publicity any more than you do,' said Bridget.

'Good. Then we have an understanding.' He held out his hand to shake hers.

Bridget kept her hand at her side. 'No. I'm afraid I can't make any kind of promise. This is a murder investigation. Your business interests must come second, I'm afraid.'

CHAPTER 10

Ffion was in the kitchen at Kidlington, making herself a mug of liquorice root tea with a slice of fresh lemon, when Jake sidled in, looking edgy. 'Hi,' he said.

'Hi.'

'Sorry I missed you last night. I read the note you left me.'

'I waited for you,' said Ffion. 'But you didn't return any of my voicemails, so I went home.'

'Sorry. I had no phone signal out at the house. And it took me and the lads ages to wrap everything up.'

Ffion nodded. On reflection she realised that she had probably jumped to the wrong conclusion about Jake and Brittany. Her imagination had got the better of her.

But she couldn't let the subject drop completely. 'So that was your ex-girlfriend, then?'

'Brittany, yeah.'

'And you didn't know that she worked there?'

'I'd forgotten.'

Forgotten. Was that really the kind of thing you forgot?

He seemed to realise that his explanation didn't really

make the grade. 'I mean, I knew that Brittany worked for Nick Damon, but I'd never been to the house before. And it was all such a long time ago.'

'Six months.'

'Right.'

That didn't seem very long to Ffion. She knew that Jake's ex-girlfriend had shared his life for years, long before Ffion had appeared on the scene. And she could easily understand Brittany's appeal, with her pleasing looks and easy-going personality.

'Brittany hadn't forgotten you. She seemed happy to see you.'

'Yeah, well. I wasn't happy to see her. Listen,' he said, coming over to take her hands in his, 'you know there's nothing between me and Brittany anymore, don't you? That's all finished. It was over before I met you. You're my girlfriend now, and nothing's going to change that.'

She let him kiss her lightly on the forehead, then turned away. 'I've got to get back to work,' she told him. 'I've got Gina's phone to look at.'

'But we're good?' he insisted, keeping hold of her hands.

'Sure, we're good.'

She carried her mug back to her desk and settled down to work. The sooner this case could be wrapped up, the sooner Brittany Grainger would be out of her life forever. Then she and Jake would be able to return to where they'd been before. With that in mind, she unwrapped Gina's phone from its bag and prepared to search for any evidence that would lead to the killer.

The first thing she checked was Gina's address book. There were no surprises there, just friends, family and – of course – the ubiquitous Brittany Grainger, plus the number of the driver, Tyler Dixon. There was no entry for Dr Nathan Frost, which seemed to back up the tutor's claim that he had never spoken to Gina before the party.

She worked through the messages and phone calls that Gina had made in the days and weeks prior to her death, and checked them against the records that the phone company had supplied. Again, there was nothing that stood out as unusual or suspicious. The only relevant entries were a series of exchanges with Tyler arranging for him to pick her up separately from Miranda and Poppy. But Ffion already knew about that.

Instead she began to explore the various photos and videos that Gina had recorded. There were plenty of them. Lots of selfies, plus photos of Miranda, Poppy and others, presumably all students judging from the locations. Gina appeared to have no shortage of friends. None of the guys in the photos appeared to be boyfriends and none of the photos stood out as relevant to the investigation.

The first item of real interest was a video timestamped late on Friday afternoon just after Miranda and Poppy had left with Tyler to go to the party. Judging from the bookcase in the background and the arty posters on the wall, Ffion guessed that Gina had recorded it in her room in college. The confident and vivacious young woman spoke directly to the camera, which wobbled slightly as she held it at arm's length.

Okay, I'm all ready to go and do my waitressing thing. Very excited because Tyler told me there are going to be some important people there tonight. He sneaked a look at the guest list when Brittany was out of the room. The guests are all supposed to be incognito of course, but the local MP is going to be among them, which is really hypocritical given that he's always banging on about the importance of family values. I wonder if his wife knows he's going to be there.

It seemed odd that Gina had simply spent that time in her room getting ready for the party and recording videos. She hadn't been to a tutorial or finished off an essay before going out. There seemed no reason why she had needed to arrange for Tyler to come back to the college and take her separately from the other two girls. A second video taken half an hour later showed Gina standing outside the college gatehouse, wearing her waitress uniform of short black dress. Her wild corkscrew curls had now been corralled into a more formal updo. She seemed very excited by the prospect of the evening to come.

Just waiting for Tyler to come and collect me. Miranda and Poppy left over an hour ago, so he should be here any minute now. Very excited to see what I can uncover tonight. This could be my big break. Wish me luck!

The video ended with a smile and a wink. It was hard to believe that the girl who had been so full of life and energy was now lying cold in a mortuary refrigerator.

That was the last video on the phone, but Gina had also made an audio recording at the party itself. The file was almost ten hours long. Ffion donned a pair of headphones and sat back to listen to it at double speed, a skill she had acquired listening to podcasts while out running. If you trained your mind to relax and block out all other thoughts, you could absorb information at a much faster rate than normal.

The recording began just before Gina entered the house and was greeted first by Brittany and then by Nick Damon himself. Afterwards much of the audio was indistinct and meaningless, consisting of background music, laughter and inaudible chatter. More often than not it was Gina's voice that came across most clearly.

Another glass of champagne, sir?
Have you finished with that plate?
The bathroom is just down the corridor on the right.
Let me fetch you another.

It must have been tedious work, but Gina engaged the guests in a bright, cheerful voice that never seemed to tire. Ffion could imagine her charming all the men with her pleasant manner and striking looks. With her flame-red hair, she must have had eyes following her around the room.

Ffion pressed the pause button and replayed at normal

speed a snippet of conversation that had taken place between a young woman with an East European accent and an older, somewhat pompous man. Only the man's booming voice was fully intelligible.

I enjoy riding, of course. Do you like horses? What's that, my dear, you've never ridden a horse? Perhaps I could show you around my stables some time. Shooting's one of my passions too. It's a shame that fox hunting's been banned. Damn shame. It's the fault of those bloody city folk. What do they know about real country life, eh?

Ffion wondered if this was the elusive member of parliament that Bridget was trying to track down. It sounded like he was enjoying himself. She noted down his words, and resumed listening at double speed. There were still hours left to listen to.

Sometimes Gina returned to the kitchen to collect more drinks or food. It was quieter away from the main party and Ffion was able to hear the snatched conversations between the three waitresses more clearly.

Have you seen that guy in the jester mask? (Ffion recognised Miranda's voice.) *What a jerk! He keeps grabbing my bum.*

They think they can get away with anything, like no one knows who they are behind those masks.

You should complain to Brittany, they're only supposed to get off with the escorts.

Brittany doesn't care about that, just as long as the guests stay happy. (Ffion's ears pricked up with interest at that.)

That plague doctor's giving me the creeps. He stares at me every time I walk past.

You'll never guess who's here. (This was clearly Gina's voice.)

Who? Someone famous?

Dr Frost.

Who?

You know, the German lecturer at college.

Oh, him. (Disinterested.) *What's he doing here?*

Brisk footsteps were picked up on the recording and then Ffion heard the voice of Brittany sounding cross and bossy.

Come on, hurry up. What are you all doing in here? There should only be one of you in the kitchen at a time. You need to keep the guests supplied with food and drink.

So, thought Ffion, with some satisfaction, the personal assistant's own mask was beginning to slip. She wasn't quite as nice as she pretended to be.

From the change in background noise, Ffion knew that Gina had moved back into the main room. The murmur of multiple conversations was growing louder as the guests imbibed more alcohol and began to relax. For a long while, Ffion could make out nothing of any significance, then she hit pause again, and replayed another section.

There was a clink of glasses, and then Gina whispered something indistinct to one of the guests. A man's voice – it was recognisably Dr Frost's – replied, 'What was that?' His voice was muffled, as if he had a mouthful of food.

'I said, you should leave,' said Gina emphatically. 'You don't belong here.'

There was no reply, and after a minute Ffion surmised that Gina had returned to the kitchen. The clink of glasses and cutlery being loaded into a dishwasher temporarily drowned out all other sounds.

Ffion paused the recording again and made a note of the time at which this exchange had occurred – at approximately ten thirty.

Then she resumed her double-speed listening.

For the next hour or so, the party became increasingly raucous, and conversations grew even more difficult to decipher. If Gina had been hoping to use this recording as the basis for a newspaper article, she would have been disappointed with the results. So far Ffion had written less than a page of notes.

After a few more trips to fetch fresh supplies, Gina found herself in the kitchen once again with Miranda and Poppy, despite Brittany's instructions.

I think that if I get the chance (Gina was saying) *I might stay over.*

What for?

None of your business. And don't worry, if I get caught, that's my problem.

Gina, if you get caught, it will become our problem too. We don't want to lose our jobs.

Well, I'll make sure I don't get caught, then. But don't come looking for me when it's time to go. It will just draw attention to me.

This was presumably the argument that Miranda and Poppy had described. Ffion noted the time. It was about twenty minutes before midnight.

The party continued, becoming ever noisier. Then Gina must have run into someone in a side room, because the background noise noticeably lessened. Once again, Ffion resumed normal listening speed and wrote down what she could hear.

'What are you doing here?' asked Gina.

The response to her question was inaudible, but Ffion assumed that she was once again speaking to Dr Frost.

'You shouldn't be here!'

Now Gina sounded cross. She was evidently annoyed that Frost hadn't heeded her earlier warning to leave. Whatever the German lecturer said in reply was lost, but Gina quickly returned to the crowded hall, where those guests who had not yet retired upstairs were now making even more noise than before. After a few minutes Gina must have gone back to the kitchen, where she was accosted by Miss Brittany Bossy-Boots Grainger. 'Give me that tray and take a bottle of champagne and two glasses upstairs to Apollo. He's in the room at the end of the corridor on the right. Hurry now, he won't want to be kept waiting.'

Ffion wondered which of the guests had had the hubris to name themselves after the Greek god of the sun whilst she listened to Gina's footsteps ascending the wooden stairs. When Gina reached the upstairs landing her steps were deadened by a carpet. It was much quieter up here away from the party and Ffion imagined Gina glad of a few minutes' respite. She'd been on her feet for hours. Ffion heard the clink of crystal as if Gina was setting the champagne and glasses down, and then a knock on a door, presumably Apollo's.

Suddenly Gina let out a cry. It was soon muffled as if someone had put a hand over her mouth. There were sounds of a struggle: inarticulate grunts and the drag of feet over the carpet. A door opened and closed. Was it the one Gina had just knocked on – Apollo's door? Or another one? It was impossible to say. More gasping breaths. A thud. Some indistinct movements.

The audio continued, but now there was only silence.

CHAPTER 11

Bridget listened with the rest of the team as Ffion replayed the key snippets of Gina's audio recording. It was shocking to hear the actual murder taking place. After a morning dealing with the raw grief of Gina's bereaved parents, and an afternoon struggling to extract information from Nick Damon and his lawyer, this grim reminder of why they were all working so hard on a Sunday did little to raise Bridget's spirits. With nothing but an insipid coffee from the dispensing machine to energise her, her buoyant start to the day felt like an age ago.

'So, do we think that this man, Apollo, is Gina's murderer?' she asked.

'It's possible,' said Ffion. 'Gina was taking a bottle of champagne up to his room. We heard her knock on his door, and then she was attacked.'

'So if we can find out who Apollo was, we have our killer,' said Ryan.

'Except,' Jake pointed out, 'that Gina's body was discovered in Frost's room. And that's not the room at the end of the corridor.'

'So, did Gina go to the wrong room? Or was she attacked while she was at Apollo's door?' Bridget rubbed her temples with her fingertips. So many questions. And each new piece of information just seemed to raise more. She needed to start pinning down some hard facts. 'Who is this Apollo, anyway? Why didn't people use their real names?'

'It was all part of the game,' said Jake. 'Like the masks. Concealed identities.'

Bridget had long since lost patience with masks and concealed identities. 'We need to find out what alias all the guests used. Especially this Apollo character. Jake, speak to Mr Damon's PA first thing tomorrow and find out who they all were.'

'Um... yes, ma'am.'

Bridget sensed some reluctance on his part. 'Do you have a problem with that?' she asked.

'No, ma'am. Of course not.' But his ears were glowing a tell-tale pink, and Ffion was glaring at him with obvious displeasure.

Bridget sensed invisible undercurrents in this exchange, but had no appetite to delve into the matter this evening. 'Right now, I want to get hold of this MP, Hugh Avery-Blanchard. It's high time he gave an interview and provided us with a DNA sample. We've spoken to everyone else who was at the party. He's been giving me the slip for far too long.'

'It's Sunday evening, ma'am,' pointed out Jake.

'Well, he should have thought about that earlier,' snapped Bridget irritably. 'I'm going to call him now.'

She had given Mr Avery-Blanchard a fair chance to get in touch with her, but leaving a message with his secretary had yielded no results. It was time to give him a call on his direct line. She looked up his mobile number on the police database, and dialled. The phone rang three times before an imperious voice answered.

'Avery-Blanchard here. Who am I speaking to?'

'Good evening, Mr Avery-Blanchard. This is DI

Bridget Hart from Thames Valley Police.'

The MP exploded in rage. 'Bloody hell! Are you the woman Cynthia mentioned? You can't just call me on my private line, you know.'

Bridget held the phone away from her ear until the outburst was over. 'You didn't return my message from yesterday,' she said calmly.

'I'll return messages when I damn well choose!' bellowed Avery-Blanchard. He paused for breath. 'I've been very busy. Do you think I have nothing better to do just because it's a Sunday? There are far more demands on my time than most people imagine.'

Bridget thought it best not to mention the fact that police officers often had to work at the weekend too, as she was doing right now.

'Sir, I'm investigating a murder and I need to speak to you as a matter of urgency about a party you attended on Friday evening at the home of Mr Nick Damon. Would you be willing to come to the police station to give a statement?'

'Are you mad!' shouted Avery-Blanchard. 'What if someone sees me?'

'Then can I come and see you at home?'

'Certainly not!' He was practically spitting down the receiver.

'Then where would be convenient?'

The MP was breathing hard like a man on his way to an early heart attack. 'Look, if you must see me, I'll get Cynthia to open up the constituency office. You can meet me there.'

'This evening?'

'If we must.'

'I'd appreciate that very much, sir.'

'Meet me there in half an hour. And don't call me on this number again.'

The line went dead.

Bridget looked up at Jake, who was eyeing her with an expression of amusement. 'Jake, I think I'll take you with me, if you don't mind.'

'That sounds wise, ma'am. Just in case he causes you any bother.'

'What about the rest of us?' asked Ryan.

'It's too late to do anything more this evening,' said Bridget. 'I suggest you go home and get some rest. I need everyone in bright and early tomorrow.'

★

Hugh Avery-Blanchard's constituency office was located in the town of Witney, a drive of around half an hour from Kidlington. At this time on a Sunday evening, traffic was light, and Bridget made good progress in her Mini.

'So, what do we know about this Hugh Avery-Blanchard?' Jake asked, as they sped along the dark country roads, his long legs folded double in the Mini's constricted interior. Next time, Bridget really ought to suggest they take his car.

'Apart from the fact that he has a filthy temper, and is terrified of any kind of bad publicity?' she asked.

'And that he has a completely ridiculous name.'

Bridget chuckled. Hugh Avery-Blanchard's predecessors had owned land in Oxfordshire since the Norman conquest, and the family could apparently trace their ancestry back to 1066. In feudal times, Bridget's forebears had probably worked as serfs on his ancestors' estate. And people like Hugh Avery-Blanchard never forgot that.

'Why don't you look him up?' she suggested.

'Good idea.' Jake pulled his phone from his pocket. His typing wasn't quite as rapid as Ffion's, but it was still a lot more proficient than Bridget's own.

'Here we go. He's forty-five years old, married with two children, educated at a minor public school. He's been the Member of Parliament for Witney since the last election, and he's currently a Parliamentary Under Secretary of State in the Ministry of Housing, Communities and Local

Government. Doesn't tell us a great deal.'

'Oh, I don't know,' said Bridget. 'As I understand it, a Parliamentary Under Secretary of State is just about the lowest rung of government minister, but from the way he talks, you'd think he was next in line to be Prime Minister, which suggests he has a greatly inflated opinion of his own importance. Anything else?'

Jake did some scrolling. 'Well, he sounds like your typical rural MP, with strong views on family values, as well as an interest in field sports. He seems to enjoy killing animals and telling other people what to do. But this is interesting. He appears to be tangled up in some controversial building project that's planned for one of the local villages.'

'What sort of controversy?'

Jake read on for a moment. 'It's the usual stuff. NIMBYs trying to stop a housing development of one and two bedroom apartments and three bedroom starter homes because they think it will destroy the green belt and reduce the value of their own properties.'

Bridget knew that Jake was struggling to get onto the housing ladder and had little sympathy for the kind of people who blocked new developments. In fact, it wasn't long before they were driving through the village in question. A large banner strung up between two trees invited them in hand-painted red letters to 'Save Our Village. Save Our Greenbelt.' Bridget wondered just how far the middle-class residents of this quiet corner of rural England would be prepared to go. Would they lie down in front of bulldozers? Somehow she doubted it.

A thought occurred to her. 'Does it say who the developer is?'

Jake did some more scrolling. 'Damon Developments. Hang on, Damon Developments is one of the companies owned by Nick Damon.'

'Now why doesn't that surprise me?' said Bridget.

They soon arrived in Witney High Street with its assortment of eighteenth-century buildings housing an array of small, independent retailers including a butcher's, a hairdresser's, numerous estate agents, family-run restaurants and an exclusive home-furnishing store. Bridget grabbed a parking space between two oversized SUVs, and she and Jake walked the short distance to the constituency office.

The door of the Georgian building was opened by a woman introducing herself as Mrs Cynthia Duckworth. From her overbearing voice, Bridget immediately recognised her as the phone dragon she'd spoken to the previous day. She was older than Bridget had imagined, probably in her mid-sixties, but Bridget hadn't been wrong about the pearls that adorned Cynthia's ample bosom, which was firmly encased in a checked jacket with large brass buttons. She was taller than Bridget by some six inches and held herself very upright.

'Mr Avery-Blanchard is an extremely busy man,' she said in lieu of welcome. 'You're lucky that he's agreed to make time for you.'

Bridget bristled at the implication that a murder enquiry was less important than whatever a Parliamentary Under Secretary of State normally got up to on a weekend, but she kept her tongue. It was quite apparent that access to the MP was closely guarded by this woman, whose voice betrayed a note of fondness whenever she mentioned his name.

Cynthia knocked briskly on a panelled door and opened it without waiting for a response. 'The police are here to see you, sir.'

'Thank you, Cynthia,' said Avery-Blanchard brusquely.

'Would you like me to bring tea or coffee?' asked Cynthia.

'No. I don't think this meeting is going to take very long. I need to get home to prepare for the week ahead. I'll be back in the House of Commons for an important debate tomorrow,' he added, as if Bridget had no idea how a politician might spend his working week.

'Very good, sir,' said Cynthia, withdrawing and closing the door behind her. Bridget wondered if she was the sort to listen at the keyhole.

'Now, what is this about?' demanded Avery-Blanchard from behind his desk. He was a tall, broad man, whose hair was receding rapidly. Though only in his mid-forties, he looked considerably older. His flabby face was flushed an unhealthy claret, and his nose was riddled with a spider's web of broken capillaries. His generous eyebrows ascended and swooped as he spoke.

It didn't appear that Bridget was to be offered a seat, but she didn't mind that. It wasn't often that she had the chance to look down on witnesses while interviewing them. She stood in front of the desk, with Jake at her side.

'I understand,' she began, 'that you attended a party on Friday evening at the home of Mr Nick Damon.'

Avery-Blanchard's eyebrows immediately knotted together in indignation. 'And what evidence do you have to support that claim?'

Bridget hadn't anticipated a direct challenge to what seemed like an uncontroversial opening statement. 'Your name appears on the guest list, and several witnesses reported seeing you there.'

'Hmm, well, I shan't deny it,' conceded Avery-Blanchard with bad grace. 'What of it?'

'At that party, a woman was murdered. Her name was Gina Hartman.'

'Never heard of her,' declared Avery-Blanchard. 'What are you implying?'

'I'm not implying anything,' said Bridget levelly. 'I am simply interviewing you as a potential witness.'

'A witness? Not a suspect?'

It was a peculiar response, and Bridget wanted to say, *not at this stage*, but she knew she had to avoid antagonising this prickly individual. 'As a witness,' she repeated. 'We're interviewing all the party guests.'

'I see.' Her reassurance seemed to have dialled the politician's temper down a notch. 'What is it you want to know?'

'Perhaps you could tell me how you came to be at the party in the first place? What is your connection to Mr Damon?'

Avery-Blanchard's brows rushed to the offensive again. 'What business is that of the police? Mr Damon is one of my constituents, and a major employer in this region. He's exactly the kind of man that I ought to be associating with, don't you think?'

'I see. So you have no personal connection with Mr Damon?'

'I have personal connections with a lot of people. As I already told you, he's one of my constituents.'

'Have you been to any of his parties before?'

'Is that a relevant question?'

'I don't know at this stage, sir.'

'Well, then let's leave it for now, shall we?'

Bridget decided to focus in on the specific facts she needed to find out. 'We understand that the guests at this party assumed an alias for the evening. What alias did you use?'

'That doesn't seem to be the least bit relevant to me. I refuse to answer.'

'Then can you at least confirm that you stayed overnight at the house?'

Avery-Blanchard seemed to be calculating whether he could feasibly deny it, or refuse to answer. Eventually, he said, 'Yes. I stayed overnight in one of the guest bedrooms, then left first thing in the morning. Work to do.'

'Were you alone in your room all night?'

The red spots in Avery-Blanchard's cheeks turned brighter. 'If you or anyone else suggests that I wasn't alone, I promise you, I'll sue for slander. What do you take me for?'

There was a knock at the door, and Cynthia entered. 'Is everything all right, sir?'

'Yes, thank you, Cynthia. Detective Inspector –'

'Hart,' supplied Bridget.

'– Inspector Hart is just about to leave.'

'I'm not finished yet,' said Bridget. 'So if you could close the door on your way out, Mrs Duckworth...'

Cynthia withdrew, reluctantly pulling the door behind her.

'We won't take up more of your valuable time than is absolutely necessary,' said Bridget. 'Now, to the matter in hand. The woman who was found dead on Saturday morning was a student at Oxford called Gina Hartman. She was working as a waitress at the party. She had very distinctive curly red hair. Do you remember seeing her?'

Jake produced a photograph of the murdered student and placed it on Mr Avery-Blanchard's desk.

He studied the photo casually. 'Pretty girl. Yes, I think I do remember her.'

'Did you speak to her at any time?'

'Of course not. She was just a waitress.'

'Did she speak to you?'

'No.'

'At around midnight, Gina was given the task of taking champagne and glasses upstairs to one of the bedrooms. Did you see her then?'

'No, I already told you. I spent the night alone. Why would I have ordered champagne and glasses to be brought up to my room if I was alone?'

'Then what time did you go to bed?'

'I don't remember.' Avery-Blanchard looked to be on the verge of standing up and showing them the door. 'Now, do you have any more questions, or can I go home to see my wife?'

'Not quite yet,' said Bridget, holding up a hand to forestall him. 'I'd like to ask if you'd be prepared to supply a DNA sample to help us eliminate you from our enquiries.'

'A DNA sample?' The MP made it sound as though she'd asked him to donate one of his vital organs. 'I'm perfectly within my rights to refuse, and in fact I do refuse. I'm sorry to hear that one of the waitresses died, truly I am, but I can assure you I had absolutely nothing to do with her death. Now, I really must insist on bringing this interview to a close.'

'Before we do that,' said Jake politely, 'I have a question, if you don't mind.'

'What is it?'

Bridget was also curious to find out what her sergeant wanted to ask.

'Does your wife know that you attended a masked party at which professional escorts were paid to entertain the guests?'

At that, Avery-Blanchard blew his top. 'This is an outrage. How dare you bring my wife into this! You have no right to make such accusations, and if any word of my presence at this party gets out, then I'll have you both in court for defamation. Now get out of my office!' He stood up abruptly.

'Well, thank you for your help,' said Bridget.

Avery-Blanchard stood behind his desk, bristling with rage. He said nothing in reply.

They passed the secretary on their way out, and Bridget wondered how much of the conversation she'd overheard. Most of it, she guessed.

'And thank *you* for your help,' said Bridget.

Peering at them over her reading glasses, Mrs Cynthia Duckworth succeeded in radiating a great deal of righteous indignation as they left.

'Well, that was interesting, don't you think?' said Bridget to Jake, as they emerged onto the High Street. 'It would seem that Mr Avery-Blanchard is very afraid of something, and I don't think it's just his wife.'

CHAPTER 12

D r Nathan Frost wasn't ordinarily a religious person, but after the recent shock he had endured, he found himself in need of comfort and solace. There was something about choral evensong in the college chapel that was most soothing, whether it was the organ music, the familiar ritual or just the pleasing symmetry of the building's Gothic architecture.

He took a seat at the very back of the chapel, hoping to remain inconspicuous, but the wooden pews which faced each other across the black and white chequered aisle soon filled up with students and staff, so that everyone was forced to squash up in close proximity. It seemed that Gina's tragic death was drawing the college community tighter together. Yet Frost, who had found himself at the centre of this horrible drama, had never felt more like an outsider.

Miranda and Poppy, the other two girls who had worked as waitresses at the party, entered the chapel arm in arm, looking forlorn, as if the fate of their friend could so easily have been theirs. And perhaps it could have been, for Frost was still none the wiser about why Gina Hartman had met her death. Students flocked to embrace the two friends, offering their condolences, and Frost turned away in ignominy.

Lizzie and Lucy, the German students he'd been teaching on Friday evening, just hours before his world had turned so catastrophically upside down, glanced at him awkwardly before moving further down the aisle. He could hardly blame them for wanting to avoid him. What was the essay he'd set them? *By making his bargain with the devil, is Faust responsible for his own downfall?* How horribly ironic.

The Classics tutor, Dr Slater, sat in the pew directly opposite, his arms folded, his eyes fixed sternly on him, as if in judgement. Frost wondered if he would ever be able to bring himself to sit at high table again, or if he would have to take his meals in his room henceforth. All eyes seemed either to be turned his way in disapproval, or else averted in embarrassment.

The warden of the college took his place in the seat reserved for him at the very back, facing down the length of the chapel. Frost caught his eye briefly but Lord Bancroft was adept at not letting his feelings show. He gave no sign of acknowledgement, and Frost had no idea what he was thinking.

The service was about to begin when Dr Ashley, Gina's tutor, rushed into the chapel at the very last moment. Astonishingly, on spotting Frost, he made a bee-line for him.

'Do you mind if I squeeze in here?'

Dr Ashley was sweating slightly as if he'd been running. He fanned himself with an order of service. 'I just dropped Gina's parents off at the railway station. They wanted to go home as soon as possible. I don't blame them.'

Frost squirmed with discomfort. He had no idea why Dr Ashley was talking to him, when everyone believed he had killed one of the man's own students, but at least he had been spared the torture of meeting Gina's parents, a small blessing.

'The police released you, then?' said Dr Ashley.

'Yes.' Presumably everyone knew he had been arrested and held in custody overnight. 'There was no evidence to charge me. I was simply in the wrong place at the wrong time.'

'Then it's true that you were at the house where Gina died?'

'Yes.'

'And you found her body?'

'I did.'

Dr Ashley nodded gravely. 'I do hope she didn't suffer. You know, at the very end.'

Frost didn't know what to say to that. He could only imagine that Gina had suffered terribly. The image of her lifeless body would haunt him until the end of his days. He was relieved when the chaplain, a youngish woman who was very popular with the students, rose to stand before the altar and welcome everyone on this sad occasion.

Frost closed his eyes, barely hearing a word she said. He wished now that he hadn't come. There was no solace to be found in this place. He should have stayed at home in Headington, and kept away from college for a few days. In fact, he wondered if he might get away altogether. But the police had told him to stay in Oxford. He felt slightly feverish and wondered if he was sickening with something.

His thoughts drifted, as they so often did, to German literature, and in this case to Thomas Mann's *Death in Venice*, the novella in which the writer Gustav von Aschenbach's obsession with a young Polish boy leads to the destruction of his dignity and ultimately costs him his life. Frost's own dignity had now been thoroughly destroyed. He wasn't sure he would ever recover.

*

After returning from Witney, Bridget dropped Jake at the police station so that he could collect his car. She wondered if he'd be heading off to see Ffion this evening. There'd definitely been some tension between the two of them when Brittany Grainger's name had cropped up earlier, and she wondered what exactly was going on there. But it was no business of hers to ask. The trials and tribulations of young love, she mused.

She was about to drive off when she suddenly broke out in a cold sweat. She was supposed to have gone round to Jonathan's house in Iffley for dinner this evening at seven. Worse, she was supposed to have picked up Chloe from Vanessa's house after lunch. But she'd been so consumed with tracking down and interviewing Hugh Avery-Blanchard that she had totally forgotten.

She turned off the engine, pulled out her phone, which she had put on silent, and thumbed through the notifications. Oh God, she had a ton of missed calls and voicemails: one from Jonathan and half a dozen from Vanessa. Hating herself in equal measure for being such an inadequate mother and lover, she listened to Vanessa's messages first, enduring the unmistakable and progressively more pronounced tone of rebuke in her sister's voice.

Are you there? I wish you'd pick up the phone, Bridget. I must say I was very disappointed you didn't tell me yourself that you weren't coming to lunch today. Jonathan was very kind to collect Chloe and bring her here. I do think you take him rather for granted. And perhaps you should take more interest in what your daughter gets up to.

Bridget wondered what that last barbed comment was supposed to mean. Vanessa had a habit of dropping cryptic remarks instead of saying out loud what was on her mind. Bridget wondered what particular aspect of Chloe's life she had neglected this time.

Vanessa here again. If you could just give me a call to let me know when you're coming to collect Chloe, that would be much appreciated. I'm not surprised that she gets herself into trouble when you're hardly ever around. By the way, lunch with her and Jonathan was lovely. It's a pity you couldn't make it.

Now Bridget's mind began to imagine the worst. What kind of trouble had Chloe got into? They had spoken just this morning, and Chloe had been around at Olivia's house last night, so Bridget had no idea what Vanessa was alluding to. Why couldn't her sister just speak plainly?

Hello? This is Vanessa again. Jonathan's gone now and Chloe's waiting to be picked up. Are you going to be much longer?

Vanessa's clipped tones left little doubt that she was now fuming with Bridget. But there was still one more message to go.

Bridget, I suppose you must be dreadfully busy with this new case you're working on, but if you've got a moment maybe you'd like to pick up your daughter. Of course, she's more than welcome to spend the night here. I've got a spare toothbrush in the bathroom. But she's got school tomorrow so she'll need to go home to get her uniform. Toby and Florence have early morning tennis practice tomorrow…

There was more, but Bridget had grasped the underlying message. She was a useless mother, and Vanessa was much better at looking after Chloe than she was. It was a fair criticism. Her sister probably kept spare toothbrushes in her bathroom cabinet for precisely this sort of situation and had just been waiting for an opportunity to demonstrate her superior organisational skills. Although she resented Vanessa's accusation, Bridget felt suitably chastised.

Jonathan's message was far more conciliatory, but that didn't make Bridget feel any better as a person.

Hi, hope you're okay. I realise you've got a lot on at the moment so don't worry if you don't have time to reply. I just wanted to say, no worries about missing dinner this evening. I can always cook again another night. Take care, speak soon.

Oh God. She sank forward and let her head drop onto the steering wheel, imagining poor Jonathan alone in his kitchen, the food spoiling in the oven, wondering what on earth had happened to his date for the evening. Perhaps Vanessa was right, and Bridget really didn't deserve him. She did deserve Vanessa's comments however, even though she still didn't understand what Vanessa was talking about with regard to Chloe being in some kind of trouble.

Although she was desperate to call Jonathan to apologise, she knew that she had to phone Vanessa first and check on Chloe. Much as she dreaded her sister's inevitable rebukes, her daughter always came first.

Vanessa sounded exasperated when she answered the call. 'Bridget, at last. Where have you been?'

'Vanessa, I'm so sorry I missed your calls. I was stuck in Witney interviewing a witness. I know I should have contacted you, but I'm on my way now.'

'Well, all right. I'll make sure that Chloe's ready for you.'

'Thanks. But what did you mean in your message about Chloe being in some kind of trouble?'

'Well. Perhaps she ought to explain for herself. I expect she would have done if you'd been around to see her this morning.'

'Vanessa, please just tell me,' said Bridget through gritted teeth.

'Do you know where she was last night?'

'Yes, of course. She stayed over with her friend, Olivia.'

'And do you know what they got up to?'

'She told me they were getting a pizza and then staying in.'

'Well,' said Vanessa, 'what they actually did was go out to a party where Chloe drank vodka and stayed out late. Honestly, Bridget, I don't know what kind of girl this

Olivia is, or what kind of parents she has, but if Chloe was my daughter I'd be thinking twice about letting her go out with this girl again.'

'Oh God,' said Bridget. 'How is Chloe? Is she all right?'

'She looked pretty rough when she first arrived. I don't think the vodka agreed with her very well. But a couple of paracetamol soon fixed that. No harm done.'

'Oh, thank you, Vanessa, and I'm really sorry. Tell Chloe I'll be there for her in fifteen minutes.'

Before setting off, she called Jonathan.

'Jonathan, I'm so sorry. I've been incredibly busy today and I forgot I'd arranged to come over to your place and… what can I say? I'm hopeless.'

To her relief he didn't sound angry. 'Bridget, you're not hopeless. Well, not completely. You're doing a difficult and important job, and I understand that.'

'You're not angry with me?'

'No. And how is Chloe? Is she all right now?'

'I think so. I'm just about to go and fetch her from Vanessa's house.'

'Okay.'

'So I won't be able to see you tonight, but let me take you out for dinner tomorrow to make amends.'

In Bridget's experience most problems could be solved by a large plate of pasta and a bottle of Pinot Noir. And even the most intractable of difficulties could be put right with the addition of a chocolate panna cotta.

There was a pause at the other end of the line.

'Listen, Bridget, I'm sorry but I can't do tomorrow night…'

His voice trailed off and she wondered what was wrong. 'Jonathan?'

'Tomorrow is the anniversary of Angela's death, and I always visit her parents and go to the cemetery with them.'

'Oh.' Angela had been Jonathan's wife. She had died of a brain tumour three years earlier. Bridget could hear the pain in his voice and didn't know what to say.

'Perhaps we can see each other again in a few days,' he

said.

'Of course. I'm sorry.'

'Yes, speak soon.'

The line went dead.

Bridget sat in her car, in the dark, staring blankly at the wall in front of her. She had let everyone down today. Her daughter, her sister, and Jonathan too. And for what? Was she really any closer to uncovering Gina's murderer? It didn't feel like she'd made much progress.

She wondered if she'd taken on more than she could handle. For the first time since her promotion to detective inspector, she felt the weight on her shoulders becoming too much for her to bear. She was leaning on her team, on her sister, and on Jonathan for support. She was even leaning on her own daughter.

If she'd been around more to spend time with Chloe, she'd have found out for herself what she was really up to, instead of hearing it second-hand from Vanessa. And if she'd been around more, perhaps Chloe wouldn't have felt the need to lie to her, or to go out drinking in the first place.

Perhaps Bridget had been too greedy, wanting it all – a fast-paced career, a family, a new relationship. Perhaps by chasing all of those things, she'd taken on too much. But if that was the case, what was she prepared to give up? Certainly not her family. And she was desperate not to lose her career either, having fought so hard and for so long to get to where she was now. But that only left Jonathan.

Like Vanessa had told her, she'd taken him for granted. And she knew that she'd let him down badly this evening. It wasn't just dinner she had missed, it was an opportunity for him to talk about the past, and perhaps to begin a new stage in his life, a chapter he could share with her. Now all that felt in jeopardy.

It was obvious that he still felt a strong attachment to Angela, and especially on the anniversary of her death. How could he not? From what he'd told Bridget, he and Angela had enjoyed a perfect relationship until her life had been cut cruelly short. She had supported him in setting up his gallery, travelling to London with him whenever he went to auctions to buy and sell paintings. Somehow, Bridget felt certain that Angela would never have forgotten dinner with Jonathan. Maybe she was fooling herself to think that she could ever replace Angela in Jonathan's life.

With a sigh, she started the engine. The luscious strains of Puccini's *La Bohème* poured from the car's speakers, but she turned the music off, hardly in the mood to listen to tales of unrequited love. She drove despondently to her sister's house in leafy North Oxford in silence.

*

It was late when Jake phoned Ffion. Driving all the way to Witney for the interview with Hugh Avery-Blanchard had taken ages, and now he was tired and hungry. He wondered if she was waiting for him at his flat, or if she'd already gone home.

'Hi,' she said, when she answered his call. Her voice was cool, and he sensed that the issue of Brittany Grainger had not yet gone away. The look she'd given him when Bridget told him to give Brittany a call to find out about the party guests' aliases had seemed unnecessarily harsh. It wasn't as if he'd volunteered for the job.

'Hi there,' he said, injecting as much cheer into his voice as he could. 'I've just finished interviewing the MP with the boss. Now I'm on my way back. I'm starving. Fancy grabbing a takeaway and going back to my place?'

'A takeaway? Again?'

There was no disguising her lack of eagerness at his suggestion. She'd already made it known that she didn't share his enthusiasm for his dietary preference of tasty meals involving dead animals and saturated fat.

'I could cook for you instead, if you prefer,' he offered.

'No thanks.'

Well, his cooking might not be the best, but she'd never refused it before.

'Then, would you like to cook for me?' he suggested.

He was even willing to eat a plate of falafel and bean sprouts if that's what it took to keep Ffion happy. He could easily grab a quick bite to eat on the way over to her place to make sure he didn't starve.

'Not tonight. Perhaps some other time.'

Her flat refusal left him feeling rejected, almost shunned.

I haven't done anything wrong, he wanted to tell her.

'All right, then. See you tomorrow at work.'

On his way back down the Cowley Road he stopped his car and called in at the local fish and chip shop for an extra-large portion of haddock and chips, liberally doused in salt and vinegar. Under the circumstances, he felt more than justified in his choice of evening meal. Fish was supposed to be good for you, wasn't it? Even if it was doused in beer batter and deep-fried in fat.

He took the food back to his flat, found a football match on the telly, and opened a beer. As he began to devour the greasy chips and battered haddock, he couldn't help but be reminded of a long weekend in Scarborough he'd once spent with Brittany. Now there was a woman who never complained about eating proper food. She had a healthy Yorkshire appetite. He began to wonder what Brittany was doing right now, and whether she was also alone.

*

Dr Nathan Frost lay in bed in his small house in Headington.

After coming face to face with Dr Ashley in the college chapel, he'd foregone dinner in college that evening, unwilling to endure the continued scrutiny and side-long glances of his fellow dons. Instead he had cycled home and, with little enthusiasm, removed a ready-meal from the freezer and placed it into the microwave.

He'd eaten the food on his lap watching the news on television. War in the Middle East; the plight of refugees; a host of looming environmental disasters. The various crises paraded before him, brought into sharp focus by the faces of the victims, each turned despairingly towards the unflinching gaze of the camera. He knew he should have some sympathy for the catastrophes engulfing the planet, but his own personal tragedy consumed him to the exclusion of all else. He chewed his food, one mouthful after another, tasting nothing, until it was gone.

Now, at half past eleven, he lay awake, listening to the endless sound of traffic on the London Road. An ambulance on its way to the John Radcliffe Hospital sped past, siren blaring. A group of men on their way home from the nearby pub staggered past his house, their voices loud and belligerent.

He closed his eyes and tried to fall asleep. But he was afraid of what that might bring. Sleep meant dreams.

He was reminded inevitably of Arthur Schnitzler's novella, *Dream Story*, which had been turned into the Hollywood film *Eyes Wide Shut*, with some famous actor and his wife in the leading roles. Just like the antihero of that grotesque tale, he had willingly and foolishly entered into a world of decadence. A dangerous world, where the normal rules of society no longer applied. Of all people, he should have been forewarned. What use had all his reading and studying been, if he had failed to heed such obvious warnings?

He willed his eyes shut and waited for sleep to come.

He awoke some while later, enveloped in a cold sweat, the wisps of a dream still reaching out to him. Disturbing images of masked figures crowded around him, leering at him, accusing him of murder. Telling him he would have to pay for what he'd done.

But what had he done?

If only he could remember.

CHAPTER 13

After collecting Chloe from Vanessa's house the previous evening, an argument had inevitably taken place between mother and daughter during the car journey home to Wolvercote. Bridget's frustration after her interview with the recalcitrant Avery-Blanchard, followed by her telling-off by Vanessa, her feelings of guilt at abandoning Chloe and discovering about the late-night partying, and finally her misunderstanding, or whatever it had been with Jonathan, had left her frustrated and short-tempered.

'Why couldn't you have told me you were going out to a party?' she'd demanded of Chloe.

'Because I knew you'd totally freak out!'

'I'm freaking out now!' Bridget protested.

'Well, that just proves it then!'

Chloe appeared to have convinced herself that the vodka-drinking episode had somehow been Bridget's fault. And now, this morning, she seemed determined to punish Bridget further for her negligent parenting by lying in bed until long after the deadline for a school day had passed.

'You'll be late, and you can't blame me for that!'

Bridget declared. 'You're fifteen years old, and you can get yourself out of bed!'

By the time she'd finally prised Chloe from beneath her duvet, retrieved her unwashed school sports kit from the laundry bag – 'Mum! I'm going to stink wearing this stuff?' – 'Well you could learn to use the washing machine yourself!' – and battled with the roadworks on the Oxford ring road, she only just made it to the John Radcliffe hospital in time.

The hospital's senior pathologist, Dr Roy Andrews, had promised to make an early start, and Bridget didn't want to let him down, especially as she was the one who'd bullied him into making his promise. She burst into the autopsy suite just as he was preparing to begin the post-mortem.

'Ah, Bridget, glad you could make it. Now that the chorus has finally arrived, the concert can commence. As you can see, the soloist is ready to perform.'

The pathologist's normal hang-dog expression was partially obscured by the mask he wore over his nose and mouth, but his eyes twinkled at Bridget from beneath bushy eyebrows, and she knew that he meant no harm by his gentle teasing.

His assistant, Julie Pearson, who was laying out a terrifying array of surgical tools on the stainless steel worktop, turned and waved at her.

Bridget was always struck by the relentless cheerfulness of the people who worked in the mortuary, even if, in the case of Roy Andrews, it was a rather dour Scottish humour that predominated. Unmarried, and known to be something of a workaholic, his colourful collection of bow ties never failed to brighten up the department. Today a pattern of musical notes peeked out from under his gown.

The welcome from Roy and Julie, combined with the sobering surroundings of the morgue, helped Bridget put her own problems in perspective, and she began to prepare herself mentally for what was to come. She had arranged for Ffion to accompany her to the post-mortem, and was pleased to see that the junior detective had already arrived. The Welsh constable's natural sangfroid was a considerable asset in the presence of dissected corpses. Bridget had watched too many sergeants turn green under the harsh lighting of the autopsy room, and needed someone who wouldn't flinch at the sight of a knife slicing through dead flesh and tissue. Ffion had first demonstrated this ability during the autopsy of Zara Hamilton, a student found murdered at Christ Church back in the summer, and since then Ffion had been Bridget's go-to choice of assistant for such occasions.

Bridget herself was not immune to feelings of nausea while watching Roy Andrews mercilessly dissect a corpse, but she was usually able to steady herself with a few deep breaths. What motivated her to attend a post-mortem in person whenever possible was a fierce determination to bear witness to what remained of a human life, and to acquire first-hand knowledge of any clues to the nature of the killing. A post-mortem always had the effect of reinforcing her determination to catch the victim's killer.

Bridget changed into her protective clothing knowing that it made her look even shorter and rounder than usual, whereas Ffion managed to look alluring even in scrubs and a face mask. She shivered involuntarily in the cool, clinical environment which was devoid of colour and comfort. Roy and Julie were making their final preparations. She wondered what made someone choose to spend their working days in this soulless space with its white-tiled windowless walls, harsh strip lighting and humming ventilation ducts which seemed to sap all energy. And that was before you factored in the corpses.

In the middle of the chilly room, a body lay on a gurney, covered by a white sheet.

'Everyone ready?' The pathologist flexed his fingers which were encased in a pair of surgical gloves.

As ready as I'll ever be, thought Bridget. She nodded her assent.

Ffion was waiting eagerly, her notebook and pen in

hand.

Roy tapped a microphone which hung down from the ceiling above the body to check that it was on, cleared his throat, and began what would be largely a soliloquy, delivered in his resonant Scottish burr. Bridget was used to the way that Roy Andrews liked to make each autopsy into a performance. Not for the first time she thought he could have pursued a successful career on the stage, playing lugubrious characters in tragedies or dark comedies.

'Forensic post-mortem of Miss Gina Hartman, Monday the twenty-first of October, conducted by Dr Roy Andrews in the presence of Julie Pearson, DI Bridget Hart and DC Ffion Hughes.'

He removed the sheet to reveal Gina, who looked more like a wax model than a human being. Her mass of red curls had been tied back out of the way, leaving her face bare and exposed.

With quick, deft movements, Roy and Julie removed Gina's clothing – the short black waitress dress and her underwear – and bagged it ready to be sent to forensics. Stripped of her clothing, Gina seemed even younger and more vulnerable. Bridget took a couple of deep breaths as images of her dead sister, Abigail, sprang into her mind's eye, just as she had known they would. She swallowed as her thoughts turned inevitably to Chloe, and she said a quick, silent prayer of thanks that her daughter was currently safe at school.

Roy began to carefully inspect the body, speaking into the microphone as he proceeded to note the victim's eye colour, hair colour, skin condition, and other identifying marks. Julie cut off a sample of Gina's red hair, and took some nail clippings to be sent to the lab.

'She appears to be in very good shape,' said Roy, 'apart from the fact that she is, of course, deceased. So let's now turn to the cause of death. A cursory glance at the victim would seem to indicate that she has been strangled. Please step forward for a closer look and I will attempt to explain.'

Ffion moved nearer without hesitation, peering at the body with undisguised curiosity. Bridget shuffled forwards a couple of inches, feeling that she could already see more than enough.

'If we look at her neck,' said Roy, 'we can see patterns of contusions, and abrasions caused by fingernails.' He pointed to tiny curved marks either side of Gina's larynx, as well as some faint bruising.

'I didn't notice those on Saturday,' said Bridget.

'Don't worry, they might not have been visible then,' said Roy. 'As the skin dries out it becomes more transparent, and marks like this literally come to the surface. But it was not only the killer's hands that left these marks. The small indentations were almost certainly made by Gina herself as she tried to prise the attacker's hands from her throat.'

The image of Gina struggling in vain to save herself made Bridget's stomach turn over. She didn't think she was afraid of death itself, but she was nauseated by the idea of the fear and suffering that a victim went through in their last moments alive on this earth.

'The neck area,' continued Roy, 'shows signs of bruising caused by the pressure of the assailant's thumbs and fingers. Thumbs generate more pressure than fingers and these larger bruises at the front of the neck would suggest she faced her attacker.'

Bridget nodded.

'Death will almost certainly have been caused by asphyxiation. Do you see these pinpoint haemorrhages in the skin?' He pointed to a rash of tiny dots in Gina's cheeks. 'You can also see them here in the conjunctiva of the eyes.'

Bridget had so far tried to avoid looking at Gina's eyes, which were staring unblinkingly up at the ceiling, but now that the pathologist had drawn her attention to them, she couldn't help but notice the tiny red dots.

'They're called petechiae,' said Roy, 'and are caused by bleeding under the skin due to an increase in blood pressure. Taken on their own, they're not proof of asphyxiation, but given the other evidence so far, I think we can safely assume that's what they are.'

'I'm sure you're right,' said Bridget. She had never known Roy to be wrong.

'The internal examination will prove it, one way or the other. But before we move on to that, I want to draw your attention to other bruising on the victim's arms, shoulders and torso. This, while not serious, strongly suggests that some kind of violent struggle took place, probably before or during strangulation. I think it's fair to assume that Gina didn't go quietly.'

'Might she have screamed or cried out during the attack?'

'It's possible. But the presence of patterned contusions around the mouth indicate that a hand may have been forced over her mouth to silence her.

'Now,' said Roy, 'I expect you're going to ask me for a time of death right down to the last second.'

'You know me too well,' said Bridget.

'I shall do my best. If we work on the usual basis that a body cools down, on average, at the rate of one degree per hour, then we can work backwards to a likely time of death. When I first examined Miss Hartman's body at midday on Saturday her temperature was twenty-three degrees, which would indicate a time of death of ten o'clock the previous evening.'

Ffion, who had been about to write down the time of death in her notebook, looked dubious at this pronouncement.

'But aren't there other factors we need to take into account?' asked Bridget.

'DI Hart, I'm delighted that you've been paying attention to my lessons. Your attendance at these post-mortems has not been in vain. There are indeed other factors to consider, primarily' – he patted his own ample stomach – 'the amount of insulation the victim was carrying. In the case of Miss Hartman, who is somewhat more slender than me, we can safely assume a more rapid drop of body temperature. Therefore, I would hazard a guess that she died around midnight. The other factor which supports this hypothesis is the state of rigor mortis. She was completely rigid when I examined her on Saturday, but now you can see that the small muscles of the face have relaxed.' He prodded Gina's cheeks gently with one gloved finger.

'So we're looking at midnight, give or take, what, an hour either way?' asked Bridget.

'Give or take,' agreed Roy.

Ffion now made a note in her book. 'That tallies with the timing of the assault that we heard on the audio recording.'

Roy beamed with delight at this news. 'Then let us proceed to the second half of our performance. The internal examination.'

Bridget took a step back as Julie moved in with her scary-looking tools. She tried to mentally detach herself from the proceedings as Roy drew a Y shape on Gina's torso beneath the curve of her breasts, cut her open, and removed the breastplate to reveal her heart and lungs.

Roy kept up a running commentary as he lifted out the internal organs one by one, inspected them, and then passed them to Julie who placed them on the weighing scales as if she was working on the meat counter in Waitrose.

It was only when he came to Gina's uterus that he fell uncharacteristically silent.

'What is it?' asked Bridget.

'One moment, please,' said Roy. He removed the organ with the utmost care and passed it to Julie. The pair of them conferred with their backs to Bridget and Ffion for what felt like an age. Bridget desperately wanted to know what they were doing, and yet at the same time, she didn't. A cold feeling was creeping over her.

At last Roy turned to face her, his eyes unusually solemn. 'I'm afraid that I have bad news for you. There is evidence of a placenta in the victim's uterus.'

'You mean –'

'Yes,' interrupted the pathologist. 'It would seem that Gina was in the very early stages of pregnancy.'

CHAPTER 14

The photos on the website of Angel's Escort Agency suggested a glamorous backdrop of London's West End. The reality, however, was somewhat grubbier. Jake stopped his Subaru outside a betting shop in a commercial road in Whitechapel and peered out at the grimy-looking buildings and shops that lined the street.

'Is this the place?' he asked Ryan.

'This is the address she gave me.'

Ryan had spent an hour or more on the phone the previous day in contact with a woman called Angel, endeavouring to persuade her that it was in her best interests to allow him and Jake to interview her escorts in a place where they would feel safe. This was the result.

Jake left the car parked in the street, hoping it would still be there on his return, and followed Ryan up a steep staircase to a cramped office above the betting shop. The interior of the office was filled with a strong smell of cigarette smoke that a lemon air freshener perched on the edge of the desk did little to keep at bay. A well-tanned blonde woman of indeterminate age regarded them from behind a computer screen.

'You must be Angel,' said Ryan. 'DS Ryan Hooper. We spoke on the phone. And this is DS Jake Derwent.'

Angel regarded them with some disdain, a cigarette in one hand. 'I hope this ain't gonna take long. My girls are busy. They could be out earning money with clients right now.'

On a Monday morning? thought Jake. But he decided to let Ryan do the talking. The guy seemed to have a rapport with the woman.

'Don't worry, Angel. We'll be out of your hair ASAP.'

She tapped an inch of ash into a coffee mug. 'You can use the room at the back.'

The dingy space she indicated looked more like a broom cupboard than a habitable space. Jake coughed, and waved away the smog of Benson & Hedges that invaded his nostrils. 'Do you think we could open a window?' he asked.

'No. It'll let in all the traffic fumes,' said Angel. 'I like smoking, and if you don't, you can go somewhere else for your interviews.'

'It's illegal to smoke in the workplace,' Jake pointed out.

'I can do what I like here,' retorted Angel. 'This is my office. I don't normally have visitors. I'm probably not even insured for them.'

'You have insurance, then, do you, Angel?' said Ryan with a wink.

'You're a cheeky so-and-so, young man. Remember that I only agreed to help you out of the goodness of my heart.'

'And after I suggested sending some officers round to inspect the workings of the business,' said Ryan.

Angel sucked the last life out of her cigarette, stubbed it out, and lit up another. 'Just be nice to my girls – and boys. They're high-class, you know. I don't employ no riff-raff round here. I supply ladies and gents of distinction for dinner parties and conversation. Any other services they choose to provide is a strictly private arrangement between them and the client. Got that?'

'We've got it,' said Ryan. 'Don't you worry about a thing.'

Jake decided to let Ryan do most of the talking during the interviews. The garrulous sergeant was in his element interviewing the stream of gorgeous females who trailed in and out of the broom cupboard one by one, each with long, silky hair, flawless facial features and – Jake was pretty sure – surgically enhanced figures.

He soon began to lose track of them all. By mid-morning, Nina, Nikita, Regina, Arianna, and Mia had blurred in his mind into an amorphous mass of hair, teeth, pouting lips and sultry eyes. But none of them had proven to be very cooperative.

The truth was, despite the distraction provided by the escorts, his thoughts remained firmly fixed on Ffion. After spending the previous night alone, brooding over their relationship, he was determined to bring his disquiet out into the open. It was time to put an end to this simmering stand-off that had come between them, and to talk properly about where they stood and what they each wanted. As far as he was concerned, nothing had changed. So, he had bumped into his ex-girlfriend during an investigation. But there was nothing between him and Brittany. After the way she had treated him, there could never be anything between them. Ffion needed to know that. And she needed to trust him, and to accept what he told her as the truth. Without trust, the relationship would never last. Nodding to himself, he resolved to raise it with her when he got back to Oxford.

'Next!' called Ryan. The door opened and a good-looking young man entered the back office. Ryan seemed slightly surprised, but stood up and shook the guy's hand. 'DS Ryan Hooper and DS Jake Derwent. And your name is?'

'Josh. Very pleased to meet you, Ryan and Jake.' He shook both their hands, holding onto Jake's in particular for rather longer than seemed necessary.

'So, you were at the party on Friday night?' began Ryan.

'I was,' said Josh. '*What* a house! Have you been there?'

'Um, yeah,' said Ryan.

'Seventeenth century,' gushed Josh. 'Jacobean. All those lovely long galleries and mullioned windows. I can't get enough of that kind of thing.'

'Right.'

'Yeah, I'm studying for a degree in Architecture, you see. Working as an escort at weekends pays for my tuition fees.'

'I see, and have you been to that particular house before?'

'Ooh, loads of times. And always with someone new to spend my evening with.'

'Did you spend Friday night with anyone in particular?'

'I most certainly did. But you'll never guess who.' He waited expectantly.

'No,' agreed Ryan. 'I'll never guess. So perhaps you could just tell us?'

Josh frowned petulantly. 'A *judge*!'

'Did he tell you that he was a judge?'

'He didn't *stop* telling me,' said Josh, laughing. 'Some people like to show off, you know? I slept with a *very* famous actor once, and he just couldn't stop namedropping people the whole time I was with him.'

Jake studied his notes. 'Would this judge happen to be the Honourable Mr Justice Neville?'

'It would, indeed.'

'And did you spend the whole night with the judge?'

'What are you asking?' said Josh, looking coy.

'I'm asking if you slept with him.'

'Cheeky!' said Josh. 'But yes, since you ask, I did. Are you going to ask me how it was?'

'No,' said Ryan. 'I'm going to ask you if you saw the murdered woman, Gina Hartman, at any time during that evening?'

'She was one of the waitresses, right? I can't say I really

took much notice of them.'

'And did you see or hear any kind of disturbance? A struggle, or anything of that kind?'

'No.'

'Okay, thanks for your time, Josh. Can you send the next one in?'

'Is that all?' Josh left, looking disappointed to have the interview brought to such a swift end.

Jake glanced down at the list of names to remind himself who they were supposed to be interviewing next. It was Erika from the Czech Republic, who turned out to be a slim-waisted brunette with long legs and eyes like dark pools. Jake had flown to Prague once with his mates from Leeds for a boozy weekend. In between pints of the local beer, he'd appreciated the stunning medieval architecture of central Prague, but the drive from the airport had taken them through grim suburbs of monotonous high-rises. He wondered what sort of life Erika had escaped from to end up working for an escort agency in London.

She seemed like an intelligent young woman, although her English was heavily broken and accented. Like the other girls, she was very reluctant to talk. Ryan tried to gain her confidence with some easy questions to start.

'So, Erika, how long have you lived in England?'

'Is nearly two years now.'

'And you've been working as an escort all that time?'

Erika seemed reluctant to answer, perhaps sensing a trap.

'We're not here to cause you any trouble,' said Jake. 'We just want to see if you can help us find out who murdered Gina Hartman.'

She nodded cautiously. 'Is working as escort, yes. Is good money.'

'I'm sure it is,' said Ryan, 'for a pretty girl like you.'

She dropped her gaze to the floor.

'So, have you been to one of these parties in Oxfordshire before?' asked Ryan.

'Yes. Already twice. This is third time for me.'

'And what did you do at the party on Friday?'

'Talk to guests. Dance a little. Then go upstairs.'

'Who did you go upstairs with, Erika?'

'I go upstairs with man called Apollo.'

Jake pricked up his ears. He exchanged glances with Ryan, who leaned forward eagerly. 'Apollo? Was that his party alias?'

Erika frowned in puzzlement.

'Was that his real name?' clarified Jake. Ryan suppressed a snigger.

'Ah. No. Is not real name. Guests use other name at party… is alias, yes.'

'So who was he really?' asked Ryan, 'this fellow who thought he was a Greek god?'

Erika shook her head. 'Cannot say. He only call himself Apollo.'

'But did you recognise him? Was he someone famous?'

'Cannot say,' said Erika. 'He is wearing mask.'

'But he must have taken his mask off in bed. You saw his face, didn't you?'

'Yes.'

'Come on,' said Jake encouragingly. 'I promise that you won't get into any kind of trouble.'

She seemed to be thinking it over carefully. She glanced over her shoulder in the direction of the reception desk, where Angel was seated, another cigarette clamped between her lips.

'Anything you tell us will remain strictly confidential,' said Ryan. 'Angel won't get to hear about it.'

'Okay, then Apollo is MP.'

'Hugh Avery-Blanchard?' enquired Jake, trying and failing to picture the florid-faced MP on Mount Olympus.

She nodded.

'What time did you go upstairs with him?' asked Ryan.

She shrugged. 'Maybe ten. Perhaps little bit later.'

'Half past ten?'

'Yes.'

'And did you spend the whole night with him?'

'Yes. When I wake the next morning, he is already leaving.'

'So he stayed in the room with you all night?'

'Yes.'

'You're sure? This is important, Erika.'

'Yes.'

Ryan seemed disappointed by her answer. Jake knew what he was thinking. If Erika had been in the bedroom with Avery-Blanchard all night from ten thirty, then he couldn't possibly have murdered Gina, who had most likely been strangled at around midnight. Gina had certainly been very much alive when she'd taken the champagne up to Avery-Blanchard's room just before midnight.

A new thought occurred to Jake. 'Was Apollo alone at any time,' he asked her, 'for instance, when a bottle of champagne was sent up to the room at around midnight?'

Erika thought for a second. 'When champagne comes, I am in bathroom.'

'So you didn't see the waitress who brought it to the room?'

'No. Am in bathroom, like I say. I hear knock on bedroom door, then some kind of noise. When I finish in bathroom, champagne is in room, ready to drink. I don't see waitress.'

'What kind of noise did you hear?'

'I... maybe some shout... a woman, maybe. I don't know.'

'And how did Apollo seem after you left the bathroom?'

'Seem? Maybe... little bit red in cheeks.'

'Like he'd been in a struggle or a fight?'

'I don't know.'

'How long were you in the bathroom, Erika?'

'Little while. Few minutes.'

'Five minutes? Ten?'

'Maybe.'

'So is it possible that Apollo could have answered the door, gone out of the room, attacked Gina, and then returned?'

'I don't know. Maybe. Please, no more questions now.'

'All right,' said Ryan. 'Erika, you've been extremely helpful. Thanks for taking the time to talk to us.'

'I can go?' She stood up hesitantly, then left the room quickly, casting one last nervous glance over her shoulder with those smouldering dark eyes.

CHAPTER 15

Bridget left the autopsy in a sombre mood. The revelation of Gina's pregnancy cast a whole new light on the case. Dr Roy Andrews had confirmed that although the pregnancy had been in its very early stages, Gina would almost certainly have known about it.

Bridget remembered her own shock at discovering she was pregnant with Chloe. Staring at those two blue lines in the toilet cubicle at work. They didn't seem substantial enough to indicate the existence of a new human being. It hadn't been planned, unlike her sister's two pregnancies which had been planned and executed with the precision of a military operation, and Bridget suspected that Gina's hadn't been intended either. Having a baby would have meant a huge disruption to her academic studies, quite possibly the end of them, and she wondered if Gina had wanted to keep the baby. That decision would no longer have to be made.

The biggest question now was the identity of the father. It seemed a fair assumption that this was also the man Gina had sex with on the evening of the party.

'As soon as we get the DNA results back from the lab

we ought to know who she slept with,' Bridget said to Ffion as they arrived back at Kidlington.

'Although we haven't managed to get DNA samples from *everyone* yet,' said Ffion, as if her thoughts were running in tandem with Bridget's own.

'We're still missing the MP,' agreed Bridget.

It was hard to imagine that Gina had been sleeping with the pompous Hugh Avery-Blanchard, and yet if she had been searching for a story that would damage the MP's reputation, who could say how far she might have been willing to go?

'Have you looked at Gina's laptop yet?' Bridget asked Ffion.

'It's next on my list of jobs.'

'Good. See what you can find. She might have kept a diary, or notes for an article she was writing. Perhaps we can find out what she was working on for the student newspaper.'

'Will do,' said Ffion. 'What about you?'

'That,' said Bridget darkly, 'depends on what the Chief Super has to say.'

Detective Chief Superintendent Grayson was in his lair when Bridget went looking for him. He raised an inquisitive eyebrow as she knocked and entered his glass office. 'Progress, DI Hart?'

'Of a kind, sir.'

After she'd explained the latest development, Grayson looked even less happy than usual. 'A pregnant murder victim. The press will love this, if word gets out. Who do you think the father might be?'

'We're waiting for the results to come back from the lab, sir. But there's still one guest who's refused to provide us with a DNA sample: Hugh Avery-Blanchard.'

At the mention of the MP for Witney, the creases of Grayson's forehead deepened further. 'What do you intend to do about it?'

'He'll be in London now, at the House of Commons. He has a very important debate to attend, as he was eager to inform me. With your permission, sir, I'd like to go and see him again, and this time insist that he provides us with a DNA sample.'

'You realise that you have no authority to require him to provide one?'

'Yes, sir. Not unless I arrest him.'

She met Grayson's stare with an implacable look of her own. He had promised to help her if she ran into trouble getting any of the party guests to cooperate. Now was the time to test that promise.

Grayson nodded. 'All right, then. Go to London. Let's get this investigation wrapped up before the details start leaking to the newspapers.'

★

Although she'd enjoyed attending the post-mortem with Bridget that morning, Ffion was very happy to be left behind in the office to examine Gina's laptop on her own. Andy and Harry were in the office too, but they were both quiet workers who caused her no bother. She was glad that Ryan and his snarky humour were safely away in London for the day, and she was relieved not to have to face Jake right now. She needed time alone to sort out her feelings about him.

As she made herself a mug of chamomile tea, she thought back to the hurt look he'd given her in the kitchen the previous day, and the brief phone conversation she'd held with him late last evening.

She knew she'd treated him unfairly. He'd gone out of his way to be conciliatory, even offering to cook for her, or to come round to her place and eat whatever she wanted. And she'd turned him down.

It wasn't as if he'd done anything wrong. The fault lay firmly with Brittany Grainger, and Jake couldn't be blamed for having the misfortune to run into his ex-girlfriend. Ffion knew that he'd split up with Brittany on unfriendly terms.

So why was she so worried about Brittany's unexpected reappearance?

The conclusion she arrived at didn't make her feel proud of herself. She was treating Jake this way because of her own insecurities. She'd always felt awkward in the company of men. Her relationships with women always seemed to flow more naturally. But she liked Jake. She wanted to stay with him. And she wasn't going to let a woman like Brittany Grainger come between them. If necessary, she would fight to keep Jake. She would begin by apologising to him when he got back from London this evening. She would make it up to him, and eat whatever food he fancied. She wouldn't even complain about the mess in his bathroom.

Happy that she'd made her decision, she set to work on Gina's laptop.

She began by working through Gina's emails. There was nothing particularly unusual or enlightening about them. After discarding hundreds of spam messages from "Nigerian princes" and "technical support departments" and sifting through various online purchases, university admin messages and suchlike, there was little of note. Ffion moved on to Gina's search history.

This was more interesting. Gina had been running searches about Hugh Avery-Blanchard, MP, including his parliamentary voting record, his responsibilities at the Ministry of Housing, Communities and Local Government, and his involvement in a local planning matter that was proving to be controversial. There were also searches into Nick Damon's various companies and business interests, as well as the judge, Graham Neville, and other guests who had attended Friday's party.

After working through all of Gina's search history for the past two months, Ffion refilled her empty mug with more chamomile tea, and began to go through the various documents stored on the laptop. In addition to essays, lecture notes and other student work, Gina had been writing several articles intended for publication in the student newspaper. Some of these were music and theatre reviews, but one folder was dedicated to Hugh Avery-Blanchard, and in particular to the building project that marked the intersection between the MP's interests and those of Nick Damon's.

Ffion began to read from the most recent document.

MP Takes Backhanders from Local Businessman

What links the Member of Parliament for Witney, Mr Hugh Avery-Blanchard, and the millionaire businessman and owner of several construction firms, Mr Nick Damon?

Avery-Blanchard, who is a Parliamentary Under Secretary of State at the Ministry of Housing, Communities and Local Government, is expected to overrule local concerns and to give approval for the development of a massive building project that will change the shape of village life in West Oxfordshire forever. Local residents have branded the proposed housing development a blight on the landscape that fails to take into account the needs of the community.

This newspaper can now reveal that Avery-Blanchard, who is married with two children, and who has frequently spoken out about a "decline in moral values" has secretly attended masked balls at the home of developer, Nick Damon, at which "wild orgies" and "debauchery" have been reported.

Not only does this expose Mr Avery-Blanchard's shameless hypocrisy, but it also suggests a strong personal connection between two powerful men, hinting at bribery and corruption taking place at the heart of government...

After reading the full document, including the various notes that Gina had made for herself, Ffion concluded that the article was a work in progress, requiring further substantiation before the allegations could be made to stick. But Gina clearly intended to find out more, and perhaps had gone to Friday's party seeking firm evidence for her accusations. Her audio recording had no doubt been an attempt to catch Avery-Blanchard or Damon, or both, in some kind of incriminating act or admission of guilt.

From what Ffion had seen and heard, it would appear that Gina had failed to uncover any watertight evidence, but she had obviously been getting close to her quarries. It was certainly conceivable that either Damon or Avery-Blanchard had discovered what she was up to and had decided to take action to stop her.

If that was the case, it was possible that Dr Nathan Frost's theory that he'd been set up as a fall guy for the murder might hold some truth after all. Ffion tapped her teeth with her pencil, running through the various connections in her mind and testing her hypothesis for holes. She couldn't see any.

She reached for her phone and dialled Bridget's number.

★

Dr Nathan Frost sat uncomfortably in his chair, studying the familiar, yet now strangely alien surroundings of his room in college. Everything was just as before – the wooden chairs with their somewhat threadbare cushions, the sagging bookshelves, the faded curtains, the carpet worn unevenly where so many feet had trodden – but he felt that he was seeing it all through fresh eyes.

Outside, the college quadrangle stood unchanged, much as it had done for centuries. Yet the gold stone buildings and striped green lawn couldn't hide the fact that something vital had been extinguished. There was an absence in the world, a void where a wide, happy smile framed by long red hair had once faced the future, full of hope, and was now gone. The ghost of Gina Hartman would linger in his heart for as long as he lived.

'Dr Frost?'

He jerked in his seat, startled out of his introspection by the sudden interruption of the voice.

'Dr Frost, are you all right?'

Two girls sat opposite him. Lizzie and Lucy. He still had no idea which was which.

'Yes,' he mumbled. 'I'm fine. Do continue.'

The girls exchanged glances. 'Dr Frost,' said Lizzie or Lucy, 'we're waiting for you to begin the tutorial.'

'Ah, yes. Of course.' He sat up straighter, struggling to remember what he was supposed to be doing. Simple everyday actions seemed, for some inconceivable reason, to be beyond him at present. 'Please, read out the title of your essay.'

Nervously, one of the girls cleared her throat and began to read from the sheaf of papers she held in her lap. 'By making his bargain with the devil, is Faust responsible for his own downfall?' She paused, glanced up at him for confirmation, and then began to read her essay aloud.

Frost twitched in embarrassment as the girl proceeded to answer the question he had set. At the time – just a few days earlier – he had felt it to be a good question, designed to tease out the essence of Goethe's play even from the pen of the least able student, and yet to offer room for the more gifted to give full rein to their analytical powers.

Now it seemed so trite, so obvious.

In view of his recent experience, the answer to the question was abundantly clear to him. He wondered how on earth he could have posed it to so many of his students for so many years. What had he been thinking?

He began to squirm in his chair as he listened to Lizzie or Lucy speak. He raised a hand. 'Stop!'

She looked up, startled.

'Stop,' he said more gently. He had no wish to alarm her. He knew that he must have already caused enough trouble in his young charge's mind.

The two girls watched him, puzzled.

'Let's talk about something else,' he began. 'Yes...'

A thought was taking shape in his mind, coalescing out of the cloud of confusion that had surrounded him since he had woken up with Gina's cold corpse beside him. He blinked to rid himself of the image and to focus his powers of concentration. Yes, another question was forming – one that felt far more urgent and compelling.

Vital, in fact.

He leaned forward eagerly. 'Let's talk about this instead. Having accepted Mephistopheles' bargain and set the disastrous train of events in motion, what might Faust have done differently to avoid his fate, or was his downfall inevitable?'

The words seemed to flow naturally from his lips. After thirty years of setting the same essay, year after year, he was surprising himself with uncharacteristic novelty. Only a few days had passed, yet everything had changed. He was no longer the man he had been. He could never be that man again. Was it possible that what had at first seemed like a catastrophe was in fact an opportunity to reinvent himself?

'Dr Frost?'

The two girls seemed embarrassed by his behaviour, but he didn't care. He repeated the question, then dismissed them with a wave of his hand. 'Go on. Write it. Come back next week and tell me what Faust might have done to avoid his downfall.'

Tell me what I might yet do, he could have said. *Tell me how I can save myself.*

CHAPTER 16

After getting the Chief Super's permission to travel to London and interview Hugh Avery-Blanchard for a second time, Bridget drove directly to the railway station and just managed to catch the fast train from Oxford to Paddington.

Once installed in her seat, she sent Chloe a quick text to say that she'd be late home, again. Chloe replied to say that was no problem, and that she was planning to go into Oxford anyway and get a pizza with friends. Bridget resisted the urge to caution her daughter not to get into any trouble, and to nag her about homework. Instead she told Chloe to take care, and to make sure she was back by nine.

There had been no further communiqué. And nothing at all from Jonathan. But then Bridget hadn't really expected anything. He would be focussed on Angela today, visiting her parents in Angela's home town of Cheltenham, and laying flowers at her grave. Bridget wondered if it would be appropriate to send him a message of goodwill or sympathy, but it was impossible for her to think of the right words. In the end she decided it was best to let him be. She didn't want to seem as if she was staking her claim to him, today of all days. No doubt he'd get in touch himself when he returned.

As the train hurtled through the picturesque villages of Goring and Pangbourne, Bridget tried to put her personal concerns aside and to think about how she was going to handle Hugh Avery-Blanchard, MP.

Before setting off she'd made a rather laborious phone call to Cynthia Duckworth at the MP's constituency office, who, after some effort on Bridget's part, had eventually yielded the information that Mr Avery-Blanchard would be spending the afternoon at the Ministry of Housing, Communities and Local Government on Marsham Street. Cynthia had been at pains to stress how busy Mr Avery-Blanchard was and that it would be impossible for him to make time to see her at such short notice. However, a call to the Ministry had proved more helpful, and the person in charge of his diary, a much more obliging assistant called Ahmed, had conceded that the Under Secretary of State had a thirty minute window available between five and five thirty, and that if Bridget arrived promptly, he would make sure that she was able to see him.

Bridget checked her watch. The train was due to arrive at Paddington at four thirty-six. It would take too long to get to Marsham Street in central London using the notoriously unreliable Circle line, so she decided to take a cab and charge it to expenses.

It might have been easier to get the Met involved and ask them to obtain a DNA sample from the MP, but Grayson was adamant that involving another force would risk leaking details of the case to the wider world, something he was at pains to avoid. Besides, the last time the Met had got involved in one of her cases, Bridget had found herself working alongside her ex-husband, Ben, an experience which had left her very keen to keep everything in-house.

She knew that Grayson was putting his neck on the line in allowing her to proceed. The Chief Constable wouldn't be happy if word got back to him about what Bridget was about to do.

'I'll be as discreet as I can,' Bridget had promised. 'But it's really up to Avery-Blanchard whether or not he chooses to cooperate. If I'm forced to arrest him, then discretion flies out the window.'

But she was determined to obtain the DNA sample she needed, especially after receiving a phone call from Jake, who informed her that Apollo was the alias that Avery-Blanchard had used at the party, which meant that it was his door that Gina had been knocking at when she was attacked. A subsequent call from Ffion confirming that Gina was investigating possible corrupt dealings between the MP and Nick Damon identified him as prime suspect.

After a short delay outside Slough due to engineering works, the train finally pulled in to Paddington only five minutes late. Bridget made a dash for the taxi rank, jumped in the back of the first cab and gave the driver the address. As London cabbies were known for their talkative and inquisitive nature, especially where anything to do with politics was concerned, she busied herself with her phone to dissuade casual conversation about why she was travelling to the Ministry of Housing, Communities and Local Government, and was rewarded with a largely conversation-free journey, punctuated only by occasional maledictions from the front of the cab directed at other drivers.

After a convoluted trip across London, skirting Hyde Park and Green Park, the taxi pulled up outside a large modern building. With its louvered horizontal slats, the ministry building resembled a multi-storey car park.

Bridget paid the driver and got out. She was already fifteen minutes later than she'd hoped to arrive. On arrival in the building, which the ministry shared with the Home Office, she was forced to wait patiently while her bag went through an airport-style security scanner. On clearing security, she went to the desk where she was asked to fill out a form, and was issued with a lanyard to wear around her neck.

She checked her watch again and saw that her window with the MP was perilously close to closing. But after all this effort, there was no way she was going back to Oxford empty-handed.

Ahmed, who had been encouragingly helpful on the phone, was waiting for her in reception. Now the look on his face at her late arrival seemed much less accommodating. Bridget wondered if his boss had censured him for agreeing to the meeting in the first place. The thought of having Hugh Avery-Blanchard as a boss made her feel a pang of sympathy for the young assistant, even though he now seemed determined to put her off.

'I'm not sure the minister will be able to see you, after all,' he muttered as he led her through a maze of corridors and open-plan work spaces. 'Perhaps it would be better to come back another day?'

'No,' said Bridget. 'I don't think so.'

Eventually they came to an office with a plain wooden door. Ahmed gave his watch a final pointed look, but under Bridget's stern gaze, he knocked rather hesitantly.

An abrupt voice said, 'Enter.'

Ahmed opened the door nervously. 'Detective Inspector Bridget –'

'I know who this woman is,' snapped Avery-Blanchard from behind his desk. 'I don't have time to –'

'Mr Avery-Blanchard,' interrupted Bridget, 'or should I refer to you as Apollo?'

The MP closed his mouth rather suddenly as Ahmed looked between the pair of them in bewilderment. 'Close the door,' commanded Avery-Blanchard, dismissing his hapless assistant with a wave of his hand.

'What are you doing here?' he demanded of Bridget. 'I thought we had concluded our discussion yesterday evening.'

Bridget took a chair, though none had been offered, and sat down. 'Since then, further information has come to light. The alias you used at Mr Damon's house party, for instance.'

'I see. What of it? Are you planning to arrest me for assuming a false identity?'

'No, but I would like to know if you were aware that Miss Gina Hartman was investigating your relationship with Mr Damon, and in particular your involvement with a planned housing development in your constituency.'

The MP took on the look of a startled hare. 'She was what?'

'You didn't know?'

'What was there to know?' he blustered. 'I have nothing to hide about my dealings with Mr Damon.'

'And yet yesterday you threatened to sue me for slander if word got out that you'd attended his party.'

'I... may have been a little over-defensive about that. With hindsight –'

'Mr Avery-Blanchard, provided that you cooperate fully with the police investigation, there is absolutely no reason why anyone needs to know about your private affairs. Your wife included.'

'Good, I –'

'All I need from you today is a sample of your DNA.'

The MP glowered at her mutinously. 'And what if I refuse?'

'Then I shall have no choice but to arrest you on suspicion of murder.'

The MP's red cheeks flushed crimson with indignation. 'You wouldn't dare!'

Bridget smiled sweetly at him. 'Do you really want to put that to the test?'

Five minutes later she was back outside the building, the DNA swab safely in her bag.

'Paddington station, please,' she said to the driver of a waiting cab. 'As quick as you can.' There was a fast train back to Oxford in twenty minutes and she intended to be on it.

★

Jake was glad to leave the smoke-filled offices of Angel's Escort Agency behind and to drive back to Oxford with Ryan.

'You know that the air quality is seriously bad when even the motorway smells fresh by comparison,' remarked Ryan. 'Still, it was worth it to get another look at those girls, don't you think?'

'Mm,' said Jake, distractedly.

'Wishing you could take one home with you, eh? Or are you busy thinking about another girl? Things not going so well between you and Ffion?'

'It's complicated,' said Jake, not the least bit inclined to discuss his love life with Ryan.

'Yeah, she can be a real harpy, can't she?' said Ryan. 'I don't envy you, mate.'

'Thanks for your sensitivity,' said Jake. 'I knew I could count on your thoughtful input.'

'Just ask if you want some more where that came from.'

'I will.'

After dropping Ryan back at the station, Jake debated what to do next. He really wanted to speak to Ffion face to face, but didn't want to risk another argument by dropping in on her unannounced. Instead he picked up his phone and called her.

'Hey,' she said, her voice sounding less abrupt than last time they'd spoken. 'How was London?'

'It was all a bit sleazy, really.'

'The escorts, you mean?'

He laughed. 'Ryan, mainly. How was your day?'

'Interesting. I went to the post-mortem with the boss, then spent the afternoon ferreting out information from Gina's laptop.'

'Okay,' said Jake, hoping she wouldn't tell him anything about the post-mortem. The thought of slicing up dead bodies always made him feel queasy. 'So, what would you like to do this evening?'

He was fully prepared to go round to her place and eat

a plate of lentils, if it meant they could talk properly and openly. He wanted to explain to her once again that Brittany meant nothing to him, and to get Ffion's reassurance that she trusted him.

'Shall we go out for a meal?' asked Ffion. 'Maybe we could get a takeaway and eat it back at your place.'

'A takeaway?' Jake couldn't believe his ears. 'I thought you didn't like them.'

'I just want to do whatever you want.'

'Okay. Great.'

'And then I can tell you what I discovered about Gina,' she added.

'What was that?'

'That she was investigating Nick Damon and Hugh Avery-Blanchard,' said Ffion excitedly. 'I think she may have been onto something.'

'You think those two were up to no good?'

Jake pictured the rude, unhelpful politician and the smooth-operating businessman, and it was easy to imagine them involved in some kind of crooked dealings together.

'Gina certainly thought so,' said Ffion. 'And what's more, I think that Brittany Grainger may have known about it, too.'

Jake cringed, wondering why Ffion had chosen to mention Brittany, just when all seemed to be going so well between them again.

'What makes you say that?' he asked guardedly.

He could feel the conversation beginning to slip from his grasp. He wanted to talk about him and Ffion, not Brittany or the murder enquiry. But Ffion didn't seem able to stop herself, as if the discussion itself was drawing them both under by its own weight.

'Well,' she said, 'Brittany is Damon's PA, so she must know all about his business affairs.'

'Not necessarily,' he said.

'Well I reckon she's been lying to protect her boss.'

'What?' said Jake with growing dismay. 'Why do you say that?'

Ffion sounded dismayed too. 'Why are you defending Brittany?'

'Why are you accusing her of lying?'

'I always start with the assumption that people are lying.'

'Do you?' Jake demanded angrily. 'Is that the assumption you make about me?'

'No, of course not. I didn't say that.'

'Well, it sounded like it.'

A long silence ensued. When Ffion spoke again, her voice was cold. 'I've changed my mind. I think I'll make my own arrangements for food tonight after all.'

'Okay,' he said. 'Perhaps that's for the best.'

★

When Bridget finally got home to Wolvercote, it was late. But she was delighted to find that Chloe was back as promised, and that she'd even done some homework.

'I'm sorry I shouted at you last night,' Bridget told her. 'I was worried, that's all.'

Chloe shrugged. 'There was no need to be.'

'Maybe not, but that's what mothers are like. Especially when they don't know what their daughters are doing.'

'I wasn't doing anything bad,' said Chloe. 'Well, apart from drinking the vodka, I suppose. I didn't really like it, if that helps.'

'I would just prefer to know what you're doing in advance, rather than finding out afterwards from Aunt Vanessa.'

'I'm always sending you texts,' protested Chloe.

'But you didn't tell me you were going out to a party. If you had, I wouldn't have worried so much.'

'Wouldn't you?'

'Well, maybe not.'

'What you really want is for me to act like a robot and do exactly what you say,' said Chloe.

'I just want to know that you're safe.'

'Well, I was. So stop worrying.'

Stop worrying. It was an easy thing to say, but impossible to do. Worry wasn't something that you could turn on and off at will. It was always there in the background, gnawing away relentlessly, and it would never go away. All Bridget could do was try to live with it.

There was still no word from Jonathan either. Bridget wondered how he had got on, visiting Angela's parents, and whether he might call her later. Maybe she should call him. But she didn't want to come across as needy. No man liked that.

On an impulse she dialled his number anyway. She just wanted to say 'hi' and to hear his voice again. She was missing him desperately. But the call went to voicemail and suddenly she didn't know what to say.

'Oh, hi, it's me. I mean it's Bridget. Just wondered how you got on today.'

Stupid thing to say. Makes it sound as if he's been visiting a car showroom or something.

'Anyway, hope you're all right.'

Of course he's not. He's just spent a day visiting his dead wife's grave.

'I'm fine.'

That sounds insensitive.

'So, er, give me a call when you're free and maybe we can... meet up or something.' After a pause, she added, 'Bye, then.'

Oh God, she thought, as she put her head in her hands. Why was she so crap at this relationship stuff?

CHAPTER 17

Bridget arrived at work on Tuesday morning keen to find out whether her journey to London the previous day had been worthwhile. She had asked forensics to fast-track Hugh Avery-Blanchard's DNA sample through the lab overnight, and a lot was riding on the result, especially since the Chief Super had gone out of his way in lending her his support.

A brown envelope was waiting for her on her desk when she arrived, and she quickly tore it open and read the letter it contained. She was pleased to see that the MP's results were included along with all the other men they had taken samples from. But after reading the letter through twice, her head began to spin.

'What is it, ma'am?' asked Andy Cartwright, who was also in early.

'These are the results from the lab comparing the semen sample that was recovered from Gina's body with the DNA samples from the various suspects.'

'So which one of them was it?' asked Andy.

Bridget held the letter in front of her, still not quite believing it. 'None of them.'

Andy looked confused. 'You're saying that none of the men at the party slept with Gina?'

'That's right,' agreed Bridget, her sense of triumph at persuading not only Hugh Avery-Blanchard, but also Nick Damon to provide DNA samples, turning to dismay. 'But it's even worse than that. The DNA sample from the placenta has been analysed too, and it shows that the father of Gina's child isn't the same man who had sex with her before the party. And even worse, none of the samples provided by the men at the party match the placental DNA either.'

Andy's eyes boggled. 'So now there are two men we're searching for, and neither of them was at the party?'

'That's correct.'

The mood at the morning briefing quickly turned despondent after Bridget broke the news to her team, despite the input from Ffion, who explained that Gina was investigating a possible link between Hugh Avery-Blanchard and Nick Damon over planning permission for the proposed housing development, and the report from Ryan and Jake that the escort who had spent the night with the MP had confirmed that he had used the alias "Apollo", and that she was unable to provide him with a full alibi.

'So let me get this straight,' said Ryan, scratching his head. 'You're saying that we still have no idea who Gina slept with before the party, or who the father of her child is?'

'That's right,' said Bridget. 'And just to be clear, the person she slept with before the party is not the father of the child.'

Jake looked mystified. 'So where do we go from here?'

'We're just going round in circles,' said Bridget. 'But someone close to Gina must know about her personal life. I suggest we start with the other two waitresses, Miranda and Poppy. Ffion, you and I are going back to the college to speak to them again.'

★

It was mid-morning by the time Bridget and Ffion arrived at Wadham College. The quadrangle was largely deserted, with most students at lectures, in tutorials, in the science labs or in one of the many college or university libraries.

Finding neither Miranda nor Poppy in their rooms, Bridget decided to call in on Dr Ashley, the Psychology tutor who had been so helpful previously.

'You could try the college library,' said Dr Ashley. 'Shall I point you in the right direction?'

They followed him through a stone archway and into an open quadrangle facing a modern, three-storey hexagonal building that, to Bridget's eye, resembled a concrete fortress.

'This is the new library,' explained Dr Ashley. 'It doesn't have quite the charm of the old library, but it's very practical.'

'Yes, I'm sure it is,' said Bridget, who had fond memories of the ancient library of Merton College, with its barrelled ceiling, sixteenth-century fittings, and stained-glass windows.

After introducing them to the librarian, Dr Ashley wished them well and returned to his room. The librarian was happy for them to look around, and Bridget was willing to concede that, as Dr Ashley had said, the library was very well designed inside. The building was light and airy, with rows of neatly stacked shelves, and spacious tables at which students sat surrounded by piles of books.

The students glanced up at the detectives with cursory interest as they passed, then returned to their studies. Bridget remembered her own student days spent in the college library or the Bodleian. Apart from the architecture, the main difference between then and now was that these students were all using laptops and tablets whereas Bridget had written her essays laboriously by hand until her fingers cramped up and she couldn't hold the pen anymore.

Having established that Miranda and Poppy were not

on the ground floor, they climbed a short flight of stairs to the mezzanine level. This was a more informal space, incorporating a bean bag area, something else that would have been unheard of in Bridget's day, but she thought it was rather a nice idea.

Miranda and Poppy were slouched on black leather bean bags, books on their laps, in front of huge glass windows with a view across the lawn of older, more traditional college buildings. They looked up when Bridget and Ffion approached.

'This is my boss, Detective Inspector Hart,' said Ffion in a hushed voice. 'Could we have a word with you? Somewhere where we can talk in private?'

The girls looked at each other then nodded silently.

'My room's the nearest,' said Poppy. She led them outside and back to the front quadrangle. On entering the room she hastily straightened the duvet cover and stuffed a pile of dirty clothes into a plastic bag before sitting down on the bed.

Miranda took the chair by the desk, while Bridget and Ffion remained standing.

'What's going on?' asked Miranda. 'Do you have news about Gina?'

Bridget decided to let Ffion talk, since she had previously interviewed the two students.

As was her style, Ffion dispensed with any unnecessary preamble. 'Were you aware that Gina was pregnant?' she asked them bluntly.

'What?' said Miranda. 'No way.'

Poppy stared wide-eyed in amazement. 'She was pregnant when she died?' A tear began to form in one eye.

'That's correct,' said Ffion.

From the girls' reaction, Bridget deduced that the news had come as a complete surprise to both of them.

'I can't believe it,' said Miranda, shaking her head.

'Nevertheless,' said Ffion. 'The forensic evidence is clear.'

'Well, I don't know what to say,' said Miranda after a

moment. 'Gina didn't even have a boyfriend.'

Poppy nodded her agreement. 'We told you that before.'

Bridget wondered what the girls would say if they found out that Gina had at least two recent sexual partners. 'Was there anyone who Gina was particularly friendly with?' she asked. 'Can you think of any man she might have slept with, even if it was just once? Perhaps after a party? If she'd had too much to drink?'

'Gina never mentioned anyone,' said Miranda. 'And I can't think of anyone here in college who she might have been shagging.'

'What about a boyfriend back in Manchester? Or a holiday romance during the summer?'

'She didn't say anything,' said Poppy.

'But she could be secretive at times,' said Miranda darkly. 'She didn't tell us everything.'

'Can I just ask a question?' said Poppy, as Bridget prepared to leave.

'Of course.'

'Gina's baby. Was it a boy or a girl?'

Bridget shook her head. 'I'm sorry. I don't know. The pathologist's report didn't say.'

For some reason she couldn't quite put her finger on, her answer made her feel even more sad.

CHAPTER 18

After the investigation had run into a dead end, Bridget had asked Jake and the other detectives to go through the witness statements one more time in the hope of turning up a fresh lead. But the task seemed futile.

'This is a complete waste of time,' announced Ryan to the room at large.

Jake looked up from his desk where he'd been poring over an account by one of the party guests, the owner of a business specialising in building supply products, of how he'd spent his evening seducing a beautiful young woman. The guy seemed genuinely not to understand that the woman in question worked for an escort agency and was paid to be seduced by overweight middle-aged men such as himself.

Ryan ran his fingers through his hair so that it stood up in tufts. Witness statements were scattered over his desk as if he'd turned the file upside down and let them fall in random order. Ffion would have a fit at the chaos, thought Jake.

'If neither of the men who Gina slept with was at the

party, what are we expecting to find here?' moaned Ryan. 'We don't even know what we're looking for.'

Andy, who had his head down at the next desk, engrossed in the statements of various other guests who presumably had seen and heard nothing, merely grunted.

'Maybe it's time to grab another coffee,' suggested Jake. By his reckoning, coffee – or beer – was often the way to go when all else failed.

'Can't disagree with you there,' said Ryan. 'Where's DC Harry Johns when you need him? Harry! Time for you to go to Starbucks again.'

The young constable, who Ryan enjoyed tormenting, scowled. 'You can get a drink out of the machine here if you want one,' he said.

'We can't be expected to drink that dishwater.'

'Then you can go to Starbucks yourself,' said Harry. It seemed that the junior detective had finally had enough of being treated as Ryan's lackey.

'Go on, Ryan,' said Andy, smiling. 'The exercise will do you good.'

Ryan made no sign of getting up from his desk. 'Come on, Harry,' he cajoled, 'I'll buy you a beer at the pub tonight.'

'I don't drink beer.'

'Then it's about time you started. We'll make a man of you yet,' said Ryan, stretching his arms behind his head. He swung his chair to face Jake. 'Are you going to join us tonight, Jake, or you seeing Ffion?'

Jake felt his colour starting to rise. It was typical of Ryan to broadcast his enquiry to the whole room, knowing that the topic was a sore spot for Jake right now. Andy looked up from his pile of paper, mildly curious.

'Go on, spill the beans,' said Ryan. 'Are you two still together?'

The phone on Jake's desk began to ring and he grabbed the receiver as if it were a lifeline.

'DS Jake Derwent speaking.'

It was the duty sergeant. 'I've got a young lady in

reception who says she needs to speak to you urgently about the Gina Hartman case.'

A young lady. Jake's mind grappled to work out who it might be. Did the duty sergeant mean Erika or one of the other escort girls? But they were surely all in London.

'Did she give you a name?' he asked, picking up a pen.

'It's Miss Brittany Grainger.'

Shit, thought Jake. Brittany was the last person he wanted to see. But at least it would give him an excuse to avoid Ryan's obtrusive questions.

'All right,' he told the duty sergeant, 'tell her I'll be straight down.'

Brittany was waiting for him in reception, seated beneath a noticeboard covered in leaflets about crime prevention and drug abuse. She'd put her hair up in a French plait and was wearing a beige trench coat belted at the waist, with a silk scarf around her neck. She rose to her feet as soon as she saw him approaching.

'Brittany.'

She seemed upset. 'Oh, Jake, thank you so much for seeing me.'

'Couldn't you have phoned me if you had something to tell me?'

'I had to see you in person.' She laid a hand on his arm.

Aware of the duty sergeant watching from behind his desk, Jake turned aside to free himself from her grasp.

'We'll find an empty interview room,' he said.

'Of course,' breathed Brittany.

With her hair put back off her face, he noticed she was wearing a pair of silver heart-shaped earrings he'd bought her once for her birthday. He wondered if this was a deliberate move on her part to remind him of their former relationship.

'We can talk in here,' he said, pushing open the door to interview room two. 'Can I get you a tea? Coffee?'

'Tea would be lovely,' said Brittany, smiling at him.

He fetched two pale teas in plastic cups from the machine in the corridor and placed one on the table in front of her. It was a good job that Brittany wasn't as fussy as Ryan about what she drank.

'Thanks,' she said, taking a sip. 'I needed that.'

'So, what's happened?' asked Jake. He sat down opposite, glad of the solid table that separated them, and took out his notebook and pen.

She clasped her hands together on the table, her eyes downcast. 'I wasn't sure if I should come,' she said. 'This isn't easy for me.'

'Take your time.'

She drew in a deep breath and breathed out slowly. 'Okay, so, you know the gatehouse at the entrance to Nick's property?'

Jake pictured the small stone cottage located next to the gate leading into the estate – the one she now shared with Tyler Dixon – and wondered where she was going with this. If she'd come here to talk about the state of her relationship with her new boyfriend, then he'd have to politely ask her to leave.

'The one you share with Mr Damon's driver?'

Brittany shot him an agonised look. 'Please, I told you this wasn't easy for me. Just listen to what I have to say.'

'Okay. Go on.'

'So, Tyler's been living in the gatehouse ever since he started working for Nick. He needs to live on site so that he's always available if Nick needs him at short notice, and it means that Tyler can look after security too. It's not a big house, and it's quite cold in winter, but still it's one of the perks of the job. And after you and I split up, I had nowhere else to go, so I moved in with him.'

She gazed up at him, appealing with her eyes for him to understand.

Jake stayed silent and waited for her to continue.

'So, anyway,' said Brittany, tucking a stray strand of golden hair behind her ear, 'I was changing the sheets on our bed this morning and I found this.' She reached into her handbag and pulled out a small white envelope which she pushed across the table to him.

'What is it?'

'Look inside.'

Jake lifted the flap of the envelope. Inside lay a dangly silver earring in the shape of a leaf. He didn't touch it.

'What's this?' he asked, unable to stop himself glancing again at the silver earrings she was wearing.

'Isn't it obvious?' said Brittany, her voice wobbling. 'It doesn't belong to me. It's hers.'

'Hers?'

'Gina's. She was wearing earrings just like this when I interviewed her for the job.'

She reached into her bag and took out a small pack of tissues. Extracting one, she dabbed at her eyes which had started to leak tears. 'All this time, I've been blind to Tyler's faults, but now I know. He's been having an affair with Gina behind my back.'

Her lower lip began to tremble.

Jake sat still, finding himself torn between a desire to wrap his arms around her shoulders and hold her tight, and a firm longing to keep the safety of the table firmly between them. Now you know how it feels, he thought, and instantly despised himself. No matter how cruelly Brittany had treated him, he wished her no ill-will.

'I'm sorry,' he said.

Now that Brittany had started crying, the floodgates had opened. She scrunched up one sodden tissue and extracted another from the pack.

'I was busy up at the house all evening on Friday' – sob – 'getting everything ready for the party' – hiccough – 'and I wondered why Tyler didn't collect all three girls at the same time' – she paused to blow her nose – 'but now I know it was so that he could... he could shag that little slut in our bed.'

Jake maintained his silence, not trusting himself to say a word. He didn't know what to think. Was he glad that Brittany had finally realised that her new boyfriend was a jerk? Was he pleased that she had come to him shamefaced and chastened? Or should he be handing her over to one of the female police officers and keeping himself as far away as possible from her treacherous wiles?

Brittany blew her nose again. 'I'm the one who's truly sorry, Jake. Now I understand how much you suffered when I… when I cheated on you. You have every reason to hate me for what I did then.'

She reached across the table but he drew his hand away as if it had been burned.

His reaction seemed to sober her. 'So, what are you going to do now?' she asked.

'Do?'

He realised that she was speaking to him in his role as a police detective. Snap out of it, mate, he told himself. Pull yourself together. Whatever his personal feelings about Brittany, she had just handed him a new piece of evidence that might prove crucial.

The silver earring lay on the table between them. He pulled out an evidence bag and scooped it up, being careful not to touch it with his fingers.

'We'll send it to forensics and have it tested,' he told her. 'They'll be able to confirm that it's Gina's.'

Now his mind began to work through the implications. If Gina had been sleeping with Tyler immediately before the party, then he was clearly one of the two men they had been trying to track down. And if Tyler was in a relationship with her, might he also have been her killer? From what Jake had seen of the guy, it seemed a real possibility, especially if he'd found out that she was pregnant with another man's child.

Brittany nodded. 'Do you think it's important?' she asked.

'Well, it certainly helps to fill in a key blank in our investigation.'

'I suppose so.'

Jake wondered if she had really been asking a different question. How important was the revelation that Tyler had cheated on her to him personally? If she was asking whether the two of them might possibly have another chance at a relationship, then...

She slid her hand across the table again, and this time he grasped her fingers, holding them more out of kindness than anything more.

Just for a moment he was reminded of the good times, when they'd held hands across restaurant tables or gone for long walks together in the countryside.

'If only I could go back in time and live my life again,' said Brittany. 'I'd do it differently, Jake, I promise I would.'

There was a short, sharp knock on the door and it opened before Jake could free himself. Ffion stood there, taking in the scene with her green eyes, and Jake imagined how it must look: the pile of sodden tissues, Brittany's tear-stained face, their intertwined fingers.

'The duty sergeant said I'd find you in here,' said Ffion.

To Jake's ear it sounded like an accusation. He freed his hand and held up the evidence bag. 'Brittany, I mean Miss Grainger, has just brought in some new evidence. This might be the breakthrough we've been waiting for.'

'Really? That's good.' It was clear that in Ffion's view, the bag might just as well have contained evidence of Jake's own guilt.

'It's not what you think,' he said.

'You have no idea what I'm thinking,' said Ffion.

Brittany was hastily gathering up the tissues into her bag. Her tears had stopped as suddenly as they'd started. 'I'm sorry. I should leave,' she said.

'Would you like me to show you out?' asked Ffion.

'I'll do it,' said Jake. He had no desire to leave the two women together. That could be explosive. And he had no wish to face Ffion's wrath either. Much as he hated to admit it, right now the person he most wanted to be with was Brittany. He folded away his notebook and pen and stood up. 'And I'll take this earring over to forensics,' he added. 'Then I think we need to bring the boss up to speed.'

CHAPTER 19

There was definitely a strange mood apparent in the incident room when Bridget returned to Kidlington for a lunchtime debriefing on the morning's activities. Ffion was stony-faced, even though she'd been fine during the car journey back from Wadham, and Jake was quite obviously avoiding her gaze. If this behaviour carried on, she would need to have a quiet word with the two of them, although Bridget could hardly call herself a world expert in relationship problems, especially given the fact that she hadn't spoken to Jonathan since the weekend.

Ryan, Andy and Harry also looked thoroughly fed up, and she suspected they had no progress to report. The interview with Miranda and Poppy had led nowhere, and she was acutely conscious that Grayson would very shortly be demanding to know the results of the DNA tests she had obtained from all the party guests, Hugh Avery-Blanchard included. When he found out that none of them matched, he would no doubt go through the roof.

'Right, what have you all got for me?' she asked, forcing herself to adopt an optimistic tone.

To her surprise, Jake had big news. 'I think I've found who Gina slept with just before the party.'

'Really? Who?'

She listened with growing excitement as Jake filled her in on Brittany Grainger's visit.

'Can we be sure that it was definitely Gina's earring?'

'I've sent it off to the lab for testing,' said Jake. 'We should know by tomorrow one way or the other.'

Bridget sighed with relief. Progress at last! 'So, if Tyler is the man who slept with Gina before the party, we need to bring him in for questioning. And we need to get a DNA sample from him too.'

She looked at her team, deciding who to choose for the task. Jake and Ffion were clearly in need of some time apart, and from what she'd heard about Tyler Dixon, some muscle might be of use.

'Jake, Ryan, I'd like you to go and fetch him.'

★

There was a knock on the door and Dr Nathan Frost took a deep breath. 'Come in!' he called, with as much bonhomie as he could muster.

The door opened and two of his final-year students entered, clutching books and folders to their chests. Jodie and Gemma – or was it Gemma and Jodie? – were both fourth years, having spent their third year in Germany working as foreign language assistants in schools, or whatever it was that language students did these days during their year abroad. They glanced at each other as if they'd just been having a private conversation. He could imagine what they'd been talking about.

The warden had suggested that Frost might want to take some time off – 'Why not let things cool down a bit, eh?' But Frost, who had no idea what he might do with himself if he wasn't working, had protested that he had nothing to hide, and that staying away from college would only fuel the rumour mill even further. Besides, he had a teaching schedule to keep up.

'Do sit down,' he told the two students, who appeared uncharacteristically hesitant in his presence. He knew what they must be thinking about him. He was a monster. A killer.

He was doing his best to behave normally but it was difficult when people crossed to the other side of the quadrangle to avoid you. In the Senior Common Room, Dr Slater, the Classics tutor, had persisted in making veiled references to the Emperor Nero's more murderous antics, so much so that Frost had stopped going there, preferring to keep to the safety of his college rooms. In the evenings he cycled home to his house in Headington. He had no visitors.

As Jodie and Gemma took out their essays, Frost checked his notes to remind himself what question he had set them the previous week. Ah, yes. *Discuss the discord between genius and sanity in the works of Thomas Mann.* Not an easy topic by any measure. The question would require reference to many of Mann's greatest works, but principally his novel *Doktor Faustus*.

'Whose turn is it to read their essay?' he asked.

'It's mine,' said Jodie or Gemma. He noted that the girl had brought a copy of *Doktor Faustus* to the tutorial with her. A bright girl, Jodie – or Gemma.

'Please proceed.'

He put his head back in his chair and closed his eyes, the better to concentrate on what the girl was saying. He didn't expect too much from this first essay of the new term, but hoped for just one or two original insights into the work of one of Germany's greatest writers of the twentieth century.

In Mann's reshaping of the *Faust* legend, the fictitious composer Adrian Leverkühn strikes a demonic bargain, gaining unparalleled creative genius in exchange for the madness brought on by syphilis. He is propelled to fame and glory, before being reduced to a state of incoherence, living out his final years as a helpless invalid.

The thought made Frost shudder with dread. It was yet another reminder of how far he had fallen, and how much further he might still fall.

Sanity was a fragile thing, easily lost. Thomas Mann had understood this. As Jodie/Gemma regurgitated well-worn ideas on health, sickness, genius, madness and the moral disintegration of Germany in the 1930s, he wondered if he himself was losing his mind.

He had lain awake every night since what he now thought of as "the incident", plagued by fears, tormented by doubt. Sleep, when he was able to snatch it, did nothing to help, simply amplifying his worst terrors. He didn't believe he could have killed that girl, but how could he be absolutely sure? The blanks in his memory were torture. He had contemplated asking Dr Ashley, the Psychology tutor, if hypnosis might be of some use in recovering his memory. But Frost couldn't bear to speak to the man, so acute was his embarrassment.

'... for example in *Death in Venice*, ...' said Jodie/Gemma.

Frost had missed most of what she'd been saying for the last few minutes. But the mention of Thomas Mann's novella sparked a sudden recollection of the Venetian mask he'd worn to the party. The police had confiscated it as evidence, and he was glad it was gone. It was a hateful thing to him now. The masks worn by the guests had not only concealed their faces but had also hidden their humanity. When you lost sight of yourself, you could become anyone. You could do anything. That was what he'd wanted, of course, but now he saw all too clearly his mistake. If only he'd never met that damnable Nick Damon. If only he'd declined the invitation to that accursed party.

You shouldn't be here!

His eyes snapped open. Had Jodie/Gemma said that? He didn't think so. The girl was still ploughing gamely through her essay, now moving on to a discussion of *The Magic Mountain*, Mann's exploration of love and death amidst sickness and decay. But the words had come to him as clearly as if they had just been whispered in his ear.

They were Gina's words, spoken at the party on Friday night. He could hear her sweet voice as if she were here now. He had remembered them! The dark void of his amnesia had offered up this one brief recollection at last.

Just as he'd told the police, she had warned him to leave.

You should leave. You don't belong here.

He wished he'd taken her advice. Gina had known there was danger at the party and had tried to warn him. But like a fool, he hadn't listened.

You shouldn't be here!

But wait, had she been speaking to him that time? He had a feeling she had been talking to someone else. But if so, who? And why?

He struggled to remember, but the black abyss that had swallowed his memory refused to yield any more.

★

Jake was relieved to escape from the claustrophobic confines of the office, and to get away from Ffion's murderous glares. Out on the open country road he put his foot down, and even Ryan seemed impressed by his driving. The marked police car accompanying them just about managed to keep up.

'This Subaru can shift, can't it?' said Ryan. 'But can we switch the music off?'

Jake reluctantly silenced the heavy guitar riffs and pounding drumbeat of the Kaiser Chiefs. 'I was enjoying that,' he complained.

'Well there's no accounting for taste.'

'What do you like to listen to, then?' asked Jake.

'I'm more of an Eminem guy.'

'Really?'

'Yeah, I enjoy a bit of rap. Anyway, speaking of differences of opinion, you can take it from me that a bit of rivalry in a relationship never did any harm.'

'Is that right?' said Jake sceptically. He had no doubt that Ryan was referring to him and Ffion. Ryan never missed a trick, and he'd clearly picked up on the fact that there was something going on between himself, Ffion and Brittany, even though as far as Jake could recall he'd never mentioned to Ryan that Brittany was his ex-girlfriend. 'You're speaking with your deep and insightful knowledge of what women want, no doubt?'

'That's right,' said Ryan. 'What I'm saying is that if Ffion's a bit jealous, then it's a signal that she must really care about you.'

'I suppose so,' said Jake, brightening at the thought.

'And you can hardly blame her for being jealous, can you?'

'What do you mean?' asked Jake indignantly. He'd gone out of his way to discourage Brittany's attentions, and it was only her dogged persistence, and the unlucky arrival of Ffion in the interview room just as he was holding Brittany's hand that gave Ffion any valid reason to feel jealous.

'Don't be such a dope,' said Ryan. 'Brittany Grainger's hot. No wonder Ffion's always staring daggers at her. I'll tell you what, if you get tired of dancing to Brittany's tune, I might just ask her out myself.'

'Would you?' For some unaccountable reason, the idea of Ryan asking Brittany out on a date made Jake feel quite angry. He switched the Kaiser Chiefs back on. 'Next time I want your advice, I'll ask for it,' he said.

They arrived at Nick Damon's property just as the black Mercedes S-Class was also pulling in at the gates. The darkened windows of the car made it impossible to tell who was inside. Jake waited while the electric gates slid silently open, then followed swiftly on the Merc's tail before they could close again. The black car swept up the drive and swerved to a halt in front of the big house, kicking up a cloud of dust.

Three figures emerged: Nick Damon, his lawyer Mr

Gold, and the driver Tyler Dixon.

Today Damon was dressed in an immaculate charcoal suit, with a crisp white shirt and blue tie. He strode over to Jake and Ryan, a look of thunder on his face. 'What's going on? I don't take kindly to strange cars trespassing on my property.'

The marked police car that had been following pulled up behind the Subaru, and two uniformed officers emerged. Tyler Dixon and Mr Gold watched from a distance.

'I'm sorry, sir,' said Jake, 'but we'd like to ask your driver to come back to the station with us to answer some questions.'

'You want to speak to Tyler?' said Damon, his face clearing. 'Can't you do that here?'

'It would be more convenient down at the station. Will that be a problem, sir?'

'No, I don't think so, just as long as you don't keep him too long.' The businessman jerked his head at his driver. 'Hey, Tyler, the sergeants here want to ask you a few questions.'

'What about?' growled Tyler. He stood with his hands on his hips, his feet spaced apart in a confrontational pose. A sober suit had replaced the jeans and T-shirt Jake had seen him wearing previously, and a pair of dark sunglasses hid his eyes. 'I'm not going anywhere with *him*.'

Damon narrowed his eyes. When he spoke, it was with the authority of a man who expected to be obeyed. 'I think it would be best if you cooperated with the police, don't you, Tyler? I'll send Mr Gold to accompany you. I'm sure there won't be a problem.'

Tyler looked mutinous, but reluctantly he came over to the police car, with Mr Gold following a step behind him. One of the officers opened the rear door, but still Tyler hesitated before getting in.

'There's nothing to fear,' Mr Gold told him. 'You've done nothing wrong.'

Tyler's stony face stared back at Jake, his eyes hidden

behind his dark glasses. Eventually he made an inarticulate noise in the back of his throat, which Jake took as a grudging acquiescence, and climbed inside the car.

Back in the Subaru, Jake put his foot to the floor and the car sped off, back the way it had come. The police car followed close behind.

CHAPTER 20

When Bridget entered interview room two, it was immediately obvious that Tyler Dixon's mood was not propitious for a successful interview. He sat with his chair pushed back, leaning forwards with his hands placed flat on the table. His strong jaw moved rhythmically up and down as he chewed gum. He had removed his jacket, loosened his tie, and rolled his shirt sleeves up to reveal heavily tattooed and muscular arms. He looked like a cornered animal ready to pounce at the slightest provocation.

Bridget was glad of Jake's reassuring presence as she took a seat opposite.

Mr Gold the lawyer sat next to Tyler, steely and impassive as a waxwork in his pinstriped suit, shirt and tie. Bridget knew that he would do his best to shut down any line of questioning that risked getting Tyler into trouble.

Well, Bridget had dealt with obstructive lawyers before. She would worry about Mr Gold when the time came. Right now, her first challenge was persuading Tyler to open up and start talking. She knew that if she played this next part wrong he would probably refuse to answer any of her questions.

'Mr Dixon,' she began, once the preliminaries were out of the way, 'thank you for agreeing to come in and speak to us.'

She waited patiently for Tyler to respond. Eventually he grunted in acknowledgement.

First point to me, thought Bridget. Even a grunt was better than stony silence or the dreaded words, "no comment".

'You are currently in the employment of Mr Nick Damon. Is that correct?'

Tyler chewed gum in silence, as if considering whether he might plausibly deny the assertion. An almost imperceptible nod from Mr Gold swayed him towards an answer. 'Yeah.'

Bridget suppressed a smile. Now that Tyler had answered her first question she knew that she could keep him talking as long as she chose her words carefully.

'How long have you worked for Mr Damon?'

'About five years, I guess.'

'And how would you describe your job exactly?'

'Driving mainly. Nick likes to be chauffeured about.'

'Anything else?'

Tyler shrugged. 'Whatever needs doing. Car maintenance. I'm good with my hands, see?' He opened and clenched his large fists. 'Anything needs fixing around the house, Nick gets me to see to it.'

'What kinds of things?'

'Electrics mostly. Lights, thermostats. I'm in charge of security too.'

'Security? What does that involve?'

Tyler turned the question over in his mind, apparently searching for a trick. 'Gates, alarms, outside lighting. Plus I accompany him when he goes out.'

'I see. Does Mr Damon often require a bodyguard when he leaves his house?'

'That isn't what my client said,' interjected Mr Gold.

'Then perhaps he could explain for himself what he

meant,' said Bridget. She turned to Tyler with an expectant look on her face.

'Nick's an important man,' said Tyler. 'He's rich. A man like that needs protection.'

'Protection from who?'

'No one in particular.'

Bridget knew that if she pushed this line of questioning further she would probably lose the cooperation that she had won. 'Do you have any other duties at the house? Perhaps you help out during Mr Damon's parties?'

'Yeah.' Tyler seemed proud to acknowledge it. 'Like I said, I'm in charge of security. I stand on the door and make sure that people give the correct password before I open the gate for them.'

'On Friday, did you stand at the door all night?'

'Until the last guest arrived.'

'Which was when?'

Tyler shrugged. 'Around ten, I guess.'

'And then what did you do?'

'Helped myself to some food in the kitchen. I might have grabbed a quick beer.' He glanced sideways at the lawyer. 'Nick doesn't mind if I have just one. I wasn't due to be driving again for at least a couple of hours.'

'So you must have seen the waitresses going about their work?'

'I saw them. So what?'

'Did you speak to them?'

'Nah.' He shook his head.

'What about Gina?'

'I just said I didn't have anything to do with any of them.'

'And how did you spend the rest of your evening?'

'I just hung around until it was time to drive the girls back.'

'Can anyone vouch for your movements?'

'No.'

'Tell me again about when you fetched the three waitresses from Wadham College. You picked up Miranda and Poppy first. What time was that?'

'About six.'

'But you didn't collect Gina then. Why was that?'

'She wasn't there. The others said to go without her.'

'Were you expecting her to be there?'

'I guess.'

Bridget recalled what Ffion had told her about Gina's phone containing an exchange of messages arranging for Tyler to pick her up separately from the other two girls. 'We happen to know that Gina arranged in advance for you to pick her up later.'

'Right,' said Tyler, not missing a heartbeat. 'I forgot about that.'

'So you were in regular phone contact with Gina?'

'Not regular. Only when we needed to make arrangements for the parties.'

'So you saw her only when collecting her from college and returning her after the parties?'

'That's right.'

'Why did she ask to be picked up separately on Friday?'

'She didn't say.'

'And you didn't ask? Even though you'd been obliged to make a round trip of over an hour to accommodate her?'

'I get paid to not ask questions.' He winked at Mr Gold. 'Nick likes his staff to be discreet.'

'I see. So you always do what people tell you? Is that the kind of man you are?'

Anger flickered across his dark brow. It was obvious to Bridget that Tyler Dixon had an extremely short fuse, and the smallest thing might turn him to violence.

He chewed vigorously at his gum, working to bring his emotions in check. 'I do what Nick tells me.'

'Well, what a star employee you are,' said Bridget sarcastically. 'Tell me, what time did you collect Gina from college?'

'Must have been about half seven.'

'And what time did you arrive back at Mr Damon's house?'

The chewing gum was working overtime now. 'It was just after eight o'clock, I suppose.'

Bridget referred to her notes. 'The two other waitresses say that she didn't get to the house until nine. That's a whole hour unaccounted for.'

'They must be mistaken.'

'Really?'

'Yeah.'

Bridget produced the evidence bag containing the silver leaf earring. The lab had pulled out all the stops to examine it quickly. They were still running tests to see if they could match fragments of skin removed from the earring to Gina's, but they had already recovered a strand of hair that looked like it belonged to the murdered girl. That long red hair was very distinctive, and Bridget had no reason to doubt that Gina had worn the earring. She removed it from its plastic bag and laid it on the table.

'What is this?' asked Mr Gold.

Bridget didn't answer him. Instead she looked directly into Tyler's eyes. 'Do you know what it is, Tyler?'

He barely glanced at the earring before looking away. 'Nah. Never seen it before.'

'Take a closer look, Mr Dixon. Are you sure you haven't seen it before?'

'Well, it's not mine, is it?' he joked.

No one laughed.

'Did it belong to Gina Hartman?'

'How should I know?'

'Well then, let me ask you a different question. Does it belong to your girlfriend, Brittany Grainger?'

His gaze shot back to hers. 'Why would you ask that?'

'Does it?' she persisted.

'I don't know. It's not the kind of thing I pay much attention to.'

'Well,' said Bridget, choosing her words with care, 'It was found in your bed at the gatehouse. And we have evidence that it belonged to Gina Hartman. So how did it come to be in your bed, Mr Dixon?'

'How the hell should I know?'

As Bridget watched him, gears seemed to be turning slowly in Tyler's head.

'Did Brittany give you this earring?' he demanded. 'That bitch!' He clenched his fists. 'It was her, wasn't it? I'll –'

'Hey, cool it, mate,' said Jake, half rising out of his seat.

Mr Gold rested a hand on his client's shoulder and gave him a warning look. Tyler had long since shed any unwillingness to talk and was now speaking far too openly for his lawyer's liking.

With clear reluctance, Tyler settled back into his chair and Bridget continued with the interview.

'Were you having an affair with Gina?'

'Of course not,' he said. But his eyes remained resolutely on the earring now, as if he were trying to calculate how much the police already knew. It was the obvious tell of a man who was lying to save his skin and trying desperately not to trip himself up in the process. Bridget decided to push her luck a little further.

'In that case, Mr Dixon, I'm sure you won't mind providing us with a DNA sample?'

'What the hell for?'

'So that we can eliminate you from our enquiries.'

'No bloody way.' He crossed his arms in front of his chest and leaned back in his chair. 'They can't force me to do that, can they?' he added nervously to Mr Gold.

The lawyer scratched the back of his head, apparently also engaged in some calculations of his own. 'I think you might find,' he said, speaking slowly and deliberately to Tyler as if to a child, 'it might be in your best interests to cooperate with the police.'

'What the...?' Tyler turned on the lawyer angrily. 'That's crap advice, that is. Aren't you supposed to be protecting me? Can't you see what they're doing? They're trying to pin the blame on me. This is a bloody stitch-up!'

'A DNA test would, as they say, eliminate you from their enquiries,' said Mr Gold reasonably.

Tyler looked unconvinced by this logic. 'No. I won't.'

The silver earring still sat on the table, the only bit of hard evidence they had on him. But Bridget knew she was close to finding more. She didn't believe for one millisecond Tyler's denial about having an affair with Gina. The earring in his bed, his inability to account for Gina's late arrival at the party, his general behaviour under the pressure of questioning… all pointed to him being the man who had slept with Gina before the party. And if he'd later discovered that she was carrying another man's baby… it didn't take much imagination to picture a hothead like Tyler Dixon losing it and carrying out a violent assault. A DNA test would show one way or the other whether he was telling the truth.

'Then you give me no choice,' said Bridget. 'Tyler Dixon, I am arresting you on suspicion of the murder of Gina Hartman on the eighteenth of October.'

CHAPTER 21

By the time the interview with Tyler Dixon was finished, it was late in the day, but Jake's spirits were higher than they'd been for some while.

We've nearly got him, he thought, as he returned to his desk after handing the suspect over to the duty officer to be processed. After a night in the cells the cocky bastard might change his tune about his relationship with Gina, especially once the result of the DNA test was known.

The rest of the team had gone home and the incident room was dark and empty, but as Jake dropped his paperwork onto his desk, a voice called out behind him.

'What are you looking so smug about?'

He spun to face Ffion, standing in the open doorway in her green motorcycle leathers, the light of the corridor illuminating her short, blonde hair.

'I thought everyone had packed up for the night,' he said.

'I waited behind.'

'For me?' he asked hopefully. He wondered if she had calmed down now after their row the previous evening. If she had, maybe they could talk properly and get things sorted out. But then he remembered how she had caught him in the incident room this morning, Brittany's hand in his.

'I hear you've arrested Tyler Dixon,' she said.

'Yes, that's right. It's a good result.'

'Is it? Or do you just dislike the guy because your girlfriend preferred him to you? Perhaps this is personal.'

Jake was stung by her accusation. 'If you're suggesting I somehow set up Tyler just because I don't like him...'

'But you don't like him, do you? You hate him. He makes you feel threatened.'

A bunch of possible retorts all popped into Jake's head at once, but he held his tongue. If Ffion was trying to provoke him into a fight, he wouldn't rise to the bait. 'That earring didn't find its own way into his bed,' he said quietly.

'Maybe not, but I still think you're refusing to face up to the truth.'

'Which is what, precisely?'

'That Brittany Grainger probably knows a lot more about Nick Damon's activities than she's admitted.'

'Oh, does she, indeed? And now who's jealous?'

Ffion regarded him with composure. 'If I'm jealous it's only because you've given me good reason to be. She levelled a green fingernail at him. 'The problem is that you're blind to her faults because you're still partly in love with her.'

'I am not!' he declared.

In love with Brittany? Of course he wasn't! After the way she had treated him...

'And don't you think you should have declared to Bridget that you have a serious conflict of interest in this case?'

'I do not!' But did he? His head was starting to spin.

'Just think about it,' said Ffion. 'And call me when you've made up your mind whether you want me, or if you still want her. Because right now you seem to want both.' She grabbed her biker's jacket from the back of her chair and left the room.

Jake stayed where he was, glaring at the empty doorway where she had stood. His heart was racing, his breaths coming in short gasps. He knew that he was on the brink of losing her.

He didn't want that. And yet, he knew there was a germ of truth in what she'd said. Brittany still had a power over him. There was a physical magnetism to her that simply drew him in, and the only way he could ever truly free himself of that force was to get her out of his life once and for all.

He switched off his computer, locked the paperwork in his desk drawer, and headed outside, resigned to yet another night alone eating takeaway food in front of the telly.

He was halfway across the car park when he heard a woman's footsteps behind him.

'Jake, I'm so glad I've caught you.'

'Brittany, what are you doing here?'

She gave a helpless shrug. 'I've been sitting in the café across the road from the police station all afternoon. I didn't know where else to go. I couldn't go home, could I? It's over between me and Tyler now.' She began to weep, a single tear running down the curve of her cheek.

'Shit, yeah.' Jake hadn't really thought that through. He'd been too caught up in Tyler's arrest and his argument with Ffion.

'So, did you bring Tyler in for questioning?'

He nodded. 'He's under arrest.'

'Oh my God.' Her voice cracked and she wiped her eyes with the back of her hand.

Jake stood inert, willing himself not to take her in his arms. 'I understand,' he said. 'This must be really hard on you.'

She offered him a small, watery smile. 'I knew you would, Jake. You were always such an understanding person.'

'So, er, where will you go if you can't go back to the

gatehouse?' he asked her.

'I don't know. I haven't really thought about it. I suppose I'll have to check into a hotel for a few nights until I can get myself sorted out. It'll cost money, but what choice –'

'No, don't do that.' The words were out of his mouth before he could stop himself.

Brittany looked at him with her wet eyes. She looked lost and vulnerable.

'My flat's not very big,' said Jake, 'but I don't mind sleeping on the couch. Just until you get yourself back on your feet.'

He refused to think what Ffion would say if she found out what he was doing.

Or Bridget for that matter, if she knew that he was accommodating one of the key witnesses in the investigation. But Brittany wasn't just any witness. He couldn't stand by when she was suffering like this.

'Oh, Jake, I don't know what to say. You're so kind. But I don't want to cause any trouble… what about that other detective? I got the impression you and she were…'

'Just good friends,' said Jake, although the words felt like a betrayal in his mouth.

The truth was, he didn't know where he stood with Ffion anymore. But he knew that Brittany needed his help.

'Well, in that case,' she said, her smile brightening. 'Thank you very much.' She kissed him lightly on the cheek.

*

There had still been no communication of any kind from Jonathan, and Bridget now regretted the garbled message she'd left on his voicemail the previous night. With hindsight, it would have been much better to give him some space. It was still too early in their relationship to be sure of what they each wanted, but it seemed that what Jonathan wanted from her right now was silence. He had been out of touch for two whole days. Maybe visiting Angela's grave had sown doubts in his mind about Bridget's suitability as a partner. Perhaps, after comparing the idealised memory of his wife to the glaring reality of Bridget, with all her hang-ups, preoccupations and failings – not to mention her appalling timekeeping – he had found her sadly wanting. In a fit of gloomy fatalism, she wondered whether they would both be better off apart. Perhaps Bridget was destined to spend the rest of her life single.

After checking her phone once again for missed calls or messages, she poured herself a large glass of Pinot Noir and took it through to the lounge. There, she turned up the volume on *Madame Butterfly* and began to work her way through some rather congealed leftover Bolognese sauce that she'd reheated in the microwave, which she ate with a slice of toasted bread straight out of the freezer. Vanessa would have been horrified, but Vanessa wasn't around to see. To Bridget's gratification, the wine/toast/sauce combo worked surprisingly well together.

Chloe was out with friends yet again, and Bridget lacked the energy or willpower to try to make contact. On the face of the available evidence, her habit of bombarding her teenage daughter with an endless stream of electronic messages had succeeded only in driving her further away. As Chloe grew older a gap was opening up between mother and daughter and Bridget didn't know how to bridge it. Everything she did seemed to open it even wider. She reflected that she might be better off giving Chloe her own space, just as she ought to have left Jonathan alone to grieve in private. It so often seemed that every time she intervened in a tricky situation, the result was the opposite of what she intended.

She took another large gulp of wine and discovered that her glass was almost empty already. She topped it up from the bottle – might as well finish it off now.

As Puccini's love duet soared to its heart-rending climax, her phone rang. She almost missed it over the swell of the music, but leaned over to grab hold of it just before it went to voicemail.

'Hello?'

'Bridget, it's me, Jonathan. How are you?'

'Jonathan,' she said, almost breathless with relief at the sound of his voice. 'Hang on, let me turn the music down so I can hear you.'

She stumbled off the sofa and turned the volume down. 'That's better. Listen, I'm so sorry about that message I left earlier. I was stupid. I should have given you some space and I don't want you to think –'

'Bridget, stop,' said Jonathan, interrupting her. 'There's no need to apologise. I'm the one who's sorry. I should have called you earlier, but the traffic was terrible driving home – there was an accident on the A40.'

'Oh.'

'But that's really just an excuse. I should have phoned you back yesterday.'

'There was no need,' she said quickly.

'There was. I really ought to have returned your call. It's just that I've been doing a lot of thinking since visiting Angela's grave, and –'

'Yes?' Bridget felt a hard lump in her throat, as if her whole heart had leapt out of her chest in anticipation of the realisation of her worst fears. Was Jonathan about to tell her that it was all over? She wondered what she might yet say to make him change his mind, but she could find no words.

There was a moment of silence, then Jonathan said, 'And I realised how much I missed you.'

'You did?' Her heart jumped back into its usual place, and she felt its firm and steady beat against her ribcage. 'You missed me?'

He laughed. 'Don't sound so surprised!'

'I've missed you too, Jonathan. More than I can say.'

'So, when can I see you again?'

'How about tomorrow evening?'

CHAPTER 22

Oh God, Oh God, Oh God. What a total idiot he'd been.

Jake stood beneath the shower, letting hot water pummel him awake. He lathered himself with shower gel, trying desperately to scrub away all traces of Brittany's perfume. But the scent seemed to cling to him like a second skin, bringing back unwelcome memories of the night before. It must be all over the sheets and pillow cases too. He'd have to take the whole lot down to the launderette and put them on a high temperature wash. And then carry out a forensic search of the flat for any long blonde hairs she might have left behind. Oh God, Oh God, Oh God.

How had it happened?

He knew perfectly well how it'd happened. He'd been weak and vulnerable after his latest row with Ffion, and Brittany had been upset following her break-up with Tyler. They'd gone to the Indian restaurant next to his flat – another mistake, because the waiters there all knew him well, and had made no secret of their interest in this new woman in Jake's life, no doubt wondering what had happened to the elfin Ffion. He wondered if he could persuade them to keep quiet about it. And there, over a couple of lamb biryanis, garlic infused naans, and however many bottles of Cobra beer, they had consoled each other, reminisced over past times, and then, almost inevitably, ended up in bed together.

I was powerless to stop it, he told his reflection in the shaving mirror after emerging from the shower, but the Jake in the mirror regarded him with a stern and sceptical look.

The truth was, Brittany was so much more relaxed than Ffion. When he was with her, things just seemed to flow effortlessly. In this case, they had flowed effortlessly into bed.

You promised to sleep on the couch, his reflection rebuked him.

Yeah, but –

Whatever had happened, he needed to put it right. The sooner he fixed this, the better. Damage limitation, that was the best he could hope for now. And he might as well get on with it.

Brittany had still been fast asleep when he'd crept into the bathroom, full of shame and self-loathing. When he returned to the bedroom, she was up and dressed. Considering that she was wearing yesterday's clothes and hadn't yet showered, she was looking remarkably fresh and pretty.

'Morning,' she chirped. 'Sleep well?'

'Um, yeah. Look, about last night –'

'Fun, wasn't it?'

'Well, yeah, but –'

'What?' She smiled at him, relaxed and innocent of the troubles running through his mind.

'The first thing is, I'm supposed to be with Ffion...'

'I didn't see Ffion with you in the restaurant last night.'

'No,' he admitted.

'But I do remember you telling me all the ways that the two of you were incompatible and how the relationship wasn't working.'

Jake cringed at the thought of how much he'd revealed to Brittany after a few beers. 'Yes, all right, but the second thing is, you're a witness on a murder case I'm working on, and we really shouldn't have –'

'Relax,' she said, giving him a kiss on the cheek. 'You always worry too much. I promise I won't tell your boss.' She gave him a smile. 'So, what are you doing this evening?'

'I'm probably going to have to work late,' he said hurriedly.

'No problem. I have to work too. But first I'm going back to the gatehouse to fetch my things while you've got Tyler safely under lock and key.'

'Your things?'

'Yeah, I can't leave them at the gatehouse, can I? Is it okay if I bring them back here for now?'

★

Bridget was in a positive mood when she arrived at work. Talking to Jonathan on the phone the previous evening had calmed her down and made her realise how she'd been getting everything out of perspective. Chloe had come in at ten o'clock and gone straight to bed, so there had been no squabbling between them for a change. And for once she hadn't had to wake her daughter up to get her to go to school. Chloe had been up and out of the door before Bridget had even finished her breakfast.

She took a coffee to her desk and was pleased to see that Tyler Dixon's DNA results had arrived back from the lab. Everything seemed to be going her way. She opened the envelope and quickly scanned the results. Bingo! The test proved that Tyler Dixon had indeed slept with Gina Hartman on the night she died. He could continue to deny it all he liked, but the evidence was conclusive. And if Tyler had lied about this…

'Have you got a moment, ma'am?'

She looked up. 'Sure, what is it Andy?'

The sergeant was hovering near her desk clutching a printout. 'It's about the guy we're holding in the cells, Tyler Dixon.'

'What about him?'

'I've been running a background search and his name cropped up in the database. Five years ago he was charged with Assault occasioning Actual Bodily Harm under Section 47 of the Offences Against the Person Act following a brawl outside a pub in Banbury.'

Bridget's interest was greatly aroused by this new fact. The weight of evidence against Tyler Dixon was steadily accumulating.

'And did it go to trial?'

'Yes…'

'I sense a "but" coming.'

'He was tried in Oxford Crown Court but the judge threw the case out.'

'On what grounds?'

'Insufficient evidence.'

'That sounds odd. The Crown Prosecution Service don't usually let something go to trial unless they're convinced they've got a good case. Why did it go to the Crown Court? Section 47 cases are usually tried by a magistrate.'

'In this case, the magistrate referred it to the Crown Court because of the serious nature of the injuries caused. The victim was knocked unconscious and lost several teeth as a result of the attack.'

Bridget was reminded of the look of murderous anger that had flashed across Tyler's face several times during the interview yesterday. It was easy to imagine him doing some serious damage to anyone unlucky enough to stand in his way.

'So, the thing is…' said Andy.

'Yes?'

'I had a chat with the sergeant in Banbury who dealt with the case. He made it clear to me that his comments were strictly off the record, but he thinks the trial wasn't conducted fairly. He says there was plenty of evidence and a couple of good witnesses, but in his opinion the judge was biased from the outset.'

'That's quite an allegation. Who was the presiding judge?'

'Graham Neville.'

'Is that so?' The Honourable Mr Justice Neville, to give him his correct title, was one of the guests at Nick Damon's party. This was certainly an interesting turn of events. 'Well done, Andy. Good work.'

The sergeant returned to his desk looking pleased.

Bridget remained at her desk digesting this latest nugget of information. If, as the sergeant from Banbury was suggesting, the presiding judge had rigged the outcome of the trial, it seemed quite feasible to conclude that the judge was in Nick Damon's pocket and had been bribed or otherwise influenced to get Tyler off the hook. Bridget had seen for herself the subtle power a judge could wield in court by excluding evidence or blocking certain lines of questioning. It seemed that the full extent of Nick Damon's web of influence might extend beyond Hugh Avery-Blanchard to include all manner of powerful men.

She took Tyler's DNA test results to show to Jake. 'All right,' she said, 'it's time we had another crack at Tyler Dixon. He's not going to be able to simply deny everything this time.'

'No. I guess not.'

'You okay, Jake?' she enquired. He seemed distracted this morning, and Bridget wondered again what was happening between him and Ffion. Her own love life might be back on track, but it looked as if Jake's was spinning well and truly off the rails. But whatever was happening in his personal life, she needed him to focus on work now.

'I'm good,' he said, standing up.

On the way to the interview room she quickly filled him in on the story of Tyler's assault charge.

'I can't say I'm too surprised that Tyler got into a fight,' he said. 'But this business about an unfair trial is a serious matter… do you think we should go and talk to this judge?'

'No point,' said Bridget. 'He'll only deny everything. We don't have more than a rumour to go on.'

When they arrived in the interview room, they found Tyler Dixon looking the worse for wear after a night in the police cells, but no less hostile in his attitude. He was conferring gruffly with his lawyer, Mr Gold, but the two men fell silent as Bridget entered and took her seat.

'Right, let's get started shall we?' she said brightly.

Taking Tyler's sullen silence for a yes, she placed the report of the DNA tests on the table where he and the lawyer could see it. 'So, we now have conclusive proof that you did have sex with Gina Hartman on the night of the party.'

'I did not,' said Tyler, not even bothering to look at the report. He leaned forward menacingly. 'I already told you that.'

Mr Gold laid a restraining hand on his client's arm – an action that seemed rather rash to Bridget, having learned about Tyler's history of violent behaviour. 'Tyler, DNA evidence doesn't lie. Why not admit you had sex with her? It doesn't mean you killed her.'

Bridget nodded to Jake, who produced once again the evidence bag containing Gina's earring and laid it on the table as a reminder of why Tyler had been arrested in the first place.

Tyler glanced at the earring, then looked first at Mr Gold and then at Bridget, as if trying to assess which one he trusted least. 'All right, then, I admit it. I did sleep with her.'

'Good,' said Bridget. 'Now we're getting somewhere.'

'But it wasn't in the gatehouse.'

'What?'

'I never took her there.'

'Where then?' asked Bridget, mystified by his response.

'In the back of the car.'

Out of the corner of her eye Bridget saw the lawyer pull

a face of disgust. It was perhaps the first emotion she had seen him express.

'So how did Gina's earring find its way into your bed?' asked Jake.

'How the hell should I know? And what's it got to do with you, anyway? Why do you keep going on at me?'

'Tyler,' warned Mr Gold. 'If you don't want to answer a question, please just say "no comment".'

Tyler leaned back in his chair, his arms folded, defying his lawyer by saying nothing.

'Let's see if we can get to the bottom of this, shall we?' said Bridget. 'You admit to having sex with Gina on the day of the party. When did it happen exactly?'

'After I picked her up.'

'At approximately seven thirty?'

'Yeah. I drove her to Nick's place and parked next to the gatehouse. We did it in the car.' He smirked at Jake.

'And then what?'

'Gina went into the house to start work, and I took up my post at the front door, ready to admit the guests.' He grinned. 'I only just made it in time. The first guest was already waiting at the gates when I said goodbye to Gina.'

Beside him, Mr Gold's expression turned sour.

'Let's move on,' said Bridget. She wasn't clear why Tyler was spinning this rather fanciful yarn about having sex in the car, but there seemed little to gain from pursuing it further right now. 'When did you find out that Gina was pregnant?'

The question delivered the shock that Bridget hoped it would. Mr Gold in particular appeared startled by the revelation.

'What?' said Tyler. He gazed at Bridget with fury. 'You're lying!'

'So you're saying you didn't know she was pregnant?'

'No. Of course I bloody didn't.'

Bridget ignored his denial. 'Were you jealous of the fact that she was expecting another man's child? Did it make you angry to think that someone else was sleeping with her?'

'No!'

'Did she tell you about it that evening? Is that why you strangled her?'

'I bloody well didn't! I didn't even know she was pregnant!'

Now Jake leaned forward to engage the suspect.

'Mate, it's easy to see how it could happen. You and Gina had been sleeping together for a while, yeah? You thought you meant something to her. And now, this news felt like a slap in the face.'

Tyler shook his head, too angry to form words.

'You didn't mean to hurt her,' continued Jake. 'You just needed to tell her how you felt. But perhaps she wouldn't listen. She told you she didn't love you. She said it was over between the two of you.'

'No. None of that happened. I didn't know she was pregnant. I didn't even see her again after we had sex.'

'We think you did, though,' said Jake. 'So tell us what happened. Did you get into an argument with her? You didn't mean for it to go any further. You just lost control.'

'Because,' said Bridget, picking up the thread, 'we know you have a history of violence. Five years ago you were charged with Actual Bodily Harm following a fight outside a pub in Banbury. The assault was serious. The victim was badly hurt.'

'My client was acquitted of that charge,' said Mr Gold swiftly.

But Tyler wasn't listening to his lawyer anymore. 'I never killed her! How many times do I have to say it?' He banged the table with his fists, making the earring jump in its plastic evidence bag.

'Calm down,' said Gold. 'She's only trying to rile you. Rise above it.'

But Tyler was well and truly riled. He looked about desperately, as if searching for a way to escape. 'I didn't kill her!' he yelled again. 'Check her phone. Gina was recording all night. Listen to the recording. It will prove it wasn't me!'

'Gina was... what?' said Mr Gold. For a moment the lawyer's professional demeanour slipped before he recollected himself. 'That's impossible. Tyler, it was your job to keep the girls' phones safe while they were at work.'

'Yeah, well,' sneered Tyler. 'I didn't take Gina's phone, did I?'

'Any such evidence,' continued Mr Gold, '... if it even exists... would be inadmissible in court. Use of mobile phones by staff attending the party was clearly prohibited under the terms of their employment.'

'Really?' said Bridget. 'Did they sign contracts saying that no audio recordings were to be made? Was their employment contract that formal? Did they even have a contract?'

From the lawyer's stony look Bridget surmised that the students hadn't been asked to sign any such contract. It seemed that the lawyer hadn't been quite as diligent in protecting his client's interests as he might have been.

'For the record,' said Bridget, seizing the opportunity, 'I can confirm that we are in possession of Gina's audio recording from the party, and that it contains evidence of her attack. But I'm sorry to have to inform you, Tyler, that there's nothing in that recording that exonerates you of her murder. On the contrary, it confirms that she was attacked when she went upstairs at around midnight, and you've already admitted to us that you were present in the house at that time and have no alibi.'

She paused, watching his reaction. She almost felt a stab of pity as the last trace of hope visibly faded from his face.

'Tyler Dixon, I will be contacting the Crown Prosecution Service and recommending that you should be charged with the murder of Gina Hartman. Is there anything more you would like to say?'

Tyler stared at her dumbfounded. 'I didn't kill her.'

'Do you understand what I just said?' asked Bridget.

'I didn't kill her,' he repeated.

★

Feeling pretty satisfied with the way the morning's interview had gone, Jake went into the kitchen to grab himself a well-deserved cup of tea. Tyler Dixon might still deny murdering Gina Hartman, but he was looking about as innocent as a gangster at a kiddies' birthday party. Even with the evidence they had already collected, they had enough to put him away for life, and the forensics guys hadn't finished yet.

Jake whistled a tune to himself as he waited for the kettle to boil. He chucked a teabag into his Leeds United mug, adding a couple of spoonfuls of sugar for good measure. Ffion had nagged him to cut down on the sugar, or better still to give it up entirely, but she wasn't around right now. And what she didn't know about...

Oh God, he thought. Brittany.

Ffion didn't know about what had happened the night before, and she mustn't ever find out. Bridget, too, must never discover that he'd slept with a key witness. If she did, he'd be back in uniform and would probably spend the rest of his career responding to burglaries on the Blackbird Leys estate.

But how was he going to fix the hole he'd dug for himself? One thing was clear – there was no way Brittany could move in with him like she clearly intended to. He would have to put a stop to that before things got even worse than they already were. In fact, the next time he saw Brittany, he would tell her what he'd decided. That he had made a huge mistake in sleeping with her the other night, that it was all over between them, and she would have to move her gear out of his flat and into a hotel. Yes, that's what he'd do. And then he could talk to Ffion and try to...

'You look happy about something,' said a musical Welsh voice from behind.

He jumped, sloshing scalding water over himself from the kettle. 'Shit!'

Ffion narrowed her eyes, cat-like. 'What's the matter with you? You're jumpy today.'

'Sorry, you just surprised me, that's all.'

He ran his hand under the cold tap and dabbed it dry on a tea towel.

'So, what's new?'

'New?' He stared at her, wondering how much she knew. Had she somehow guessed that he'd spent the night in bed with Brittany?

'With Tyler Dixon?'

'Oh, Tyler!' he said.

Ffion's eyes followed him suspiciously as he moved around the kitchen. 'What did you think I was talking about?'

'No, nothing.'

'So?'

'Tyler... yeah. Turns out, it was right to arrest him. The DNA results proved he slept with Gina, and in fact he eventually admitted it, although he's insisting on some ridiculous story about having sex with her in his car instead of in bed.'

'In the car?' said Ffion. 'Classy.'

'Right,' said Jake, 'he's a real creep. Andy also found out that he has form for violence. He was charged after a pub brawl, but it looks like Damon bribed the judge to let him off.'

'Nice guy, huh? So, do you think he did it?'

'Sure. Bridget's going to charge him with the murder.'

'Is she?'

'Why, don't you think he's guilty?'

'Maybe,' said Ffion. 'The guilty always give themselves away eventually'

She held Jake's gaze and he felt his ears beginning to burn. Suddenly all he could think about was himself in bed with Brittany the night before. He wondered if his own guilt was written all over his face, just as obvious to Ffion as Tyler Dixon's was to him. How much did Ffion know? And how much might she guess? 'I –' he began.

'You slept with her!' accused Ffion.

He wondered how she could possibly have deduced that when he hadn't said a thing.

'I –' he tried again, but he knew that the one word was as good as a signed confession.

'You bastard!' she yelled. 'You're as much of a slimeball as Tyler Dixon. And I'll tell you what, Brittany Grainger deserves both of you!'

CHAPTER 23

'DI Hart, a word, please.'

Bridget glanced up from her desk to see the dark and baleful figure of Chief Superintendent Alex Grayson beckoning to her from the open doorway of his glass-fronted office. Abandoning the charge report she was preparing, she entered the Chief Super's domain fully expecting to be reprimanded for some dreadful oversight on the case. Most likely Hugh Avery-Blanchard had made good on his threat to sue her for slander.

'I was just about to come and see you, sir. Is there a problem?'

'Sit down, DI Hart.'

To her surprise, Grayson offered her a grudging smile, a rather unusual state of affairs. Bridget was immediately wary. Somehow she preferred Grayson when he was his normal gruff self.

'I understand that congratulations are in order,' he continued. 'That was very quick work on the part of you and your team.'

She realised that he must already know about the

outcome of her latest interview with Tyler Dixon. The Chief Super had ears everywhere.

'Thank you, sir.'

'So, you're ready to charge the suspect?'

'Yes, sir. At least, I think so, sir.'

As she'd suspected, her lukewarm response was met with displeasure. 'You think so?'

'Well, the thing is, sir, I still have one or two unanswered questions.'

'Such as?'

'For one thing we don't know who the father of Gina's unborn child was. All the DNA tests have come back negative.'

Grayson's face clouded over as he absorbed this unwelcome information. 'Is that relevant? If this driver killed the girl in a fit of jealousy, then it hardly matters who he was jealous of.'

'Well, maybe not. But I'd like to know for sure.'

Grayson tapped the desk with his fountain pen, always a sign that he was frustrated or impatient. 'Thorough, aren't you, DI Hart?' he said reluctantly. 'Well, it's good to be thorough.'

'Yes, sir.'

'Is there anything else bothering you?'

Bridget knew that her next answer would only make Grayson even less inclined to support her, but her conscience wouldn't allow her to duck the issue. 'Well, it's becoming evident that the real purpose of these parties that Nick Damon hosts is to influence people in positions of authority so that they are obliged to help him with his business dealings.'

'Bribery?'

'I don't have any evidence of money actually changing hands. But favours are supplied. Sometimes of a sexual nature.'

Grayson's brows furrowed in annoyance. 'Who are we talking about? Do you have names?'

'Yes, sir,' said Bridget with a sinking heart. With every

reply to Grayson's questioning, she felt like she was hammering nails into her own coffin. 'The MP, Hugh Avery-Blanchard, and a judge, a Mr Justice Neville.'

'Graham Neville? Hmm…'

The name seemed to have struck a chord with Grayson. Bridget wondered if the two men's paths had crossed before.

'I'm no fan of Graham Neville,' said Grayson. 'What do you have on him?'

Bridget explained the accusation of trial-fixing that had been made by a sergeant at Banbury.

'Interesting,' said Grayson. 'Do you have sufficient evidence for a conviction?'

'Not yet, sir.'

The Chief studied her for a few seconds more before dismissing her. 'All right, DI Hart. Carry on. See what you can dig up. But remember –'

'Yes, sir. I'll keep you informed.'

Bridget wondered what her next move should be. She knew that she didn't have much time, but she really wanted to pin down the identity of the father of Gina's baby. But having eliminated everyone who was at the party, she didn't know where to turn. Perhaps she should start considering guests who had attended previous parties at Damon's home, and start testing them, but that might prove to be a long list of suspects. Like Grayson said, it might not even be important.

The chance of finding firm evidence that Nick Damon was involved in corruption also seemed remote. The judge and the MP weren't likely to admit anything that might incriminate themselves, and neither would Damon himself, nor his slippery lawyer, Mr Gold. She wondered whether it was worth bringing Brittany Grainger in for questioning, to see if she might let something slip under pressure. But she knew she was clutching at straws. The sensible move was simply to proceed with charging Tyler Dixon.

Returning to her desk she discovered a missed call on

her mobile. She didn't recognise the caller's number, but whoever had phoned had left a voicemail. Bridget's heart started to race as she listened to the message.

'DI Hart, it's Miranda Gardiner here, from Wadham College. We spoke yesterday. I was one of the waitresses at the party at Nick Damon's house. I... I think I've found something out. Something important. I think I know who killed Gina... Oh God, it's so awful I can't bear to think about it. Please call me as soon as you get this. I'm going to stay in my room in college. I'm too scared to leave...'

The girl sounded terrified. Whatever had she discovered? Bridget returned the call immediately, but it rang out and went to voicemail. She tried again, but the same thing happened. She checked the time of Miranda's call. The student had phoned ten minutes ago, while Bridget had been in the Chief Super's office.

She looked quickly around the office to see who was available.

'Ffion, come with me. We need to go to Wadham College right away. I've just had a call from Miranda Gardiner. She claims to know who killed Gina Hartman. She sounded scared, and she's not answering her phone.'

There was a strained look on Ffion's face as if she'd been crying, but Bridget didn't have time to wonder about that now. In any case, Ffion was always quick to respond to an emergency and was already pulling on her leather jacket. Bridget grabbed her bag and they rushed down the stairs together.

Bridget drove as fast as she could down the Banbury Road. In the passenger seat, Ffion sat silently, but Bridget passed Ffion her phone and told her to keep trying Miranda's number. But there was still no response.

At the entrance to the college the porter called out for them to sign in, but Bridget and Ffion dashed past, heading into the main quadrangle.

'I know where Miranda's room is,' said Ffion, and

sprinted ahead, with Bridget struggling to keep up.

Ffion reached the room first and banged loudly on the door. There was no answer.

'Miranda,' called Bridget, 'it's DI Hart. I'm here with my colleague DC Ffion Hughes. I got your message. It's safe to open the door.'

There was still no reply. Bridget tried the door, but it was firmly locked.

'Could she have gone somewhere?' asked Ffion.

'She said in her message she was too scared to leave her room.'

'All right, then,' said Ffion. 'Stand back.'

'I could fetch the master key from the porter,' said Bridget.

'No time for that, boss.'

The Welsh constable took a step back, then spun on her heel, her long leg connecting with the door. One of the wooden panels split open with a crack.

'Taekwondo?' said Bridget. 'Jake told me you did it,' she added, when Ffion nodded.

Ffion said nothing to that, but reached through the hole in the door and turned the handle from the inside. The door swung inwards.

At first glance the room appeared to be empty and Bridget felt a little foolish for having allowed Ffion to break down the door. Now they would receive a complaint from the college and a bill for repairs. She would find herself in Grayson's office once again, and this time there would be no half-smile or congratulations.

But then she noticed the desk light lying on the floor and began to feel a growing sense of dismay. Had the lamp been used as a weapon, either to attack Miranda, or in self-defence? There were other worrying signs too. A half-drunk mug of coffee had been knocked over, spilling its contents onto a pile of printed papers on the desk. A bedside locker had been knocked out of place, its drawers half open.

What had happened here?

'Look.' Ffion pointed to the door of the fitted wardrobe which was slightly ajar.

Dreading what she might find, Bridget snapped on a pair of latex gloves that she kept in her pocket and eased open the door.

Slumped in the corner of the wardrobe, amongst a pile of clothes and shoes, lay the body of Miranda Gardiner. She was lying awkwardly, her head at an uncomfortable angle, the muscles in her face slack and unresponsive. Her eyes were closed and Bridget knew immediately that she had arrived too late. She knelt down and felt for a pulse. Nothing.

'Call this in,' she said to Ffion. 'We have a second murder.'

CHAPTER 24

While Vik and the SOCO team got on with the job of scouring the murder scene for evidence, Bridget found herself once more seated opposite the warden of Wadham in his lodgings.

This time around, Lord Bancroft looked every one of his seventy years. He sat in his chair in a state of shock, his large hands spread out on his desktop as if he needed their support to hold himself upright. If his hair hadn't already been the snowiest white, Bridget feared that the news of this second murder might have turned it a shade paler.

'Tell me, Inspector,' said Lord Bancroft, passing one of his liver-spotted hands across his brow in a gesture of weariness, 'why is someone killing my students? How am I to explain this to everyone? What is going on?'

Bridget saw no reason not to tell the warden what she knew. 'I believe that Miranda's death is linked to Gina's. Miranda phoned me shortly before she died and left a message to say she thought she knew the identity of the person who murdered Gina. She sounded frightened and told me that she was locking herself in her room.'

And not without good reason. Miranda's body, when it

had been extracted from the wardrobe, showed extensive bruising to the arms, face and neck. A violent struggle had clearly taken place, and Dr Sarah Walker suspected another strangulation. It looked like the work of the same killer.

'So Gina's murderer came to the college with the intention of killing Miranda?' said Lord Bancroft, sounding appalled at the idea of the intruder entering college grounds.

'We can't say at this stage exactly what happened.'

'But your working hypothesis must surely be that both students met their killer at this party where they were waitressing?'

'That would seem to be a reasonable assumption,' said Bridget.

'Then what about the third student, Poppy Radley? Where is she now?'

'She's in the care of one of our female officers,' said Bridget, keen to reassure the warden that Poppy was being well looked after. 'She's been told about Miranda's death, and an officer will stay with her to make sure that she's safe.'

'That's something, at least. And what about Miranda's parents?'

'We'll be contacting them to tell them the news.'

The warden's face was stricken. 'Two young lives taken. Two sets of grieving parents. My heart goes out to them.'

Bridget nodded. She knew that the warden would do his best to assist Miranda's family when they came to Oxford to see their daughter's dead body. And Bridget resolved to accompany them to the morgue herself. She owed them that.

'After you released Dr Frost from custody,' said the warden, 'I tried to persuade him to take some time off. Feelings were raw, rumours were rife, and I was concerned about his own wellbeing. But he insisted on returning to work immediately. He was adamant. Do you think –'

'We'll need to interview him about Miranda's death, obviously,' said Bridget.

'If he had anything to do with this, I'll never forgive myself,' said Lord Bancroft.

★

Apart from the scene of crime officers, medical staff and other police personnel bustling back and forth in Front Quad, the college had become a virtual ghost town, with students and lecturers retreating to their rooms, seeking safety and comfort.

Bridget found Dr Frost alone in his room. The German tutor was obviously well aware of the day's events and looked visibly shaken. While Bridget took a seat on the sofa, Frost stood by the window, looking down at the activity in the quadrangle below.

'They tell me it was one of Gina's friends who died,' he said. 'One of the other waitresses at the party.'

'Miranda Gardiner,' confirmed Bridget. She studied Frost's agitated face. The dark rings under his eyes told her that he wasn't sleeping well. The tutor kept touching his forehead unconsciously with one hand, as if he could ward off the horror of what had taken place. He was either deeply shocked, or else a very polished actor, and Bridget was inclined to believe the former.

'I'm so sorry,' he murmured. 'So very sorry. I feel that this is all my fault somehow. If only I knew what really happened that night...' He glanced up at Bridget. 'This other girl, Miranda, was she strangled too?'

'I'm afraid that I can't tell you that right now.'

'No, no. Of course not. Foolish of me to have asked.'

'Dr Frost, I have to ask you, where were you this morning between eleven and twelve?'

Miranda had left the phone message just after eleven o'clock, and it had been nearly midday by the time Bridget and Ffion had discovered her body.

'Between eleven and twelve? Um... well, I was here in

my room.'

'Can anyone vouch for that?'

Frost shook his head sadly. 'No. I didn't have any tutorials during that time. I was alone.'

'Did you leave your room at any point, to go to the Senior Common Room, for example?'

'I avoid going there these days. The other tutors, you know, they…' He tailed off miserably.

'I understand,' said Bridget. 'This must be difficult for you.'

'Yes,' he said. 'Yes, that's right. You're the first person to…' He stopped again, his forehead frowning in concentration. 'No one understands. They all think I did it. And now… this second murder… I won't be able to show my face.'

'Miranda telephoned me shortly before she died,' said Bridget. 'She told me she had guessed the identity of Gina's killer. Do you have any idea who she might have suspected? Did you speak to her at all since the party?'

'Speak to her?' Frost stared at Bridget in alarm. 'Good gracious, no. I wouldn't have dared go near her, not after … no, I'm sorry, I have no idea. It's not like I haven't been thinking about that question myself, you know. In fact, I've been struggling for days to remember something that might provide a clue.'

Bridget had the impression that Frost had more to say. 'And have you remembered anything?'

'Well, yes, I've started to have flashbacks. Things come to me, sometimes when my mind is elsewhere. Fragmented images, mostly. Nothing conclusive.'

'What sort of images?'

'I remember something that Gina said to me at the party. *You shouldn't be here.* I have a feeling she was speaking to someone else, but I don't know who. But I do recall some of the masks people were wearing. There were a number of Pierrots, and several cats. And I'm sure there was a jester too. The designs come from the Venice Carnival, you know. Most of them go back centuries. They derive originally from the *commedia dell'arte* tradition.'

Frost was beginning to display a typical academic's enthusiasm for quirky historical facts and tangential details. Bridget's own History tutor, Dr Irene Thomas from Merton College, had always had a fascination for the darker aspects of the human experience and had recently given Bridget an extensive guide to Jacobean revenge tragedy while she was working on another murder case. Bridget suspected that if she let him, Dr Frost would now start expounding on the significance of different sorts of Venetian masks. Fascinating though that might be, she didn't have time for it now.

'Have you remembered anything else?' she asked.

'I remember the stairs.'

'What about them?'

'They were carved from dark oak. The newel post was in the shape of an acorn. I remember standing next to it, being intrigued by the skill that had been required to produce such an elaborate piece of craftsmanship.'

'Anything else?' asked Bridget, beginning to wonder if the man was simply trying to waste her time.

'I was tired. I was feeling sleepy after someone gave me the...'

'Rohypnol,' prompted Bridget.

'... yes, the sleeping drug. I remember wanting to lie down, so I went upstairs.'

Bridget waited patiently, but Frost seemed to have stopped. 'And then what?'

'Nothing,' he said, shaking his head. 'Try as I might, I can't remember anything after that. Not until I woke up.'

Bridget tried not to show her frustration. 'Keep trying,' she told him. 'And call me if you remember anything else. Anything at all.'

*

Poppy Radley was in her room, being looked after by a female police constable. When Bridget arrived, she was sitting cross-legged on her bed, a mug of tea in her hands, and a look of indescribable misery on her face. She glanced up at Bridget and her lower lip began to tremble.

The constable leaned forward with a box of tissues, and Bridget deduced from the mound of soggy tissues already in the wastepaper basket that this wasn't the first time Poppy had broken down in tears since learning of Miranda's death.

A cry emanated from her now, and she buried her face in her hands. Bridget sat down next to her on the bed and waited until the wailing had subsided into a quiet sob before speaking.

'Poppy, I'm so sorry about what's happened. But I need your help if we're going to catch Miranda's killer. Can you tell me if you saw Miranda any time this morning?'

Poppy gave her nose a blow, then nodded. 'I saw her at breakfast. We sat together.'

'And what time was that?'

'About half past eight.'

'What did you talk about?'

'Oh, nothing special. Just, you know... life in college. I told her I was missing home. I don't usually. It's just that after what happened to Gina...'

'Did Miranda mention anything about Gina over breakfast?'

'No, not really. Just that we both missed her. Gina could be a bit aloof at times, but now she's gone...'

Bridget cut in before Poppy could dissolve into tears again. 'Did you see Miranda again after breakfast?'

'No. I had to finish some work for my tutorial, so I came back here to my room.'

'And what time was your tutorial?' prodded Bridget gently.

'At midday, and it finished at one. And then, when I came out, the police were here, and I heard that Miranda was dead.'

She began to cry again, and Bridget waited patiently.

Eventually Poppy looked at Bridget with tear-stained

eyes. 'But before I went to my tutorial, I had a visitor,' she said.

'Who?'

'It was that creepy guy, Mr Gold.'

Bridget could barely keep the surprise from her voice. 'Mr Damon's lawyer? He came here to see you?'

'Yes. He came to my room.'

'What time was this?'

'About half past ten.'

At ten o'clock, Bridget had only just finished interviewing Tyler Dixon in Mr Gold's presence. She calculated that Gold must have driven straight to the college immediately after finishing the interview.

'What did he want?'

'He was rather threatening, actually,' said Poppy. 'He said he knew that Gina had made an audio recording at the party. He wanted to know what else she'd been up to, and whether Miranda and I had been doing anything similar, which we weren't, obviously. I told him I had nothing to do with Gina's activities and I didn't even approve of them. He kept going on and on, asking what Gina had discovered, and whether she'd found out anything about any of the guests, but I said I didn't know.'

Bridget could have kicked herself for her carelessness. She herself had informed Gold about the audio recording at the interview with Tyler that very morning, which was presumably why he'd come straight to see Poppy. With hindsight, it had been a mistake to mention it. But, Bridget reflected, it would be far better if the lawyer representing one of the suspects wasn't himself a suspect in the case. She was growing rather tired of Nick Damon's tangled web of influence.

'Were you alone when Mr Gold saw you?' she asked Poppy.

'Yes.'

'Did he mention anything about speaking to Miranda?'

'Yes, he said he was going to speak to her next.' Poppy stared at Bridget open-mouthed as she realised the significance of what she was saying. 'I messaged her to warn her that he was coming, but I didn't wait for a reply because I needed to get to my tutorial. And Miranda's quite good at standing up for herself. I thought she'd handle him better than I had. But – oh my God – do you think he killed her?'

'I don't know, Poppy,' said Bridget. 'But I'm going to find out.'

CHAPTER 25

After leaving Poppy's room, Bridget wasted no time. She quickly rounded up Jake and Ryan and sent them off to find Mr Gold and bring him in for questioning. From what Poppy had told her, Damon's lawyer had gone to see Miranda just minutes before the murdered student had phoned Bridget to say she thought she had guessed the identity of Gina's killer.

If only Bridget hadn't been called away to account for her progress to the Chief Super, she would have been able to take Miranda's phone call, and everything might have turned out differently. One thing was clear to her – despite his undoubtedly shifty behaviour, Tyler Dixon couldn't possibly have murdered Miranda, as he'd been in police custody. She drove back to Kidlington and released him from the cells. He slouched off ungratefully, muttering something under his breath about human rights and wrongful arrest.

Bridget just had time to grab an unhealthy and unappetising lunch from the vending machine before Jake and Ryan returned from their mission to find Mr Gold. She raised a questioning eyebrow as she munched on her limp cheese sandwich.

'We got him, ma'am,' said Jake, looking pleased with himself. 'He was back at Damon's house, large as life.'

'We hoped the slimy bastard might try to make a run for it,' said Ryan, 'you know – so we could chase him for a bit, and drag him to the floor. But he agreed to cooperate fully with our request,' he concluded with obvious regret.

Bridget swallowed her half-chewed mouthful of bread and cheese. 'Where is he now?'

'In the interview room.'

'Okay,' she said, taking a last sip of Diet Coke, 'let's go and see what he has to say for himself.'

She found Mr Gold sitting calmly in interview room two in the presence of a junior officer. He now occupied the very same seat that Tyler Dixon had sat in just a few hours earlier. But there was no lawyer at his side. He had declined the offer of legal representation, evidently deciding that he would be better at defending himself than some hired solicitor. Perhaps he was right about that.

Bridget took a seat opposite and spent a minute sizing him up. As always, the lawyer was presented impeccably, this time in a dark olive suit with a matching waistcoat. And yet the man's starched collar and silk tie seemed to hide a void. Despite spending several hours in his presence, Bridget had very little clues to the real man behind the façade. Mr Gold remained an enigma. His age was indeterminate. His personality was so bland as to be non-existent. He was like a chameleon, blending into the background. In fact, he had done it so well, Bridget hadn't even considered him to be a suspect until now.

He gazed at her measuredly with dark, empty eyes. 'Good afternoon, DI Hart,' he said pleasantly. 'Perhaps you would do me the courtesy of explaining why you asked me to come here again. Is this related to Tyler Dixon?'

'No,' said Bridget. 'It isn't.'

'Then what?'

'I understand that you visited Wadham College this morning after concluding the interview with Tyler.'

'That's correct.'

Bridget was pleased that he hadn't tried to deny it. This interview would flow much more smoothly if he simply agreed with every proposition she put to him.

'While you were there, you visited Poppy Radley in her room.'

'I did.'

'According to Poppy, your behaviour was rather threatening.'

'Ah,' said Mr Gold. 'Now there I must disagree with you. I simply asked her some questions, which she answered. No threat was made, either directly or by implication.'

'What questions did you ask her?'

Mr Gold feigned a look of surprise. 'I'm sure you already know that, DI Hart. Poppy is a very intelligent girl. No doubt she told you exactly what I asked.'

'You questioned her about Gina and the audio recording she made at the party.'

'That's right. After you so helpfully made me aware of the existence of the recording, it became necessary for me to try to find out what had been recorded and whether any other recordings existed. My job is to protect my client's interests, you understand.'

'Poppy found your behaviour intimidating,' said Bridget.

'I'm very sorry to hear that. Please give her my apologies.'

'What did you do after you left Poppy?'

'I went to Miranda Gardiner's room to ask her the same questions. But there was no answer when I knocked on her door.'

'So what did you do then?'

'I left the college and returned to Mr Damon's house.'

'How convenient for you,' said Bridget.

Mr Gold gave her a puzzled look. 'On the contrary, DI Hart. It was most inconvenient. What an odd thing for you to say.'

Bridget leaned forward. 'You're telling me that you have no idea that Miranda Gardiner was murdered this morning?'

For a moment Gold lost his customary poise, but he very soon recovered himself. 'Murdered? But I know nothing about that.' He sat up very straight in his chair, as if determined to prove that he had nothing to hide. And yet the hands clasped together beneath the table suggested the opposite.

'I don't believe you,' said Bridget. 'I think you called on Miranda and she told you something which led you to kill her.'

'Inspector, no. I can assure you that is not what happened.' A slight sheen of perspiration had appeared on Mr Gold's papery skin.

'Where were you on the night of the party at Mr Damon's house?'

'Why, I was at the house myself.'

'Yes, I thought you might have been,' said Bridget. 'You didn't give a statement to police at the time, did you?'

'I don't recall being asked.'

Bridget nodded to herself. No doubt Jake and the other detectives at the house that day had made the same assumption she had made herself – that Mr Gold had arrived at the house the morning after the party in order to represent his client. In fact he had been there all along.

'So did you stay overnight?'

'I have a room where I regularly sleep when I'm doing business with Mr Damon, so yes, I spent the night there. I went to bed at around half past one.'

'Alone?'

'Yes. Certainly.'

'Did you go upstairs at any time, apart from when you went to bed at the end of the evening?'

'No.'

'Did you have any kind of relationship with Gina Hartman?'

'I don't believe I ever spoke to her.'

'What about Dr Frost?'

'I didn't speak to him either.'

'Who did you speak to?'

'I tend to keep myself to myself at these sorts of occasions.'

That didn't surprise Bridget. 'Then do you recall seeing any unusual behaviour during the course of the evening, or noticing anything that might be relevant to our enquiry?'

'I don't believe so.'

'I see,' said Bridget. 'So presumably you won't object to providing a DNA sample so that we can eliminate you from our enquiries?'

She waited to see how he would respond, wondering if it was conceivable that this man might be the elusive father of Gina's child. The idea of him sleeping with Gina Hartman was repulsive. And yet, if all other candidates had been eliminated...

'Not in the slightest,' said Mr Gold.

He held his mouth open patiently while Bridget used a swab to take a sample of his saliva.

'I'm sure you'll find that this doesn't match any DNA you might have already found at the murder scene,' he said. 'Just as I'm certain that once the forensic evidence from Miranda's room has been analysed, it will be clear that I never set foot inside her room.'

'Possibly,' said Bridget, 'if you were very careful and took steps to avoid leaving fingerprints or any other traces. But how certain can you be that we won't find one of your hairs in Miranda's room? Or some other evidence that will point to you being there?'

Mr Gold smiled nervously. 'Pretty certain,' he said. 'Although nothing in life is ever completely guaranteed.'

CHAPTER 26

On returning to her desk after sending Mr Gold's DNA sample off to be analysed, Bridget was surprised to find Jake, Andy and Harry clustered around Ryan's computer. The sound of their blokeish laughter seemed more appropriate to a pub than to the incident room.

'Whoa, look at that,' said Ryan, pointing at the screen. 'The boss is going to go apeshit when she sees this. Still, you've got to hand it to that MP, who'd have thought he'd be capable of –'

Jake gave Ryan a nudge as Bridget approached. 'What am I going to go *apeshit* about?' she asked, 'as you so delicately put it?'

'Sorry, ma'am,' said Ryan. 'Excuse my language, but you should come and see this, although I don't think you're going to like it very much.'

'What is it?'

'It's a leak, ma'am,' said Jake, as Andy and Harry scuttled off back to their desks.

Bridget groaned. She knew how dimly Grayson would view any leak of information from the investigation.

'Not so much a leak,' said Ryan. 'More like the sluice gates have been opened.' He swivelled the screen in her direction.

Bridget's stomach turned a somersault in dread of what she might see. But not even in her most fevered imagination had she anticipated anything like this. *Apeshit* didn't even begin to describe how Grayson would react when he found out.

'HOUSING MINISTER IN SEX SCANDAL,' read the headline on the news website. A rather grainy photograph of Hugh Avery-Blanchard appeared next to columns of text that seemed to swim before Bridget's eyes. She stared at them in a daze, trying to pick up their gist. Key words and phrases jumped out at her like sparks from a bonfire, each capable of igniting a media storm: *MP for Witney... private house party at home of controversial property developer... hired sex workers... blatant hypocrisy... corruption at the very heart of government.*

'The journalist who wrote this didn't pull any punches,' commented Ryan.

'That's putting it mildly,' said Bridget.

'They wouldn't have written this unless they had cast-iron proof,' said Jake. 'Remember what Avery-Blanchard said to us about suing us for slander?'

'Well, he can't sue us for this,' said Bridget. 'The newspaper must have found out something from another source.'

'Let's see,' said Ryan. He clicked on a video tagged "Breaking news" and a clip of a harassed-looking Hugh Avery-Blanchard appeared, storming out of the ministry building on Marsham Street in London. He waved away a horde of journalists who were all shouting questions and thrusting microphones at him, and climbed ungainly into the back of a waiting car, which sped off.

'Details are emerging of a scandal involving the Member of Parliament for Witney, Hugh Avery-Blanchard, and a foreign sex worker,' began the voiceover. 'Mr Avery-Blanchard, a junior minister at the Ministry of

Housing, Communities and Local Government, left London early this afternoon after the scandal broke, to return to his constituency and his family.'

The video cut to a series of shots showing a large country house with metal gates at its entrance. An aerial shot revealed the grounds of the house to be extensive with a swimming pool, tennis court and paddocks. So this was Avery-Blanchard's home – the place he had taken such great care to keep Bridget well away from.

'At the moment the MP is not making any comment about the allegations,' continued the report, 'but a reliable source has revealed that he attended a masked sex party at a friend's house where the incident took place. The house in question, belonging to a wealthy businessman, is currently the scene of an ongoing murder investigation...'

'All right, turn it off,' said Bridget, who'd heard enough. 'Let me take a closer look at that photograph.'

It wasn't a terribly clear image, but from the lavish décor in the background, Bridget recognised the location as one of the bedrooms in Nick Damon's house. The photo appeared to have been taken from a position high up, above the bed, in the corner of the room. Two naked figures were partially visible – one of them just about identifiable as the unfortunate MP, the other a woman with her face greyed-out.

'That's Erika,' said Ryan with a smirk.

'Erika?'

'A very nice Czech lady we interviewed at Angel's Escort Agency.'

'I see,' said Bridget. 'And how was this photo taken? Not with Avery-Blanchard's knowledge or consent, I'm guessing. It looks like a frame from a video. Did we check for hidden cameras in Nick Damon's house?'

'Nothing like that was present in the room where Frost and Gina were found,' said Jake. 'The guys from SOCO would have spotted a camera if there was one. But this is a different room. We didn't search every bedroom.'

'I wonder how the newspaper got hold of it?' said Ryan.

'They won't disclose their source,' said Bridget. 'Journalists never do.'

'Do you think that Gina might have planted it?' asked Jake.

'It's possible. We know that Tyler was helping her. He allowed her to keep hold of her phone during the party so that she could make the audio recording. I suppose that she might have persuaded him to plant a hidden camera.'

'But that still doesn't explain how the newspaper got hold of it,' said Ryan, 'unless Tyler gave it to them.'

'But why would he do that?' asked Jake. 'He's in enough trouble already. And he was in custody when this story broke.'

'Let me see what I can find out,' said Bridget. She was already dialling the number of Hugh Avery-Blanchard's constituency office in Witney. She didn't think that the MP would be available to talk, but if anyone knew anything about what had happened, it was his deputy and confidante, Mrs Cynthia Duckworth.

Bridget assumed that she would go straight through to the answerphone, but to her surprise, a familiar lofty voice answered almost immediately.

'Mr Avery-Blanchard's constituency office. I'm afraid that Mr Avery-Blanchard is not currently available –'

'It's DI Bridget Hart from Thames Valley Police,' said Bridget, cutting across her.

'DI Hart again.' Mrs Duckworth spoke Bridget's name with distaste, as if sucking on a lemon. 'How may I help you?'

'I'm calling about the photograph or video of Mr Avery-Blanchard that's been leaked to the press. I'd like to discover the source of the leak. I believe it may be relevant to our murder enquiry.'

'Really?' said the secretary in her headmistress voice.

'Do you have any idea who leaked the material?'

'I do, as a matter of fact.'

'And can you tell me who it was?'

'It was me,' said Cynthia, sounding quite pleased with

herself.

Bridget was stunned. 'I don't understand.'

'It's really quite simple. The video was sent in an email to Mr Avery-Blanchard, but as I have access to his emails I saw it first. I can tell you, it quite shocked me. Mr Avery-Blanchard is always quite rightly extolling the virtues of family life. I had no idea that I was working for such a hypocrite. He'll have to resign now, of course,' she added matter-of-factly. 'It's only fair.'

'And can I ask who sent the email?'

'It was anonymous, but it would appear to be a threat of some kind. The message in the email read: "Do what you promised, or this will be on the news very soon."'

'Thank you, Mrs Duckworth,' said Bridget. 'You've been very helpful.'

Bridget ended the call. Who'd have thought that the woman who had defended the MP so vociferously would turn and stab him in the back? But maybe this was what came of employing a woman of such strong principles as Cynthia Duckworth. It could easily backfire on you, as Hugh Avery-Blanchard was finding out.

She explained to the team what she'd learned.

'So, Avery-Blanchard had promised to do something, but had perhaps changed his mind,' said Ryan. 'This was a threat to make sure he made good.'

'We know that he was about to make a final decision on the housing development in his constituency,' continued Jake. 'Perhaps he was caught between pleasing Nick Damon and keeping his constituents sweet. This was a not-so-subtle push by Damon to make sure he made the right choice.'

'That sounds very plausible,' said Bridget. 'Print off a copy of that newspaper article,' she told Ryan. 'I'm going to show it to Mr Gold and see how he reacts.'

She took the printout through to the interview room, where Nick Damon's lawyer was waiting.

'Have you decided to release me?' he enquired.

'No,' said Bridget, placing the article with its lurid

photo on the table in front of Gold. 'I've come to show you this.'

For once, the lawyer's face was easy to read. He stared at the article in horror. 'Where...? Why...? How...?' he spluttered.

'Interesting that you didn't ask "who", Mr Gold,' said Bridget. 'Did you send that email to Hugh Avery-Blanchard yourself?'

'I –'

'You sent this to him as a threat, to make sure that he did what Mr Damon had asked, isn't that right?' said Bridget. 'I expect that Mr Damon gets you to do all his dirty work for him, doesn't he? I think I've finally worked you out, Mr Gold. Beneath that expensive suit, you're just a rather nasty bully, aren't you?'

He stared at her, speechless.

His silence was all the confirmation that Bridget needed. She returned to the incident room to gather her team.

'All right, listen up, everyone. That video was recorded in one of the bedrooms at Nick Damon's house. If Damon was secretly recording one of his guests, there's a good chance that all of the upstairs rooms were rigged with concealed cameras. If so, then the room where Gina's body was found must have had one too, and that means someone removed it after the murder. I want to go back to Damon's house and take it apart until we find that camera, or any record of what it recorded. If a video exists, we're going to find it.'

CHAPTER 27

The driveway leading up to Nick Damon's country house was a flurry of activity, with police cars and vans arriving and disgorging teams of detectives, uniformed officers and tech guys.

Jake stood to watch as they got to work. He was glad that both Nick Damon and Tyler Dixon were out and that Mr Gold, the dodgy lawyer, was in a police cell at Kidlington. Only Brittany was left behind at the house, and she stood helplessly to one side, looking on as the police set about scouring the premises for hidden cameras and other recording devices, and taking away laptops, desktop computers and data storage devices for examination back at HQ.

Bridget had given Jake the task of supervising the operation, but the various experts knew exactly how to do their job, and Jake's role mostly seemed to involve standing around feeling redundant. When Brittany offered him a coffee, he wasn't going to refuse.

'It's not like I can do any work,' she said. 'Your guys have taken away my computer.'

'Oh, right, sorry about that.'

'I suppose this is all about that MP,' she said, firing up the high-tech coffee maker in her office.

'I couldn't possibly comment,' said Jake, giving her a wink, 'but, yes.'

'And you're hoping to find hidden cameras in some of the rooms?'

'If there are any, we'll find them,' he said.

'I'd be surprised if you did. Nick's always very protective of his guests' privacy. That's one of the reasons for the masks. But perhaps Gina planted some. I heard that she was spying on people at the party.'

She passed him a cup of coffee, adding cream and giving it a stir so that it made a pretty swirl. Her fingers brushed his as he accepted it. 'Oh, Jake, this is all so horrible. First the murder, then finding the earring in the gatehouse, and...' Her fingers trembled as she made the second cup of coffee, and a tear formed in her eye. 'Sorry,' she said, wiping it away, 'I just keep falling to pieces.'

Jake hated to see her cry. It was instinctive for him to want to comfort anyone in distress. He supposed that was partly why he'd joined the police force. He put a hand on Brittany's arm.

'Don't worry. It's perfectly understandable. Anyone in your shoes would feel exactly the same.'

'Do you think so?'

'Of course I do.'

'It's kind of you to say so.' She finished making her coffee and took a seat close to his, crossing one long leg over the other.

'So, er, what did you do this morning?' he asked. 'Did you manage to get all your stuff from the gatehouse?'

'Yes. And then I went shopping in Oxford. I needed to buy a few things, now that I'm single again.' Her eyes began to fill with tears once more and she fished a tissue out of her sleeve and blew her nose. 'Oh look at me. I just can't seem to hold it together.'

'Don't worry,' he said, reaching out to squeeze her fingers in his hand. 'It's no surprise you're feeling emotional. You've been through a series of nasty shocks.'

'I have. I knew you'd understand. You're always so good to talk to, Jake. You're so compassionate. Oh, by the way, would you like some biscuits to go with your coffee?'

'Oh, er, yeah, that would be great, thanks.'

She fetched a packet of chocolate digestives from the desk and placed half a dozen on a plate for him. 'These were always your favourites, weren't they?'

'Yeah,' he said, helping himself to a handful and demolishing the first in two large bites. 'You know me, I'm easily pleased.'

She studied him over the rim of her cup as she took a sip of her coffee. 'I've been doing a lot of thinking in the past few days, Jake. About you and me, I mean.'

'Yeah?' he said, continuing to munch his way through the biscuits.

'I'm so sorry for how I treated you in the past. It was unforgivable of me. But I want you to know that I've changed, I really have.' She blinked her tear-stained eyes at him. 'And if you ever wanted to try again –'

She left the question dangling in the air, like a thread tempting him back to all that was familiar and safe.

Jake thought about what he'd planned to tell her – that it was over between them, that it had finished a long time ago, and that it was impossible to rekindle a flame that had been so cruelly snuffed out – but somehow the words he'd prepared refused to come. Instead, an image of Ffion yelling at him pushed itself into his mind, and resolutely refused to move aside so that he could deliver his planned speech.

'So,' he stumbled, not sure what he was going to say. 'Do you have anywhere to go, now that you've quit the gatehouse?'

She shook her head, peeping at him hopefully through her wet eyes.

What the hell, he thought. It looked like Ffion had well and truly dumped him, and somehow he didn't think that the Welsh dragon would be quick to give him a second chance. Right now, he was willing to take Brittany at her word, especially since she was so badly upset, and so obviously in need of a place to stay. He could well believe that this business with Gina and Tyler had changed her for the better, and Jake didn't believe in holding grudges.

'Come back with me,' he said. 'I know my flat's not very big, but it's better than staying in a hotel on your own.'

'It's perfect,' said Brittany, giving him a broad smile and throwing her arms around him. 'Thank you so much, Jake.'

★

Listening to the evening news in her car on the way home from work, it came as no surprise to Bridget to hear that Hugh Avery-Blanchard, MP for Witney, had resigned his seat, thereby triggering a by-election in which the opposition parties were hoping to make significant headway. The MP had made the usual noises about wanting to spend more time with his family, although Bridget doubted that his family would want to spend more time with him. The MP's wife had not appeared by his side to offer her support. She was probably on the phone to her lawyers this very minute.

Arriving back at her house, Bridget was pleased to find Chloe at home for once, and even cooking herself a meal. Bridget watched her daughter with some admiration as she removed a dish of bean and salsa nachos swimming in melted cheese from under the grill, and ladled soured cream and guacamole over the top.

'That looks nice,' said Bridget.

Chloe regarded her with some suspicion. 'What's that supposed to mean?'

'It just means that it looks nice. You're becoming a good cook. Much better than me.'

'Well, that's not saying very much,' said Chloe, but she grinned and Bridget knew that their short-lived feud was over. 'So, what are you doing this evening, Mum?'

'Actually, Jonathan's invited me round to his place.'

'Oh, yes?' Chloe raised an eyebrow.

'Just for a meal,' said Bridget hastily.

'It's no problem if you want to stay over. I'll be fine on my own.'

'I wouldn't dream of leaving you alone.'

Chloe shrugged. 'Whatever.' She began to nibble at the nachos, using them to scoop up the cheese and sauce.

Bridget hovered next to the kitchen sink, studying her daughter's familiar features – her dark glossy hair, her brown umber eyes, her pale unblemished skin. She longed to freeze time just as it was, to preserve Chloe in this moment forever. But she knew that time stood still for no one, and that Chloe was fast-forwarding inevitably towards adulthood and independence.

'I love you,' Bridget blurted suddenly, unable to stop herself. 'You know that, don't you?'

'Yes, Mum.'

She felt her colour begin to rise, but ploughed on regardless. 'It's just that I don't say it very often. I'm not good at this kind of thing.'

'No, Mum.' Chloe's dark eyes glinted back at her, a trace of amusement written in faint crinkles on her skin.

'Well, there it is. I've said it now.'

'Okay, Mum,' said Chloe, licking salsa sauce off one long finger. 'I understand. Just don't say it again. It's kind of embarrassing.'

*

After a quick change of clothing and a futile attempt to reorganise her hair into something less messy, Bridget set off to Jonathan's. His house was in the village of Iffley, tucked away in the south-east corner of Oxford next to the River Thames as it left the city. It was a charming part of Oxford and Bridget was looking forward to getting a proper look at his house for the first time.

A ten-minute drive around the ring road and over Donnington Bridge brought her to Iffley Turn. Immediately the road became tree-lined and secluded and Bridget followed the narrow route through the village towards the church of St Mary the Virgin. There, near the old church, stood Jonathan's house.

The house was built of yellow and white stone, with a somewhat rickety-looking stone-tiled roof. The starkly bare branches of a climbing rose clipped back for winter made a framework over the front door, reaching as far as the upstairs windows. Bridget longed to see its flowers bloom when summer came, and to smell their scent.

The door opened to her knock, and Jonathan stood there, dressed in his usual smart casual attire of chinos and open-necked shirt. His tortoiseshell glasses nestled beneath his strawberry blond hair, and as he leaned in to kiss her, she smelled the delicious aroma of herbs, spices and garlic wafting from the kitchen.

'Jonathan,' she said, 'it's so good to see you again.'

*

Dr Frost was just drifting off to sleep, listening to the cars passing on the London Road, when a sudden wave of terror gripped him. In an instant he was wide awake. He blinked his eyes open and saw the eerie glow through the gap in the curtains cast by the streetlight beyond his window.

His heart hammered in his ribcage as he struggled to hold onto the image that had brought him back from the brink of sleep.

A man. In a mask. Staring at him.

It was another memory from the party, he was certain of it. He closed his eyes again and tried to bring it back into focus.

Slowly, the image reformed in his mind's eye. The man, the mask, the room filled with partygoers. He could hear the music, the chatter of voices, the clink of glassware and plates.

The man was standing aloof from the crowd, just like Frost himself. Frost tried to picture the mask, but it remained just beyond his grasp. It was a sinister mask, though. And even though Frost couldn't see the man's eyes, he felt the direction of his gaze, penetrating and hostile.

The moment seemed to go on forever, captured timelessly in his broken memory.

What now? thought Frost. Think! What happens next?

And then the scene began to play again, like a film continuing after the pause button is released. The man in the mask advanced steadily towards him, weaving his way across the crowded room, and Frost shivered with trepidation beneath his bedclothes.

What had the man done next? Frost wrestled with the scene in his mind, trying to force it to continue on to its logical conclusion, but the fragment of memory refused to obey. After a moment it dissolved once again into abstraction.

Alone in his bedroom, beneath the dull glow of the streetlamp and the rhythmic rushing of the cars, Frost lay wide awake, staring up at the ceiling. He knew that he would not sleep again that night.

CHAPTER 28

Ffion knew that she was trying to distract herself with work. It was a pattern of behaviour that she was very familiar with. It's what she'd done growing up in Wales whenever she'd felt alienated from her peers or her family, which had been often. And although immersing herself in her school studies hadn't done much to develop her social skills as a teenager, it had enabled her to escape her small Welsh coal-mining village and come to Oxford. It had got her where she was today.

And where was that exactly?

On her own again.

She'd been happy with Jake, even though the fault lines in their relationship had been glaringly obvious right from the start. And despite their many differences, if Brittany Grainger hadn't appeared on the scene, they might still have made it work. Jake was a nice guy, far easier to get on with than most blokes, and there was no denying the physical attraction she felt for him, even now. But Ffion knew that she could never compete with a woman like Brittany.

No matter how confident Ffion might appear on the

outside, underneath she was sensitive and vulnerable. Brittany on the other hand exuded an easy self-confidence, and Ffion had always shied away from such overtly feminine types, knowing that she didn't belong in their world.

She was thankful that she could so easily push aside her troublesome relationship problems and find solace in her work. And there was nothing more absorbing than the kind of work she was doing now.

Bridget, being well aware of Ffion's ICT skills, had assigned her to work alongside the digital forensics team working to recover and analyse the data from the various pieces of hardware that had been confiscated from Nick Damon's house. While some of her fellow police officers found working with computers dull, Ffion liked their predictability. Computers could still challenge you, and advances in artificial intelligence and surveillance technology were moving at a staggering pace. But best of all, computers didn't do emotion, and for that Ffion was grateful.

She had come into the station early to grab some quiet time alone, and it was still only seven thirty. She'd have at least half an hour to herself before anyone else arrived.

Tapping away at her computer keyboard, she rapidly entered the commands that would unlock the latest challenge facing her – a data stick that had been recovered from Mr Gold's office. The stick was apparently blank, but that didn't fool Ffion. After a moment's typing, she was gratified to see a list of deleted video files appear on screen, and began to work her way through them, restoring the lost data ready for examination. Settling herself in her chair with a mug of matcha tea, she put on her headphones, clicked open the first of the recovered files and watched as it began to play.

The video revealed an empty bedroom dimly lit by a single bedside lamp. In the middle of the far wall was a four-poster bed covered in a satin quilt and assorted pillows and cushions. The camera must have been fixed to the ceiling, or else high up on the wall, and Ffion doubted that Gina Hartman would have been able to position it in that location herself. It was possible that Tyler Dixon had placed it for her – Ffion guessed that Gina had only been sleeping with Tyler in order to get him to do favours for her – but it was far more likely that Nick Damon himself had ordered the hidden cameras to be installed in order to give him additional leverage over his guests. While the sex parties he ran might prove to be an effective "carrot" in persuading his various acquaintances to do his bidding, the "stick" of an incriminating video would certainly provide him with a useful backup if that failed.

The video continued to play, but there was no one in the bedroom and nothing happening onscreen. Ffion fast-forwarded to twice normal speed, then five times, and then ten. Still nothing happened. She kept on watching until it came to an end.

Undaunted, she clicked on the second video, watching again at high speed until it stopped. Still nothing. Then, partway through the third video, there was a flash of movement, and she rewound and began to watch it at normal speed.

After a minute she heard a sound as the door opened, and a man stumbled into the room. He walked as if drunk or drugged, tripping over the rug before collapsing onto the bed, fully clothed. The man wore a full-face Bauta-style mask, recognisable by the black, cream and gold diamond patterning around the eyes and nose. After a moment he rolled over onto his side, dislodging the mask and exposing a glimpse of his face. It was clearly Frost.

The German tutor quickly fell asleep and began to snore softly. Ffion speeded up the video, watching as Frost slept the sleep of the dead. Fifteen minutes later, the door to the room opened a second time and Ffion slowed the video back to normal speed and re-watched as a masked figure wearing a black hat entered the room backwards, dragging somebody else along the floor.

Ffion watched intently, ignoring the other police

officers who were now beginning to arrive in the office, greeting her and engaging in the morning ritual of grabbing a coffee, switching on their computers, and discussing the latest news or sports results. She blocked out all background movement and chatter, her attention fixed entirely on the events unfolding onscreen.

This had to be it. The moment when Gina Hartman lost her life.

Ffion wasn't at all squeamish by nature. She'd always been happy to wield the knife in school biology lessons when the other girls had run crying from the room. But she had never witnessed another person actually being killed in cold blood.

The man – or woman – in the black hat dragged their struggling victim into the room and dumped her on the floor for a few seconds, as they moved to shut the door. Gina – for the woman on the floor was now clearly recognisable from her black waitress outfit and her corkscrew curls – struggled and tried to push herself up from the floor, but her attacker was back on her in an instant.

The masked assailant had their back to the camera, but their height and build suggested a man or a tall woman. Whoever it was clamped their right hand over Gina's mouth and wrapped their left arm tightly around her throat. As she was forced back to the floor, Gina tried to prise the attacker's arm from her neck, but wasn't strong enough.

With their back to the camera, the masked figure struck Gina's face, then placed both hands around her slender neck and began to squeeze mercilessly. It didn't take long for the student to be subdued. Within a minute she stopped resisting and her head dropped back, her body now as limp as a ragdoll.

On top of the bed, Frost slept on in a world of dreams, oblivious to the real-life drama taking place only feet away from where he lay.

The masked figure now stood up and turned in the

direction of the camera. For the first time the figure's masked face was clearly visible. The mask was that of a plague doctor's, showing grotesquely-distorted features with a pointed bird-like beak in place of a nose. The murderer's hair was hidden beneath their wide-brimmed hat, and it was still impossible to guess their identity.

The attacker bent down again to examine Gina's broken body. Although it would have been easier to walk away, the figure chose instead to pick her up and lay her out on the bed next to Frost's sleeping form, her face turned away from him towards the wall. In one final, bizarre gesture her killer stroked her face with a black-gloved hand, then turned to leave the room.

For a second time the figure faced the camera full on. The long, beaked nose of the plague doctor seemed to be pointing directly at Ffion. Then the figure passed out of shot. Ffion heard the door open and close again, before a spine-chilling silence fell over the room. The video played on, but there was nothing more to see.

The incident room had filled up while Ffion had been watching the video, but if anyone had spoken to her she wouldn't have known. They would probably think her even more stand-offish than usual. But Ffion didn't care. She had just witnessed a young woman lose her life.

She looked over towards Bridget's desk and saw the detective inspector about to pick up her phone. Ffion strode quickly across the office just as Bridget began to dial a number.

'Put the phone down, boss,' she said. 'You have to see this.'

★

Even though Frost had been certain he wouldn't sleep again that night, somehow he had succeeded in dropping off during the grey hours around dawn. So tired... he was always so tired now, having barely slept for days, caught in a prison between insomnia and a waking delirium that was so dreamlike in its intensity that it was impossible to distinguish fact from fantasy.

When his alarm rang to rouse him, he turned it off and returned to a fitful slumber, even though it was daylight that crept through the gap in his curtains now, not the half-glow of the streetlamp. He hoped for restful release that might begin to restore his sanity, but instead a series of nightmare images flooded his sleep, even though he knew at some level they were not dreams at all, but his lost memories finally returning.

Those memories had come at first in tiny droplets. Now they seemed to flow as freely as the drinks at Damon's party.

And he was back there now, staring once again at the man in the frightening mask across the crowded room.

A cold sweat bathed his forehead as he tossed in his bed, murmuring with agitation.

For now he remembered the man's mask. It was the plague doctor. Of course! The man's costume was hideous, with its long, bird-like nose and wide-brimmed leather hat.

But it was only a mask. No need to be frightened.

'Thank you,' Frost said to the plague doctor. It seemed that the man hadn't come to harm him after all, simply to offer him a drink. And yet wasn't that the job of the waitresses? No matter, Frost wasn't one to refuse an act of kindness from a stranger.

The plague doctor watched him as he drank the champagne. But when Frost looked for him again, he'd disappeared. Now Frost began to feel sleepy. So much champagne – it had gone to his head. And so many people. There was nowhere to sit down. All he wanted was to take the weight off his feet and rest for a while, and perhaps to close his eyes. A thought occurred to him. Perhaps he might go upstairs and find a bed to lie down on for a short time. Just forty winks until he felt better.

He headed out into the hallway where the man in the plague doctor's mask was talking to Gina. Or rather, Gina was speaking to him.

'What are you doing here?' she demanded. 'You shouldn't be here!'

That was funny. Frost wanted to stand up for the man, and to say that he was a good chap who had fetched him a drink. But he was too tired even to speak. He gripped the elaborately shaped wooden banister, pausing briefly to admire its craftsmanship, then began to climb the long staircase. It took him an age to make his way upstairs, every step a great effort. Had someone put lead weights into his shoes? He could no longer hear the noise from down below. Finally he found himself facing a door and turned the doorknob, almost falling through into the dimly lit room beyond as the door swung open. And there was the bed, just as he'd longed for. He stumbled over to it and lay down in its welcoming embrace, falling at last into the dreamless sleep he craved.

*

'Who on earth can it be?' asked Bridget.

By now the whole team had watched the gruesome video of Gina's murder but no one was able to say which of the guests had worn the plague doctor mask. The sinister-looking mask seemed a very odd choice to wear to a party, with its grotesquely distorted features.

'The plague doctor mask,' said Ffion, 'was designed by a sixteenth-century French doctor as protection against disease during later waves of the plague. You see it worn during the Venice *Carnivale*.'

'Fascinating facts, Ffion,' said Ryan drily. 'But why wear it to a party?'

'To conceal your identity. When combined with the leather hat, it's impossible to see anything of the wearer's facial features or hair.'

'Would you say it was a man or a woman?' Bridget asked, peering at the frozen image of the masked attacker on Ffion's computer screen.

But no one was willing to hazard a guess.

'So where does this get us?' she asked. It was unbelievably frustrating that they had captured the murder itself on high definition video, but still couldn't pin down the identity of the killer.

'Well, at least this proves it wasn't Frost,' said Andy. 'He's in the clear now.'

'True,' said Bridget, 'Then it must have been one of the other guests, or else Nick Damon himself, or Tyler Dixon or Mr Gold. We need to find out who was wearing that mask. I'll get on the phone to Brittany Grainger and find out if she knows.'

Bridget returned to her desk and dialled the number of Damon's PA. The call was answered immediately.

'Brittany Grainger speaking. How may I help you?'

'DI Hart here. Can you tell me if you have a list of the masks and costumes worn by the guests to the party on Friday?'

'Um, no. Sorry. But I can probably remember most of them. I was at the door welcoming everyone in. Was there someone in particular you're interested in?'

'Who wore the plague doctor's mask?'

'Ah,' said Brittany. 'I don't actually know who that was. He just identified himself as the Doctor.'

'The Doctor? So you're sure it was a man?'

'I think so.'

'But surely he must have been on your guest list,' persisted Bridget.

'Um… well, yes. Sure.'

'You don't sound certain. Was he definitely one of the guests?'

'He must have been,' said Brittany.

'But you didn't recognise him?'

'Well, his features were completely hidden behind the mask. It was difficult to tell who it was.'

More like impossible, thought Bridget. 'So how can you be certain it wasn't Mr Damon? Or Mr Gold? Or Tyler?'

'You'll just have to take my word for it,' said Brittany.

CHAPTER 29

Ffion ought to have been feeling pleased with herself after her morning's discovery. Thanks to her, they were significantly closer to discovering the identity of the killer, and Bridget had praised her work, making it clear that her contribution was valued.

But Ffion wasn't happy, and not simply because she had overheard Jake admitting to Ryan in the kitchen that Brittany had now moved back in with him.

No, there was something bothering her about the case. A niggling loose end that refused to go away. She grabbed herself another mug of tea and returned to her desk, this time navigating to the audio recording that Gina had made at the party. She put her headphones back on, blocking out the background chatter of the incident room, and began to listen to the recording again from the very beginning.

Two hours later she'd confirmed her suspicions. At around ten thirty pm, Gina had spoken to Dr Frost, telling him in a hushed whisper, 'You should leave. You don't belong here.' Then, an hour or so later, she'd given the same warning again. 'You shouldn't be here!'

Ffion had assumed that she'd been speaking to Frost

on both occasions. Certainly the man hadn't taken her seriously the first time. But listening to Gina's voice again, Ffion now began to wonder if she'd been speaking to a different person this second time.

The first message, to Frost, had been intended as a warning. But on the second occasion, the intonation and emphasis were all different. There was a sharp rebuke to Gina's tone. *You shouldn't be here!* The first person had made a mistake in coming to the party and was being warned to leave. But the second person had deliberately appeared where they weren't wanted and was being reprimanded. If Gina had been speaking to Frost again, she'd have said something like, 'I told you before, you shouldn't be here.'

Ffion's mind began to race. If the person Gina was telling to leave was the plague doctor, then it was clear from this recording that she had known her killer and thought he ought not to have been there. An unwelcome guest, perhaps, or someone who wasn't a guest at all.

★

'Let's go over it one more time,' said Bridget, standing in front of the whiteboard in the incident room. The entire team was gathered around, trying to fit together the pieces of the puzzle to make a whole.

The results of Mr Gold's DNA test had come back from the lab, and as Bridget had suspected, they showed that Gold wasn't the father of Gina's baby. Despite that, Bridget felt certain that with Ffion's latest breakthrough, they now knew everything they needed to find the killer. If only they could look at the pieces of the mystery with fresh eyes, it would become obvious how they slotted together to make a whole.

'Here's what we know,' she began, pointing to the first photograph on the board. 'Gina Hartman, final-year Psychology student at Wadham College.'

The red corkscrew hair and dazzling smile in the photo

revealed a young woman just starting to make her way in the world, unaware that her life was destined to be cut tragically short.

'According to her tutor, Gina was a gifted student, destined for a first-class degree.'

A tragic waste of a young life, Dr Ashley had told Bridget when she'd been to see him in college, and she was in full agreement with that sentiment.

'Gina was pregnant, but we still have no positive ID for the father,' she continued. 'She worked as a journalist for a student newspaper, and was using Nick Damon's parties not only as a way of earning some cash, but also to investigate wrongdoing among Damon's guests. She made a secret audio recording during the party, and we know that she was trying to find evidence of corrupt dealings between Nick Damon and Hugh Avery-Blanchard, the MP for Witney.'

'Former MP,' interjected Ryan, to some mirth from around the room.

Bridget pointed to the photograph of Nick Damon. 'It would appear that Nick Damon's true purpose in holding these parties was to nurture contacts and to gain influence over people like Avery-Blanchard who might have been able to benefit Damon's business interests in some way. Not only did he provide free drinks and entertainment, including the services of a London-based escort agency, but he appears also to have made secret videos of his guests enjoying those services, so that he could later blackmail them if they refused to help him. At least, that's what appears to have happened to our hapless ex-MP.'

Bridget paused, before pointing to the photograph of Dr Nathan Frost taken just after he'd been arrested. The man gazed out timidly from the wall, looking thoroughly out of place alongside the images of powerful men that surrounded him.

'Dr Frost appears – on the face of it – to have been invited to the party because he had influence over a planned building project at Wadham College. Certainly the project was large, and it's conceivable that Frost's vote might have been decisive. But Frost is convinced that he was invited to the party in order for Gina's murder to be pinned on him. At this stage, we can't rule out that possibility, especially since the video we've seen clearly shows the murderer deliberately placing Gina's body in bed next to him while he slept.'

Next Bridget indicated the photos of the various guests who had been present at the party, drawing particular attention to the round red face of Hugh Avery-Blanchard. 'Avery-Blanchard's name, or rather the alias that he used at the party – Apollo – cropped up again when we listened to Gina's audio recording. Brittany Grainger, Damon's PA, was clearly heard sending Gina upstairs to take a bottle of champagne to Apollo's room, just before midnight. We know that Gina was attacked immediately after knocking on the bedroom door, and we learned from interviewing the various escorts who worked at the party that Apollo was Avery-Blanchard's alias, and that Erika, the escort who spent the night with him couldn't provide a solid alibi for the time of the murder.'

Bridget moved on next to the photo of the judge, Graham Neville. 'Mr Justice Neville, the High Court judge, was also present at the party, in the company of...'

'Josh,' said Ryan.

'– Josh, who claims not to have noticed anything unusual about his behaviour during the evening.'

'Apart from the minor detail of a judge being at a sex party,' said Ryan with a smirk.

'We also believe,' said Bridget, 'although we have no firm evidence, that Neville threw a trial in order to avoid getting Tyler Dixon, Damon's driver, convicted of an assault charge.'

Bridget drew a breath. 'We still don't know which of these men wore the plague doctor's mask, although Brittany Grainger claims that he identified himself as the Doctor. She believes he was a guest, but we haven't been able to identify him from the guest list. It's possible that he was an uninvited guest – although he must have known the password to be admitted at the gate – or it's possible that Miss Grainger is covering for someone. The question then is who?'

Ffion raised a hand. 'It might not have been a man wearing the plague doctor's outfit. We can't say for sure whether it was a man or a woman who killed Gina.'

'It might not have been a guest,' said Jake. 'It might have been Tyler Dixon. He had a clear motive to kill Gina, if he found out that she'd been sleeping with another man.'

'What about the creepy lawyer, Mr Gold?' asked Andy. 'We know that he sent the video to the MP as a threat. Might he have been trying to stop Gina from carrying out her investigations?'

'We know that he went to interrogate Poppy immediately before Miranda was strangled,' said Ryan. 'I wouldn't be surprised if he did all Damon's dirty work.'

'All right, all right,' said Bridget, trying to restore a sense of order to the incident room. The fact was, they had far too much information before them. It was difficult to find a path through all the competing facts. She pointed once again to the photo of Nick Damon. The man's tanned, grinning face exuded an infuriating confidence that made her want to punch his nose.

'We mustn't forget the man at the centre of this web. Nick Damon, owner of Damon Developments and about a dozen other companies. We know that he manipulates people to get what he wants, but we don't have a shred of evidence to pin on him. Damon's too smart for that. He uses men like Tyler Dixon and Mr Gold to throw muscle around and threaten people, while he stays back, keeping himself above the fray. He generously hands out gifts to his friends, then collects favours in return. Is there any possibility he might have murdered Gina for some reason?'

'To stop her investigating his parties,' said Jake.

'And he could easily have dressed up in this plague doctor's outfit to conceal his identity,' said Ryan.

'We only have Brittany's word that the plague doctor

was one of the guests,' said Ffion. 'She might simply have been lying about this mysterious Doctor. And we know that Brittany sent Gina upstairs. She could have known that Damon was waiting there to strangle her.'

'Damon has no alibi for the time of Miranda's murder either,' said Bridget. 'And we know that Mr Gold was definitely in the college at the time of her death. In fact, he was with Poppy very shortly before Miranda phoned me to say she'd guessed who killed Gina.'

'Where was Brittany that morning?' asked Ffion.

'Out shopping in Oxford,' said Jake, shifting uncomfortably in his chair.

'So any of them might have killed Miranda,' said Bridget despairingly. 'This is getting us nowhere.'

She really needed to close this case as a matter of urgency. Grayson had cut her some slack, but with two dead students and no conclusive result, his patience would be wearing thin. And Bridget knew that this afternoon she would have to return to Wadham College to meet Miranda's parents. She would have to stand before them and tell them that she had no clear idea who had taken their daughter's life.

The memory of meeting Gina's grieving parents in college flashed before her and she recalled their quiet dignity in the face of tragic death. She thought of the cold morgue, and of Gina's marble skin and red curls, preserved in lifeless beauty. And she remembered how the warden of the college and Gina's tutor had gone out of their way to make the parents comfortable and to smooth their visit.

She thought again of Miranda's room in Front Quad, and of Frost's upstairs room that overlooked it. And now at last she guessed who the father of Gina's unborn child might be.

'Come on,' she said aloud. 'I think I know who did it, and why.'

CHAPTER 30

Frost started awake from his sleep, his forehead burning with fever, his stomach convulsing with pain as if iron bands were clamping tightly around it. His bedclothes were drenched with sweat. But he threw them aside, rising from the clammy bed with a sense of resolution unlike any he had felt before.

He had remembered!

At last, the elusive memory he had sought for so long and which told him what he needed to know had come back to him.

The voice of the plague doctor, speaking to him as he handed over the glass of champagne.

'Here, you look like you could use another drink.'

Such kind words, yet just like the man's mask, they served only to cloak the treacherous viper lurking behind them.

He knew that voice! And now he knew who had committed the terrible crime of strangling Gina, and who had sought to incriminate him as the perpetrator.

Quick as a flash he began to dress, stumbling into his trousers and pulling on his shirt, still creased from the day

266

before. He rushed downstairs to grab his shoes and bicycle clips. Shrugging a coat over his shoulders he wheeled his bicycle from its place in the hallway out through the front door. Then, pedalling furiously, he set off down the road, pushing recklessly across a line of oncoming cars that tooted their horns at him as he made a sharp right turn.

Down the long steep slope of Headington Hill he cycled, propelling the heavy metal bike as fast as he dared, feeling the cold wind tugging at him, as if it sought to hold him back. But nothing could stop him now. Like Nietzsche's *Übermensch* – or Superman, to the uneducated – he had chosen his own destiny, and was about to claim it.

At the foot of the hill a bus lurched out in front of him, but he mounted the pavement, waving his arms to shoo a pedestrian out of his way. Then, with a thud, he was back on the road, pedalling out across the busy roundabout of the Plain, weaving his way between cars and other cyclists in the direction of Wadham.

Despite the icy wind that whipped his face, despite the burning of his fever, despite the honking of irate drivers, he felt free and happy for the first time since he could remember. I am invincible, he thought to himself, as he turned right at the traffic lights into Longwall Street. Left he turned at the next junction, into New College Lane, picking up speed on his final approach to Wadham.

On arrival at the college, he dumped his bike in the lodge, ignoring the complaints of the porter, and hurried inside. He made his way immediately to Dr Ashley's room in Front Quad, and hammered loudly on the door with his fist.

'Come in,' said a voice in surprise.

Frost opened the door and pushed it wide. There, sitting behind his desk and affecting a look of startled innocence, was his quarry.

'I suppose you thought you'd got away with it,' said Frost. 'You murdered Gina, you set me up as prime suspect, and then you killed Miranda when she heard your voice and realised that you were at the party.'

The object of his hatred – his nemesis – regarded him with a cold and calculating look, just as repulsive as the mask he had worn on the night of the murder.

'You'd better come in, then,' said Dr Ashley at last. 'Close the door behind you.'

CHAPTER 31

There was no time to wait for backup. Bridget leapt into the front seat of Jake's Subaru, while Ffion and Ryan piled into the back.

'Strap in tight,' said Jake, sticking the car into gear, his right foot already to the floor.

The car pulled out of its place in the Kidlington car park with a screech of rubber, engine roaring, rev counter pushing towards the red. It sped off down the Oxford Road as fast as Jake could safely manage before crossing the ring road and entering North Oxford.

'Can you be certain it's him, ma'am?' asked Ryan from the back of the car.

'A DNA test will prove it one way or the other,' said Bridget, 'but we've eliminated every other man connected with this investigation. If none of the party guests, nor Damon nor any member of his staff was the father of Gina's child, then it was almost certainly someone she knew at college. And since Miranda and Poppy insisted that Gina didn't have a boyfriend, that only leaves –'

'– her tutor,' filled in Ffion. 'It certainly fits. If Gina told Dr Ashley about her pregnancy and then he discovered that she was sleeping with Tyler Dixon, he might have become enraged with jealousy.'

'Why kill her at the party, though?' asked Ryan. 'Why do it there?'

'Perhaps he didn't plan to kill her,' said Bridget. 'Perhaps he just went along to keep an eye on her. Gina had already told him about the parties, and she might even have told him the password. Suppose he donned a disguise and followed her to the house in order to keep watch over her, or to persuade her to come back with him. He might have taken the Rohypnol with the intention of giving it to her if she refused to cooperate. But instead, he saw her and Tyler having sex in Tyler's car next to the gatehouse.'

'Just like Tyler kept telling us,' said Jake.

'Then, after other guests started to arrive, he went inside, inventing an alias to give to Brittany.'

'The Doctor,' mused Ffion. 'Alluding to his plague doctor disguise, and also to the fact that he holds a PhD in Psychology.'

'Right,' said Bridget. 'And then, to his amazement, he found one of his colleagues, Dr Frost, at the party. He seized his chance, slipping Frost the drugged drink, so that he went upstairs to sleep, and then he confronted Gina in the hallway.'

'You shouldn't be here!' repeated Ffion. 'The words make perfect sense now.'

'He must have seen Gina go upstairs carrying the champagne,' continued Bridget, 'followed her up, and attacked her. He dragged her into Frost's room, strangled her to death, and then placed the body in the bed, knowing that Frost would be unable to provide a convincing explanation for how he'd ended up there with the body of a student from his own college. He was the perfect fall guy.'

'Except that Dr Ashley had no idea about the hidden camera that recorded a video of the whole murder,' said Ryan.

'Right. Although unbeknown to him he was rescued by

Mr Gold who deleted the video in order to cover up the fact that he and Damon had been secretly recording their guests' activities. But then later, Miranda must have bumped into him in college and heard his voice. She realised she'd heard him speaking at the party, and guessed that he might be Gina's killer. Presumably Dr Ashley noticed her, followed her back to her room, and strangled her. He was right under our noses the whole time.'

It was so often the case, mused Bridget. The truth was obvious once you'd sifted away all the distractions and false trails.

'We're nearly there, ma'am,' interrupted Jake from the driving seat.

'Okay,' said Bridget. 'Let's find him quickly and bring him in with the minimum of fuss. I don't want to create another big scene.'

★

'So, you finally worked it out,' sneered Dr Ashley, leaning back in his chair. 'I thought you were never going to remember anything about that night.'

'That's what you hoped,' said Frost. 'But you're a psychologist. You must know the marvels that the human brain is capable of.'

'Hmm, yes, even yours it would appear. You know, I quizzed you quite thoroughly that time when I sat next to you at evensong. I thought that if I sat right next to you, and you heard my voice, and that still didn't stir any recollections, then I was home and dry.'

'But you weren't, were you?' said Frost. 'Miranda Gardiner recognised your voice, and she guessed the truth. That's why you killed her.'

'Yes,' said Dr Ashley. 'And that's why I'm going to have to kill you too.'

'You wouldn't dare!' said Frost, aghast. 'How could you possibly get away with a third murder?'

'I've managed two already. I'm pretty sure I'll think of

something. Perhaps if you were to attack me, for example. Then I'd be forced to defend myself, wouldn't I? Yes, perhaps you came here acting like a lunatic, threatening violence. Everyone knows that you've been off your head this past week. Most people believe you killed Gina. And you don't have an alibi for when Miranda was strangled either. Yes, I don't think it would be very difficult to convince everyone that you're a psychotic killer. I guess you'd need to have access to some kind of weapon, wouldn't you? That way I could justify using the force necessary to break your neck.'

Dr Ashley's eyes roamed around the room. Frost looked too, wondering what kind of instrument an Oxford don might keep in his room that could hold lethal potential.

They both saw it at the same instant. An iron poker leaning against the fireplace. A black metal rod, about eighteen inches in length, with a loop at one end and a wicked spike at the other.

Dr Ashley let out an animal snarl and got up from his chair. The young man was fast and strong, and darted towards the fire iron with the desperation of a man who had nothing to lose.

But Frost had nothing to lose either, and everything to gain. Not only his innocence to prove, and his freedom to keep, but finally a chance to save his soul.

Only a week ago he had been willing to sell his soul to a devil, a man who treated human lives as commodities to be bartered and traded. And for what? A night out at a sordid party in a country house. How cheaply he had valued himself!

Not now, though. Brought face to face with his own ruin, he had risen from the ashes, ready to redeem himself through action and make his own moral rules as he chose. No longer would he hide himself away in dusty libraries, timidly shunning the material world. He would dare to take what was rightfully his, becoming the legendary *Übermensch* and doing what Nietzsche had urged us all to do – to unleash human potential to its full, uniting artistic creativity with the ruthlessness of the warrior.

Shrugging off the last of his caution, he flung himself towards the fireplace, reaching out to grasp the poker.

But Ashley got to it first.

★

The Subaru screeched to a halt outside Wadham College, and Bridget hauled herself out, aware that she was constitutionally unsuited to this kind of dynamic activity. She must look a sight – a middle-aged woman carrying rather too much weight, struggling out of a souped-up hot hatch painted an unruly shade of orange.

Ffion and Ryan were already out of the car and rushing ahead of her towards the college entrance. She hoped they would bear in mind what she'd told them: 'Play it quietly. I don't want Grayson on my back again if the college files a complaint.' She had a feeling that if they smashed down another door, the Chief Super would bill her personally for the damage.

Jake jumped out of the car too and came round to her side to help. She waved him on. 'Go on. Make the arrest. I'll catch you up.'

By the time she reached the gatehouse, Ffion had already sprinted across the quad to Dr Ashley's room and Ryan was close behind. Ffion knocked on the door and called out. 'Police! Open up!'

Bridget saw her open the door, letting out a sigh of relief that it hadn't been necessary to kick it down this time.

And then all hell broke loose.

★

Dr Ashley stood with his back to the fireplace, the black iron rod in his hand. The spike at its tip looked even more dangerous close up than Frost had feared. Ashley brandished it like a sword, a malevolent smile creeping across his features.

'So, this is how it goes,' said Ashley. 'You came to my room, and before I knew it you were gloating about the crimes you'd committed. You boasted of killing Gina, saying that you'd fantasised about her ever since she came to college. In your twisted imagination you convinced yourself that the attraction was mutual. Then, when she refused to sleep with you at the party, you strangled her, and then you strangled Miranda too... just because you'd developed a taste for it. When I tried to reason with you, pleading with you to hand yourself over to the police, you attacked me and I had no choice. I had to defend myself.'

'No,' said Frost.

'Oh, yes,' said Ashley. 'Because I really don't have a choice, do I? If I let you live, you'll go straight to the police. I had no choice other than to kill Gina too. Even though she was carrying my child, she insisted on going to those sleazy parties. She was even willing to sleep with another man whilst she was pregnant. That's the kind of woman Gina was.'

Frost stared at him, appalled. 'You were sleeping with her? You bastard! A student in your care. You had a duty to protect her. And her unborn child too!' The thought sickened him.

'You're slow to catch on, aren't you? I assumed you'd already worked out that detail,' said Ashley. 'Gina wanted to sleep with me. She was a consenting adult and she made a free choice. Don't pretend you didn't want to sleep with her too.'

'What? How dare you!'

'Don't lecture me, you hypocrite. I saw the way you looked at her from your window. Perhaps you imagined you were invisible up there? But everyone could see you, leering at Gina and drooling at the sight of her long red hair.'

'I –'

But Frost couldn't deny it. There was a kernel of truth

in Ashley's accusation. He had watched Gina from afar. He had fantasised about her. He owed it to himself to admit the truth.

As the playwright Friedrich Dürrenmatt wrote in *Incident at Twilight* – It is only in love and murder that we still remain sincere.

Now was the time for him to be sincere at last. Only the deepest truth would suffice. 'I did love Gina,' he admitted. 'I loved her, but only in the purest sense. She was like an angel. She made the world a better place.'

'You're a filthy old man, Frost,' taunted Ashley. 'And Gina was no angel. You'd never convince anyone with your declaration of pure love. You wanted her, just like I did. But the difference between the two of us is that Gina wanted me too.'

'You murderer!' bellowed Frost in rage. 'You killed her!'

He lunged forward, his fists rising in fury, but the iron poker came down to meet him.

He ducked, but the metal rod caught him a glancing blow on the shoulder, knocking him aside. He spun and saw Ashley lifting the weapon high, ready to strike again.

Then a cry came from outside, and a second later the door burst wide open. A young woman stood there, dressed in a green leather jacket that matched her eyes. 'Police!' she shouted, and in that moment, Frost saw his chance.

*

It took Ffion only a moment to take in the scene in the room. Dr Ashley himself, standing before the fireplace, an old iron poker clutched in his right hand, the weapon held high and ready to strike. Dr Frost, cowering before him, one arm raised in protection. There was a look in his eyes that Ffion couldn't quite make out – fear certainly, but also a kind of fearlessness. It was a paradox, but not one that she had any time to unravel right now.

'Police!' she shouted again. 'Put that weapon down!'

A look of startled outrage flashed across Dr Ashley's face. He seemed torn between a willingness to drop the poker to the floor, and a desire to bring it down across Frost's head.

Ryan arrived in the doorway behind her and rapidly assessed the situation. 'Drop that thing right now, mate!' he commanded.

For a moment, Ffion wondered if Ashley might be about to comply, but then she saw the expression on his face slide from shock towards loathing, and she knew that he was about to strike his victim.

Everything happened at the same time.

Without being aware of her actions, Ffion had already moved herself into a defensive posture, ready to grapple with Ashley. Her body was turned side-on, minimising the vulnerable area that she presented to her assailant. Her feet were spaced apart, ready for balance and rapid response. And she had positioned her hands before her, in readiness to strike.

Her hours of Taekwondo training at the dojang had paid off. As Ashley moved to attack, she shot out one hand and grabbed his wrist, twisting it so that the poker fell from his grasp. It clattered to the floor and he let out a wail of pain. Taking his arm in both hands, Ffion jerked him towards her, stepping aside so that he tumbled to the floor.

Ryan was lumbering into the room, ready to join the fray, but out of the corner of her eye Ffion caught a glimpse of movement.

Frost.

The German tutor shot forward, faster than seemed possible for such a fossilised relic of a bygone age, and now the metal poker was his. He rose to his feet, the weapon held out before him like a trophy.

Ashley lay on his back, screeching in pain as Ffion held onto his wrist to stop him moving. She knew she couldn't release him yet.

'Dr Frost,' said Ryan, 'put that weapon down.'

But Frost took no notice. Lifting the poker in his outstretched arm, he flung himself towards Ashley, swinging the iron rod around in a wide arc.

There was a loud crack as the metal struck the bone of Ryan's skull, and the detective sergeant toppled over backwards, his arms flailing in wide cartwheels as he went down.

Frost stood motionless in the middle of the room, surveying the unplanned outcome of his exertions with a look of surprise.

Then Jake pushed through the open doorway, his eyes wide with confusion.

'Take that poker off Frost before he hits anyone else,' Ffion ordered. 'Then check that Ryan's still breathing. Don't worry about Ashley. I've got him under control.'

CHAPTER 32

'So, are you confident that you've got the right man, this time?' enquired Grayson. 'I'm sure I don't need to remind you that this is the third arrest you've made on this case.'

'Yes sir,' said Bridget. 'Anyway it was the Banbury constabulary who first arrested Frost, and then we had good reason to arrest Tyler Dixon.'

'Yes, yes,' said Grayson dismissively, 'but you're sure about this Psychology lecturer?'

'We've formally charged Dr Ashley now. The DNA test has confirmed that he was the father of Gina's baby. And according to Frost, he made a full and detailed confession to killing both Gina and Miranda, although he's refusing to say anything to us so far. His lawyer advised him not to.'

'Lawyers,' said Grayson, infusing the word with some heartfelt loathing.

'Moreover,' continued Bridget, 'he wasn't as lucky when he strangled Miranda. SOCO picked up a couple of his hairs on her clothing, and her fingernails held traces of skin and blood that matched his DNA. She seems to have put up quite a fight.'

Bridget had met with Miranda's parents at Wadham College, and after arresting and charging the man who murdered their daughter, she had been able to hold her head up and look them in the eye. She'd phoned Gina's parents too and given them the news directly. 'I knew you'd do right by our Gina,' her mother had said, thanking her for her work.

From behind his desk, Grayson nodded in satisfaction. 'What about DS Hooper? Will he live?'

'I think so, sir.' After the struggle at Wadham, both Ryan and Dr Frost had been bundled off to the Emergency Department of the John Radcliffe Hospital, where they had been treated for minor injuries. 'He should be back at work tomorrow.'

'Good,' said Grayson. 'Perhaps I should put him down for a bravery award.'

'I'm sure he'd appreciate that, sir. And DC Ffion Hughes too. She disarmed Dr Ashley and made the arrest single-handedly.'

'Very good. What about Mr Gold, Damon's lawyer? Have we released him yet?'

'He's out on bail. But the digital forensics team traced the incriminating video that was sent to Hugh Avery-Blanchard's constituency office to an email account operated from Gold's computer, so we've charged him with blackmail. He might still wriggle out of it, as it's not clear that he made any actual demands. Being a lawyer, I suppose he's good at avoiding breaking the letter of the law. But in any case, Avery-Blanchard seems ready to testify against him, and that'll probably be enough to secure a conviction of some kind.'

'Good,' said Grayson. 'Speaking of Avery-Blanchard, I suppose you've heard the latest from Westminster?'

'I don't think so, sir. I've been quite busy...'

'The Minister for Housing has announced a review of the housing development that Damon Developments was hoping to win the contract for. In other words, they've kicked the whole thing into the long grass. There's no way they'll approve that project with a by-election taking place. And Avery-Blanchard's thoroughly in disgrace. His wife has moved out. His friends in high places have all found themselves unable to offer a word of support. The Crown Prosecution Service has launched a wide-ranging investigation into his affairs to see if there's any chance for a criminal conviction.'

'So there's some justice in the world,' said Bridget. 'Speaking of which, I just wish there was something we could do about that crooked judge, Graham Neville.'

'Ah, funny you should mention that, DI Hart,' said Grayson. 'I just happened to run into Mr Justice Neville at my golf club last night. I took the opportunity of having a cosy chat with him, during which I mentioned some of the interesting snippets of information I'd picked up recently. At the end of our conversation he wisely made the decision that it was time for him to retire from the judiciary. Of course, he'll leave his job on a full pension, and no doubt I'll be bumping into him regularly at the club in future, but at least he won't be able to do much harm from the fairway.'

'I suppose not, sir.'

'What about Damon's driver? That thug who Neville let off?'

'Tyler Dixon's prints were found all over the hidden cameras at the house. Obviously it was Damon who ordered him to install them there, but we can't prove that. Nevertheless Tyler broke the law by installing surveillance equipment in a location where people would expect privacy. We're hoping to use that as a bargaining chip to get him to incriminate his employer, but so far he's refusing to cooperate.'

'He probably thinks Damon can get him off the hook again,' said Grayson. 'I think he'll find that isn't the case. The days of pulling strings and calling in favours are over.'

'Yes, sir. But what seems most unfair to me is that Nick Damon himself looks like he might get off the hook completely. As far as I can tell he hasn't actually broken any laws. At least, there's nothing we can find convincing evidence for.'

'People like Damon are too smart to get caught out that easily. But he's had a bit of a bloody nose. He's lost that huge housing contract, as well as the contract he was hoping to win for redevelopment at Wadham College. His driver and lawyer are both in trouble, and he's lost two of his most important business associates - Graham Neville and Hugh Avery-Blanchard. All his other friends and acquaintances will be running for cover too. He'll find it a lot harder to do business in future. And there'll be no more parties at his house.'

'Even so, sir. The man's a villain.'

'DI Hart, sometimes you have to let things go. When you reach my great age, you'll understand that better. What I will say is that Damon's very much in our sights now. If he puts a foot wrong again, we'll be onto him immediately. You never know, he might even have to start playing by the rules, and for me that counts as a win.'

'I suppose so, sir.'

Bridget sighed. It pained her to think that Nick Damon was still a free man. But Grayson was right. She had to let it go. The important thing was that she had found the man who murdered Gina Hartman and Miranda Gardiner. Dr Ashley was behind bars, and the forensic evidence that Vik and his team had found would be sure to secure a conviction.

'Is there anything else, DI Hart?' asked Grayson.

'No, sir.'

'Then go home. It's late, and you've done well. You, and your team.'

★

When Jake got back to his flat, Brittany was waiting for him outside, sitting on a pink suitcase that presumably held the rest of the gear that she'd retrieved from the gatehouse.

'Have you been waiting here long?' he enquired.

'Not long.'

She gave him a warm smile, but he didn't return it.

'You'd better come inside,' he told her. 'We need to talk.'

He carried her suitcase up the stairs, then made two mugs of tea and brought them through to the living room.

Brittany was sitting on the sofa. She patted the spare seat next to her for him to join him. But this was no time for a comfy chat.

'I think I'll sit here,' he said, taking the chair opposite.

'Okay. Is there something wrong, Jake?'

He wondered where to begin. There was a lot wrong, and it had taken him far too long to work it all out. Just like when she'd first cheated on him with Tyler Dixon, he had been slow to realise what was going on. Late evenings at the office; going into work at weekends; mysterious phone messages. Simple tell-tale signs that he ought to have spotted a mile off.

But he'd been too trusting. Despite spending all his working days being lied to by criminals, he'd chosen to believe every word that Brittany told him. Perhaps it was because of his job that he'd needed to trust her so absolutely. He couldn't allow that murky world of deception and transgression to intrude into his home life.

But he'd found out in the end. Like Ffion said, liars always gave themselves away eventually. And Brittany's lies were about to catch up with her yet again.

'I've been thinking,' he said.

'About what?'

'Tyler Dixon.'

'Oh, Jake. Is that what the trouble is? I told you, it's over between me and Tyler now. I'm so sorry I ever got involved with him. I know I hurt you, but now all I want to do is make it up to you. I'd do anything to put things back to how they were.'

'Anything?'

'Anything.' She gazed directly into his eyes, her expression open.

It would have been so easy for him to trust her.

'Would you even go so far as to plant false evidence during a criminal investigation?' he asked.

'What?'

He studied her face and watched her falter, then begin to calculate. He'd seen that look so many times, but mostly in police interview rooms, on the face of suspects who'd been caught out in a lie and were working out how they might backtrack and save themselves.

'The earring you found that belonged to Gina,' he said.

'What about it? It was Gina's wasn't it?'

'Yes. DNA tests confirmed it.'

'So what's the problem?'

'You didn't really find it in your bed, did you?'

'What do you mean? Where else would I have found it? Anyway, didn't Tyler admit to sleeping with Gina?'

'He did, eventually. But he always maintained that they had sex in his car.'

She pulled a face. 'Typical Tyler. I really don't know what I ever saw in him.' She leaned forward, reaching out her hand for Jake's.

But Jake pulled his hand away.

'Dr Ashley – when he finally agreed to answer our questions – confirmed that he saw Tyler and Gina in the car before the party.'

'Well... I don't understand why you're bringing this up,' said Brittany. 'Who cares if they did have sex in the car that day? The earring could have been left in the bed some other time.'

'Not if Tyler never took Gina back to the gatehouse.'

'Well, he must be lying about that. Why would you believe him?'

'Because he has no reason to lie. And because when Gina's body was taken to the morgue, she wasn't wearing any earrings. Someone must have taken them.' He'd checked that particular fact for himself in the pathologist's report. It was a small detail, but sometimes the smallest details turned out to be the most important.

He took a sip of his tea. It was sweet and milky, and gave him the strength he needed to carry on.

'And then there's the hidden camera in Frost's bedroom,' he said.

'Creepy, yeah. Do you think Tyler installed the cameras?'

'We think he probably did. After all, he was responsible for security at the house.'

'Will he get into trouble over that? Is it illegal to spy on people in that way?'

'Yes. He might well get into trouble. And Mr Gold too, since all the cameras were linked to his computer.'

'I never liked Mr Gold,' said Brittany.

'The thing is,' said Jake, 'we still haven't found the camera that was installed in Frost's bedroom. We found cameras in all the other guest rooms, and we recovered the video footage from Frost's room, so we know there must have been a camera there. But someone removed it before the police arrived at the house the Saturday morning after the party.'

'Tyler again, I expect.'

'Possibly. Except that we're pretty sure that Tyler was in the gatehouse during that time.'

'Well, then Mr Gold, or perhaps even Nick himself? I guess they wanted to conceal what they'd been up to.'

Jake studied her closely. She was good, very good. Even now, when pushed into a corner, she displayed none of the usual tell-tale signs of lying. It was how she'd been able to fool him before.

But he wasn't going to be fooled by Brittany again.

He knew now how to tell when she was lying. It was very simple. Brittany lied every time her lips moved.

'Who dialled 999 that morning to report the death?' he asked.

'Well, I did.'

'And who went into Frost's room before the police arrived?'

'Well, me, and –'

'Anyone else?'

'Not as far as I know. Not until the police came.'

'So who removed the camera, Brittany?'

'What are you saying, Jake?' Tears began to well up in her clear blue eyes.

'I think it was the same person who planted the earring in your bed.'

The tears fell freely, drawing dark paths as they rolled down her cheeks. 'You're accusing me of that? You think I'm lying to you?'

'Yes,' he said, swallowing down his own pain. 'That's exactly what I think. In fact, I'm sure of it.'

She stayed where she was, still weeping quietly. He guessed she was trying to formulate another plan, to find some new way that might yet save her. But he wasn't going to let her make a fool of him again. He had already closed his heart to her.

'I think that you should go now, Brittany,' he said.

'But where can I go, Jake? I can't go back to the gatehouse. I can't move back in with Tyler – not after everything that's happened.'

'Honestly, Brittany, this might sound like a cliché, but I really don't give a damn.'

★

Ffion set off across the cold, dark expanse of Port Meadow, a running flashlight fixed to her forehead shining a bright, narrow beam onto the ground ahead of her. She enjoyed running in the dark, alone and free. The wild grassland was covered in frost, and her feet made soft crunching sounds in the silent night as she ran.

She had no qualms about being out alone at night. Her Taekwondo skills had been proven yet again during Dr Ashley's arrest, and she knew that she could defend herself from any attacker.

Running was always her best time for thinking, and for working out her feelings. Alone, with only the steady motion of her body across the dark expanse of the meadow, she could gather her thoughts, begin to process what had happened, and find a way to move forwards again.

Another murder case was closed, with a satisfying conclusion, and she'd been congratulated for her arrest by both Bridget and Chief Superintendent Grayson. That was a win, and went a little way to compensating for what she had lost.

Jake.

She had enjoyed their brief time together, and she looked back on their relationship with fondness, as well as regret. There was a tinge of bitterness too – she wouldn't be human if she didn't feel resentment towards Brittany Grainger and the way she'd forced herself back into Jake's life, driving a wedge between them, and causing their relationship to break up.

It had been a long time since Ffion had allowed a man to become so intimately involved in her life, and she knew that it would be a long time before she would again. Maybe never. But she knew she'd find someone one day, and if not a man then a woman. And even if that didn't happen, Ffion had the mental resilience and resources necessary to live her life alone.

Her feet moved quickly across the frozen ground as she followed the line of the black snaking river, flowing soundlessly beneath the starry sky. She was already halfway to Godstow Abbey, and was making good time.

In her back pocket, her phone began to vibrate.

She ignored it, but after a minute it rang a second time, and she slowed her pace to check it. Two missed calls. The first from Jake. The second a voicemail message. Her thumb hovered, ready to listen to it.

She'd seen Jake's face after the break-up and knew that he was just as tormented by what he'd done as she was. It was easy to picture him as a victim too. Brittany had used her considerable charms – both physical and verbal – to win him over, almost against his own will. And Ffion probably hadn't made his choice any easier by the way she'd walked out on him, throwing down a challenge for him to make up his mind. You could argue that she'd driven him straight into Brittany's arms just when he was at his most vulnerable.

But Jake wasn't a child. He'd made his decision in full possession of the facts. And now they both had to live with the consequences.

She deleted the voicemail message without listening to it, and then scrolled to Jake's number and blocked it. She slid the phone back into her pocket, and began to run again, picking up speed, her long legs moving mechanically through the cold, dark night.

It was good to be alone again, and to be free.

CHAPTER 33

It was lunchtime on Sunday, and so, inevitably, here they were at Vanessa's house. Bridget, Jonathan and Chloe, reunited once more.

A lot could happen in one week. Seven days earlier, Bridget had been deliriously happy, basking in the new-found intimacy of her relationship with Jonathan, and at peace with her daughter. Then a barrier seemed to have risen up out of nowhere between her and Jonathan as the anniversary of Angela's death briefly separated them, bringing their tentative romance to a juddering halt. Bridget remembered the agony of having Jonathan torn away from her, not knowing what to say to him, and not knowing how he felt about her.

And the war that had erupted between mother and daughter had been just as distressing. She'd thought for a moment that she might lose Chloe forever. But peace was restored, and a new bond forged, based on trust and understanding. Chloe was growing up, making choices of her own, and Bridget knew that she had to give her space to find her way in life, and yes, to make mistakes, just as Bridget had done.

Bridget had made many, many mistakes, and getting pregnant with Chloe had been one of them. Or so it had seemed at the time. Now she knew that her daughter was one of the best things that had ever happened to her – perhaps the best – and that trying to second guess the future was an impossible task.

Was this wisdom? Perhaps. Or just as likely it was the warm glow that came after consuming one of Vanessa's delicious lamb roasts and a glass or two of spicy Shiraz.

Vanessa bustled into the dining room, cradling bowls of apple crumble and a jug of steaming hot custard. The kids jumped up and down excitedly in their seats in anticipation, and Bridget was tempted to join in with them.

'Who would like dessert?' asked Vanessa, and was rewarded with a chorus of consent.

After lunch had been cleared away, Jonathan and James had disappeared into the kitchen to wash up and do men's talk, the kids had gone upstairs with Chloe, and a third bottle of wine had been opened, Bridget joined Vanessa in the front room.

'So, have you finished with your murder?' enquired Vanessa, brushing an imaginary piece of dirt from her armchair.

'You make it sound like I go around murdering people myself,' said Bridget. She knew that Vanessa would always regard the job of police detective with distaste, as if Bridget had taken a job at a sewage farm or a meat factory and had come straight from work without washing her hands.

'No, of course not,' said Vanessa. 'Although,' she added wickedly, 'I do sometimes wonder if it gives you ideas.'

Bridget chuckled. 'Who do you think I might want to murder?'

'I don't know. I could always give you a list of suggestions, if you like.'

'No thanks.' Bridget wondered who might be on her sister's hitlist. Perhaps people who misused apostrophes or split their infinitives. Or lazy cooks like Bridget who lived off microwave pizzas and ate late-night pasta straight out of the pan, with a handful of cheese sprinkled over it. In that case, it would be a very long list.

'Did you have a word with Chloe?' asked Vanessa. 'About the party, I mean?'

'Yes.'

'And?'

'We're good.'

'Mm. I hope so.' Vanessa sipped her wine and Bridget knew exactly what she was going to say next. 'It was about this age when Abigail started staying out late and going to parties, wasn't it?'

'Chloe isn't a bit like Abi,' said Bridget. 'She's much more sensible.'

'Yes, I'm sure she is,' said Vanessa. 'You know, I still wonder whether if we'd done something different she might still be alive today.'

'What could we have done?'

'I don't know. Something. Anything. Perhaps some tiny difference would have changed her course.'

Bridget shook her head. 'Abigail was the way she was. She couldn't have been any different. And it wasn't anything she did that led to her death. That was someone else's fault entirely.'

'Yes, I suppose so.'

'Anyway,' said Bridget. 'Enough talk of murder. What shall we talk about instead?'

Vanessa shot her a mischievous look. 'Well, actually, there was something else I wanted to quiz you about.'

'What?'

'Love.' Vanessa glanced over her shoulder to make sure that the men were out of earshot. 'I want to know all the latest about Jonathan. Tell me everything.'

A DARKLY SHINING STAR (BRIDGET HART #5)

Christmas. Ghosts. Murder.

It's nearly Christmas in Oxford and Detective Inspector Bridget Hart is enjoying a rare day off at Oxford's Christmas Market. A ghost tour seems like a fun way to round off the day. Until, that is, a brutal murder brings the evening to a tragic close.

Torn between work and family commitments over the festive season, Bridget soon discovers that the ghost of Christmas past is reaching out to the present with fatal consequences.

Not everyone believes in the season of goodwill to all men, and with a real-life, flesh-and-blood killer at large in Oxford, Bridget races to solve the case in time to prevent yet more murders.

Set amongst the dreaming spires of Oxford University, the Bridget Hart series is perfect for fans of Elly Griffiths, JR Ellis, Faith Martin and classic British murder mysteries.

 Scan the QR code to see list of retailers.

THANK YOU FOR READING

We hope you enjoyed this book. If you did, then we would be very grateful if you would please take a moment to leave a review online. Thank you.

BRIDGET HART SERIES:

Bridget Hart® is a registered trademark of Landmark Internet Ltd.
Aspire to Die (Bridget Hart #1)
Killing by Numbers (Bridget Hart #2)
Do No Evil (Bridget Hart #3)
In Love and Murder (Bridget Hart #4)
A Darkly Shining Star (Bridget Hart #5)
Preface to Murder (Bridget Hart #6)
Toll for the Dead (Bridget Hart #7)

TOM RAVEN SERIES:

Tom Raven® is a registered trademark of Landmark Internet Ltd.
The Landscape of Death (Tom Raven #1)
Beneath Cold Earth (Tom Raven #2)
The Dying of the Year (Tom Raven #3)
Deep into that Darkness (Tom Raven #4)

PSYCHOLOGICAL THRILLERS

The Red Room

ABOUT THE AUTHOR

M S Morris is the pseudonym for the writing partnership of Margarita and Steve Morris. The couple are married and live in Oxfordshire. They have two grown-up children.

Find out more at msmorrisbooks.com where you can join our mailing list or follow us on Facebook at facebook.com/msmorrisbooks.